learning at 40

L.B. DUNBAR

www.lbdunbar.com

L.B. Dunbar

Copyright © 2021 Laura Dunbar
L.B. Dunbar Writes, Ltd.
https://www.lbdunbar.com/

All rights reserved. No part of this book may be reproduced or transmitted in any form or by any means, electronic or mechanical, including photocopying, recording, or by any information storage and retrieval system, without permission in writing.

This is a work of fiction. Names, characters, places, and incidents are the product of the author's imagination or are used fictitiously, and any resemblance to any actual persons, living or dead, events, or locales is entirely coincidental.

The author acknowledges the trademarked status and trademark owners of various products referenced in this work of fiction, which have been used without permission. The publication/use of these trademarks is not authorized, associated with, or sponsored by the trademark owner.

Cover Design: Shannon Passmore/Shanoff Designs
Editor: Melissa Shank
Editor: Jenny Sims/Editing4Indies
Proofreader: Gemma Brocato
Proofreader: Karen Fischer

Other Books by L.B. Dunbar

<u>Lakeside Cottage</u>
Living at 40
Loving at 40
Learning at 40
Letting Go at 40

<u>The Silver Foxes of Blue Ridge</u>
Silver Brewer
Silver Player
Silver Mayor
Silver Biker

<u>Silver Fox Former Rock Stars</u>
After Care
Midlife Crisis
Restored Dreams
Second Chance
Wine&Dine

<u>Collision novellas</u>
Collide
Caught

<u>Smartypants Romance (an imprint of Penny Reid)</u>
Love in Due Time
Love in Deed
Love in a Pickle

<u>The World of True North (an imprint of Sarina Bowen)</u>
Cowboy
Studfinder

<u>Rom-com for the over 40</u>
The Sex Education of M.E.

<u>The Heart Collection</u>
Speak from the Heart
Read with your Heart
Look with your Heart

L.B. Dunbar

Fight from the Heart
View with your Heart

A Heart Collection Spin-off
The Heart Remembers

THE EARLY YEARS
The Legendary Rock Star Series
The Legend of Arturo King
The Story of Lansing Lotte
The Quest of Perkins Vale
The Truth of Tristan Lyons
The Trials of Guinevere DeGrance

Paradise Stories
Abel
Cain

The Island Duet
Redemption Island
Return to the Island

Modern Descendants – writing as elda lore
Hades
Solis
Heph

Dedication

Summer dreams and 2021.

Stay safe and well, my reader friends.

Prologue

[Zack]

July

Ben was dead.

There was no easy way to sugarcoat the truth. Our best friend had died after a short life and a brief struggle with pancreatic cancer. I'm still dressed in my funeral attire, minus my sports coat. My tie is loosened, and I gawk out the second-floor bedroom window into the yard next door. Anna's family calls this place Lakeside Cottage, but for the past year, it was the permanent residence of one of my oldest friends and his family. I used to live next door—once upon a time.

Swiping a hand through my hair, I sigh. The past eleven months have been hell. Just shy of a year ago, Ben told us about his diagnosis. He'd already been through treatment without success. Ben Kulis. *Clueless Kulis*, we teased him in college. The nickname came about because he only had eyes for one woman. That woman would become his wife, Anna. They were sickly sweet, madly in love, and now she was a widow too young. Ben was the best of men. Loyal to a fault, he saw the good in most people even when they didn't recognize it in themselves. Having been Anna's friend first, being Ben's pal happened second but was no less important.

Staring out the dark window, I'm distracted when a light from the house next door illuminates a portion of the yard. A yard that was mine once upon a time. My childhood dreams were built there until everything shattered when I was a teenager.

I hate this room. I hate that it faces what I once had. I hate that facing what I once had reminds me of all that I've lost.

A house. A home. A wife. A friend.

Ben would have told me to let it go regarding that house next door. I'm certain he said something similar to that before the phrase—*let it go*—became so popular. It was only a house, he probably said, but it had been my house. My home. As a landscape designer who loved plant metaphors, he might have added, "Home is where you plant your garden and sow your seeds." Instead of that house being a special place, I was uprooted as a teen and forced to bloom elsewhere.

Regarding my ex-wife, he told me to let her go as well, and I did.

Suddenly, a woman enters the yard, distracting me from my thoughts of shattered dreams and broken homes. Her hair appears golden in the dim light, flowing behind her like a mystical creature from a child's bedtime story. Her light dress covers her from shoulder to ankle yet leaves nothing to the imagination. In profile, I see the outline of her form. Pert breasts. Long legs. And that hair like a veil drifting behind her in the light wind.

She looks like an angel.

And I must be losing my mind.

This must be the neighbor who arrived around the time we visited last summer. Anna and Ben claim they never formally met her, only passed friendly hellos through the tall shrubbery between the homes. Anna's best guess is she's roughly our age. We all turned forty the year of the great reunion when Ben dropped the bomb about his situation. Now, we are forty-one.

Roughly loosening the remainder of my tie, I continue to stare into the mostly dark yard. The patio is illuminated by the soft glow of light coming from the house. *The kitchen.* I recall my mother cooking there, my brother doing homework at the oval table, and my father's laughter. Tonight seems to be a night of memories. My childhood home. My best friend's passing. And this woman is invading them both.

With my room on the second floor and steeped in darkness, I remain submerged in my dismal mood but mesmerized by her presence.

Why tonight? Of all the times I've visited this home in the past year, why am I seeing her tonight? And why does she look so beautiful, so peaceful, just standing in my yard—*her* yard—facing the lake off in the distance? Her head tips back, and I imagine her closing her eyes, allowing the soft breeze to coast over her face, caress her skin, kiss her lips.

I'm not a romantic at heart, but I'm definitely turned on. The idea of being the one to touch her cheeks, stroke down her nose, and stare into eyes I cannot see from this distance overwhelms me. *And that hair.* I want to comb my fingers through that spun gold and curl a fist in the silky threads. My mouth waters at the possibility of kissing the column of her throat, visibly on display with her head tilted backward, face aimed upward. Heaven is calling her.

Ben.

My eyes prickle, and my throat tightens. If I were a man who believed in something mystical, I'd think Ben placed this angel in my old yard just for me.

Mine whispers through my thoughts. *Why?*

I can't seem to turn away from the window when I know I should. Staring down upon her makes me feel like a voyeur, witnessing something private, almost intimate. I want to stand in that yard with her. I want to rub my hands over her shoulder where the edge of her dress slips downward, exposing the curve of muscle at the top of her arm. I want to kiss her there.

My reaction doesn't feel appropriate—*watching her, wanting her*—on this day, when I buried a friend. Still, I stare out the window at the stranger next door. My fingers curl into a fist on the window's trim, balancing me upright, holding me in place. I can't seem to look away.

Then she looks at me.

Her head swivels so quickly, I remain caught in eyes I can't see as her face angles toward the second floor, toward this window, toward me.

What does she see? The miserable man that I am. The shitty husband I once was. The poor father I've been.

I don't want to be any of those things, but I don't know how to change. I don't know what to do or what I want. I only know I want to be better. I want to *feel* better inside.

Staring down at her, I'm certain she sees me until I remember I'm covered in darkness. The lights remain off in my room, and I'm at the edge of the window. She can't possibly see me. I've been so good at pretending I'm something other than who I am. I don't think anyone knows the real me.

L.B. Dunbar
    Not even me.

1

[Zack]

August

"Hello?" I call out as I enter Lakeside Cottage, nearly trampled by my own two children who race around me to find Ben's teenage sons.

"In here!" Anna hollers back, her voice strained. Crossing the large entryway, I enter the open concept sitting area and kitchen combination filled with bright sunlight. It's been a few weeks since Ben's passing, and we're here for happier times. One final promise we made to Ben was to return every summer for the first two weeks of August. On the cusp of Ben's death, I worry the annual tradition is a little too new. I don't want Anna to be stressed about our return.

Standing beside the kitchen island is our friend who lived here during Ben's last year—Mason Becker. The two of them appear as if they've been fighting. Watching Mason swipe a hand aggressively through his perfect hair, I approach Anna first.

"Hey." I greet one of my oldest friends with wide-open arms, and she collapses against my chest. Anna's mother and mine were best friends. Anna's father was considered a sausage king in Chicago, and when this house came on the market, her parents purchased it as a second home. My childhood home was next door. Our mothers were thrilled to be neighbors for at least part of the year. We spent entire summers together. Anna and I grew up with the maternal hope we would one day marry and join our families. As I consider Anna like a sister, a romantic interest never arose between us, but she's been one of my best friends our entire lives. Our older brothers were friends when they were younger as well. The only hope of joining the Weller-McCaryn families would be her youngest sister, Amelia, and my older brother, Noah. But the chances of that happening are slim to never in a million years.

"How are you?" I ask, and her body stiffens.

L.B. Dunbar

"I'm getting a little tired of that question." There's a defensive edge in her voice I haven't ever heard from her. My dark brunette friend has circles under her equally dark eyes and looks exhausted. She also looks thin. Dismissing the warning in her tone, I glance up at Mason. He appears exasperated.

"Mason," I greet, releasing Anna and stepping over to him.

To me, Mason Becker is an anomaly in our circle of friends. I don't know how Ben allowed a man who loved his wife to remain close all these years. It wasn't as though Ben didn't see how Mason felt about Anna. He just chose to ignore it. The rest of us? We weren't so blind.

I trust my wife one-thousand percent, he once said to me when I questioned him. He didn't need to trust Mason because he knew Anna would never stray. He also believed in Mason in a way I'm not certain I would if it were my wife he lusted after. However, Mason hated Jeanine, my ex-wife. The feeling was mutual.

Mason is a manwhore. He's what I've heard women call model-worthy gorgeous. He has this artful hair, slicked back in wavy perfection, curling up on his neck. I swear he probably blow-dries his hair, the pussy.

He's lived the glory of bachelorhood his entire forty-one years, never taking a woman seriously, other than a blip on the map named Samantha, the mother of his now five-year-old daughter, Lynlee. Mason never considered marrying her. It's probably one of the few smart decisions he's made in his life. They would have killed each other.

To Mason's credit, he's been living here since Ben announced he was sick. He stepped up to be the physical strength eventually needed to assist Ben with his condition. He was also an extra support to Ben's family of two teenage boys and a middle-school-aged daughter. If only my friend was as great to his own child.

Mason and I clap backs before pulling away from one another.

"Where's Logan?"

Our original foursome includes me, Mason, Ben, and Logan Anders, newly married to Ben's younger sister. They live up the street about half a mile. There was discussion about Logan physically staying at the house in order to celebrate Ben's life, as we are calling this reunion of sorts; however, we don't want to overwhelm Anna, and with Logan's new baby, it's best he stays in his own home. Anna's been warned we aren't here to be catered to. For lack of a better explanation, we're here to use the place, recall good times with Ben, and get drunk. Anna is not responsible for us.

"He'll be here tonight with Autumn and baby Ben." Autumn had a baby shortly before her older brother's passing, and she and Logan decided to name their son after Ben. At forty, Logan became a father again, and it suits him. He already has a daughter from his previous marriage, and I need some serious dad advice from him as a new divorcé with out-of-control children. Not that Logan's daughter is out of control. Lorna is an angel compared to my monsters.

On that note, the two hellions race past me, and I'm suddenly wondering where they've been and what kind of trouble they've already caused. I don't remember being so . . . inventive at seven years old as these two seem to be. Oliver is the follower, while Trevor is the alpha of the two.

"Halt," I call out, sounding militant. "Where have you two been?"

They stop with their backs to me, both ramrod stiff but not turning around. *Guilty.*

"What did you do?"

Trevor slowly turns, giving me the eyes of his mother, wicked and deceptive despite his innocent age. "He didn't do anything," Thing One admits, pointing a finger at his brother, which means Oliver did do something. I direct my gaze to the smaller twin.

"Oliver." My voice threatens that I want the truth, but the truth is, my children hardly tell it. In so many ways, I'm puzzled by my own boys. They should listen. They should obey. It's not that difficult. They are my children. I love them, but I'm lost.

"He didn't do anything," Oliver claims of his brother, leading me to wonder which one did do something and what exactly did they do.

"Speak," I snap.

"I had to go to the bathroom," Oliver finally states, and I close my eyes, pinching the bridge of my nose. The bathroom leaves all sorts of open possibilities and deep concerns. Dueling swords as they piss. Items down the toilet. Clogging the sink until water cascades over the rim.

Taking hearty shits despite being such little people and leaving it for the next person to witness.

"It's not like she saw us," Trevor states.

"Who?" I bark, flipping open my eyes and glaring at my boys.

"The lady," Oliver adds.

"What lady?" I lower my hands to my sides, and sweat beads on my forehead.

"The one next door," Trevor admits.

"River?" Anna questions, giving a name to the witness of my son's exhibitionist peeing.

"Who?" I ask, turning to Anna.

"The lady next door. The new neighbor. Remember, she moved in last summer." Anna turns her attention to the boys. "Gold hair. Friendly smile. Nice laugh."

Gold hair? New neighbor? Could it be who I think it is?

Trevor shrugs. Oliver says, "She didn't laugh at me." His face pouts like he's offended that she might have, or maybe he's upset she didn't offer him the sound.

"Don't worry, little man. She's probably seen a little pecker before," Mason says, and I roll my eyes. He has no idea what he's just started.

"His pecker isn't little," Trevor defends, as if they have big dicks at seven.

"We aren't discussing our body parts," I remind them after having this discussion in the car ride from the east side of the state to the west. Three hours plus bathroom breaks included at least four discussions on how we are not talking about body parts with others. Dicks. Buttholes. Fingers in our nose.

"Wow, the cojones on that kid," Mason teases.

I turn to Mason as Oliver asks, "What are cojones?"

"Nothing," I say through gritted teeth, catching Mason holding his hand below his zipper and cupping upward. Spinning back to my boys, I see Trevor mimic Mason's motion, and then he state, "I have *cojones*."

"Oh God," I mutter while Anna quietly snickers. Facing her, I find her smile is weak while the sound is enough of a reminder that my friend needs to laugh. Maybe not at dick and ball antics, but it's good to see some kind of grin curl her lips. "Okay. No more talk of *cojones* and no showing the neighbor your pecker."

"I didn't show her my pecker. I had to pee," Oliver reminds me.

"Can I show her my cojones?" Trevor asks, dropping his voice to sound rough and gangster.

"No, and just for adding this word to your vocabulary, Uncle Mason wants to take you two to the beach."

Mason chuckles before coming forward to clap me hard on my shoulder blade. "Okay, little guys, let's take our big cojones to the beach." Mason passes me, and my boys break into cheers while racing to the car for their bags.

"I'm sorry about that," I say to Anna as my shoulders fall in defeat.

"Well, if anyone is going to teach them about big cojones, it's Uncle Mason." Her comment breaks us both into laughter, and I open my arms once again to bring her in for a hug.

This time, I think I'm the one who needs it.

+ + +

The trip to the beach is chaos. Clothing changes. Beach towels. Snacks. Water bottles. Another bathroom check.

"Please tell me one of those coolers has beer," I mumble to Mason as we descend toward the sand.

"Locked and loaded, stressed daddy," Mason teases. One hundred and fifty wooden stairs take us down the cliff to the shore with a small deck landing in the middle to view the grand lake before us. I'm hoping all the steps will deplete some of my boys' energy. It's wishful thinking, at least.

A set of Adirondack chairs stand in a circle on the beach, and I'm instantly reminded of the last time I sat here among my friends, along with Ben. We were celebrating baby Ben's birth while watching Ben's sons play football and my sons run around like the little crazy beasts they are. I shake off the sadness and offer Anna a small smile when she catches me staring at an empty chair.

15

L.B. Dunbar

"Beer?" I offer, stepping over to the cooler in desperate need of refreshment.

"No thanks," she mutters, gazing out at my boys playing on the edge of the water. Her daughter, Mila, entertains them. Being eleven, she's crossed over the line and considers the twins too young to be playmates. Instead, she shows interest in them like a babysitter might.

"They grow so fast," Anna states, still watching the three interact. Her sons are not home yet today. Calvin is seventeen and inherited Ben's old truck. Bryce turned fifteen and is off with friends for the day. The boys seemed to have adjusted well enough to the sudden move their parents decided to make while they were in high school. What's difficult to judge is how they are handling the death of their father at such vulnerable ages.

Mason takes a seat and automatically hands Anna an open beer even though she declined my offer. Blindly, she accepts it and takes a drink of the summer shandy. I tip up a brow at Mason, who just shakes his head at me. *Don't ask.*

"There they are," he calls out instead, and I twist in my chair to see Logan carrying three bags and something long under his arm. Autumn follows with baby Ben in a carrier strapped to her chest.

"Lorna. Come here, beautiful," I address Logan's daughter, who runs to give me a quick sideways hug before running off for Mila. The two girls are technically cousins now but also best friends despite a one-year age gap. I greet Autumn next, pressing a kiss to her cheek and then one to her son's head.

"I think he's finally asleep," she whispers. Her voice is strained from the effort of walking down all those stairs with an additional ten pounds attached to her. Gingerly, she lowers herself into a chair.

"I forgot how much shit babies need," Logan huffs, not so gracefully dropping all the bags onto the sand and bending for the cooler immediately.

"It's not shit," Autumn argues, pressing a kiss to the head of her sleeping babe.

"You're right. It's crap," Logan mocks, stepping over to his wife and pressing a kiss to the top of her head. "Want me to set up that tent thingy?"

"Not yet," she sighs. "But I'd kill for one of those." She nods longingly at the beer in his hand.

"I'll drink one for you," he teases.

"You aren't drinking?" I question and feel like an idiot when Autumn simply replies, "Nursing."

"Oh yes, let's discuss breasts," Mason teases before lifting his beer and taking a long pull.

"As opposed to *cojones*?" I joke.

"Why are *cojones* in opposition to breasts?" Logan questions, and Mason shakes his head.

"Don't ask," I retort. "But might I suggest when your boy grows older, you keep Uncle Mason away from him when he's six, seven, or any age where body parts are a fascination."

"We're men. All body parts fascinate us," Mason jests.

"Please let us talk about something other than body parts," I beg, tipping my head back in my seat. "Tell me more about the neighbor."

It isn't the smoothest transition, but I'm curious. Who exactly is River? Is she the golden-haired goddess who hasn't left my thoughts for weeks since I saw her the night of Ben's funeral?

"Speaking of body parts." Mason salaciously grins and wiggles his eyebrows.

Fuck. My hackles instantly rise, asking a question where I fear the answer. "Do you have knowledge of her body parts?"

"Oh my gosh, must we discuss Mason's sex life? Innocent ears here," Autumn jokes, covering baby Ben's ears.

"He isn't interested in sex yet, just boobs," Mason replies.

Logan chokes on a swallow of beer. "Those would be my wife's boobs you're referencing, and they are not up for discussion."

"Easy, baby daddy." Mason holds up both hands. "I just mean River has a nice rack."

Anna scrunches her face while Autumn shakes her head in disgust. Mentioning her *rack* reminds me of her outlined form, standing in the dim light of her darkened yard. She might as well have been naked that night.

"Did you bang her?" I crudely ask, my voice rough for some reason. My hand clenches tighter around the beer bottle in my hand. *I'll strangle him if he touched her.*

And I have no idea where the possessive thoughts come from.

"Fuck no. She's not my type," Mason gruffly answers, holding his head still as he narrows his eyes at me.

"You have a type?" Logan jests. Anna stands without a sound and begins walking down the beach. *Shit.*

"Should someone follow her?" I question, suddenly feeling bad about discussing sex, even if it is just Mason's lifestyle. Silently, he watches Anna stalk away.

"She's going to do this from time to time," Autumn answers. "She'll need to break away from the chaos to process her emotions."

"Is it too much that we're here?" I ask, loosening the grip on my beer bottle while checking on my boys, who are torturing Mila and Lorna in the water.

"She wants you all here, but it's also difficult." Autumn's statement makes sense. Still, I'm worried about my friend.

"Should we have stayed someplace else?"

"Definitely not," Autumn reiterates. "This is what Ben wanted. She knows this, and it's good for her."

I hear what Autumn's saying, but I take another glance down the beach at Anna's retreating back.

"She'll be okay," Autumn offers. It's a lie. We might never be okay. We'll all be different, but especially Anna.

"So. River?" Mason interjects, attempting to discuss anything other than Ben and Anna. "Wonder if she's getting laid in your old room." Mason wiggles his brows at me.

"You really are an ass sometimes," Logan huffs, taking a pull of his beer. I appreciate he's offended on my behalf. I hadn't thought about it before, but with Mason mentioning it, I'm curious now. Has she been in my childhood bedroom? Has she fucked someone all over the house? The thought both sickens me and excites me for some reason, and I realize I need to get laid. Since my divorce, I haven't branched out like my colleagues have encouraged. Maybe I'll find someone random on this trip and allow myself a one-night stand. Then again, the last time I had one of those, I ended up with a wife and twins.

"Is she married?" I don't want her to be, which isn't really fair. My eyes wander up the cliff in the general direction of the house where I once lived. Is she in the yard now? Unless she stood on the stairs belonging to her property, there's no way to see her.

"Why? You interested?" Mason arches a brow at me.

"Just curious," I mutter before taking a hardy sip of my beer. My eyes are still drawn up the cliff, wondering, wondering, wondering.

"Well, you know what they say about curiosity and cats?"

Please don't let him say it killed cats because talking about death isn't appropriate right now. I briefly close my eyes as Mason's mischievous voice warns us his wisdom will be anything but politically correct.

"It can lead you to some pretty kitty, and that's a direct body part reference." Mason huffs, proud of his analogy as he points at me around the bottleneck of his beer.

"You're so inappropriate." Autumn chuckles.

"That's what kitties like best about me." Mason wiggles his brows once more.

As Mason continues to be inappropriately appropriate, I can't remember the last time I saw a *kitty*, and my thoughts race back to River. What does she look like underneath that sheer dress? What would her skin feel like under my hands? What color are those eyes that looked up at me in the dark?

Yeah, I was definitely curious about her—kitty and all.

2

[Zack]

That night, Mason prepares dinner, which shocks the shit out of Logan and me.

"You can cook? Since when?" Logan questions.

"Since always," Mason mutters.

Dinner passes in chaos as it does when the number of kids almost outnumbers the adults present. Once the dishes are done and my sons put to bed, we gather around the sitting area off the kitchen. The difficult memory of Ben telling us about his illness returns, and then I recall sitting here on the day of his funeral.

My head turns in the direction of the house next door. Nothing can be seen of the structure through the sliver of the window beside the fireplace. The sun setting across the lake casts a glittery glow over the tall shrubbery, blocking out any view of the other yard from this level. I don't need to see the house to know what it looks like, though. Until I was a teenager, I lived there, so the layout is burned into my memory. It was nothing remarkable compared to this cottage—which is more like a sprawling mansion on the cliff. Our house was rather modest, just a two-story Cape Cod big enough for a family of four with a yard full of history.

"So, I have something for everyone," Autumn announces, startling even her husband. He rubs a hand up her back and cups her neck. She's finally baby free as mini-Ben is in his car seat sleeping.

"Before Ben passed away, he gave me an envelope for each of you."

"Jesus," Mason hisses.

Anna closes her eyes. "How did I not know about this?"

Now I'm the one surprised. Anna and Ben shared everything with each other.

"He explained to me the four points needed to be recalibrated every year." Four Points is the name of our collaboration. We originally had the concept when we were young, full of hope and shit, and probably drunk. As an architect, Logan would design homes while Mason would build them. Ben would decorate the outside with his landscaping genius, and I would keep us out of legal trouble. Last summer, Mason reminded us of that college-aged conversation, and after some apprehension, we signed on together to fulfill our lost dream. We're a little shaky in our first year, but we have promise. I like the direction we're going in.

"So, he left an envelope for north." Autumn stands and holds up an envelope.

"Ben was our North," Mason hisses, glaring at Autumn.

"What?" Anna asks, staring up at her sister-in-law expectantly.

"The house is True North, leading everyone home. That's how Ben saw this place." Autumn pauses to hold the envelope higher. "This one will go to Archer."

Archer?

"My brother?" Anna snaps. He wasn't a part of our group. A few years older than us, he had his own circle of friends, which included my brother for a long time until Archer slipped off the radar. Anna's face crumples in both hurt and disgust. "I don't even know where he is."

"Ben did, and I'll take care of it," Autumn states and the surprise on Anna's face is like someone just smacked her.

"How?" she asks of her husband's sister.

"Ben had an email address for him."

Anna closes her eyes, anger heating her cheeks, hinting at the fact she *didn't* have access to that address. I hate this for my friend but assume Ben had his reasons for why Anna couldn't have her brother's contact information. Autumn sadly smiles before turning to Mason.

"Technically, you lived north in Ben's compass, but he's calling you West." Autumn hands Mason another envelope. Her smile slowly widens as she adds, "The place where the sun sets."

Leaning toward me, she hands me an envelope. "East." I live outside Detroit, and this makes sense. "The place where the sun rises." Autumn winks at me.

"And South." She gives the final envelope to Logan. "Ben had this complicated explanation about the sun culminating in the south, explaining how it reaches a climax—"

"Climax?" Mason snorts.

"It reaches a high point or pinnacle," Autumn corrects, scowling at Mason before looking back at Logan. "He believed you'd reached it." She blushes before softly adding, "With me."

Logan gives her a long, accepting look before taking the envelope offered to him. His voice is a whisper as he says, "Definitely, sweetheart."

Autumn continues, "Ben suggested you open them on your own time but during these two weeks. In fact, he hoped that whatever you find on the page inside will begin during these two weeks. You have a year to fulfill his suggestion, which gives you until next summer when you meet back here. You can share your letters with each other, but he thought it best to make it a personal challenge."

Mason huffs and rolls his eyes. "A personal challenge."

"There isn't one for me," Anna remarks, staring at the envelope remaining in Autumn's hand while the rest of us avoid looking at the parchment Autumn holds. "Archer isn't here," Anna reiterates, her tone curt, her eyes searching her sister-in-law for some explanation.

"I think Ben hoped he might be."

A heavy silence fills the room.

Abruptly, Anna stands, visibly upset that there isn't a letter for her. "I'm going to bed."

Perhaps it's better that there isn't one for her. Anna has a long road ahead of her. She doesn't need Ben sending her haunting messages from the grave.

"Well, what the fuck," Mason announces, hastily opening his and pulling out a notecard roughly the size of the envelope itself. He reads what's written, then flips it over and flips it back. With the quick flick, I notice only a line of words and not an in-depth letter. Mason quickly stands, muttering under his breath. "Bastard."

A barroom just off the kitchen doubles as an exit from the back of the house. Mason grabs a bottle from the counter and forces the back door open. It slams when it retracts. He makes his way across the patio and toward the steps leading to the beach.

"Now I'm worried." Logan chuckles. His eyes meet mine as we sit perpendicular to one another on the couches arranged at a ninety-degree angle.

"Rock, paper, scissors," Logan teases.

"I don't know that I'm ready," I admit, staring at my own white envelope.

"It can't be that bad, right?" Logan says, although concern fills his voice.

"You don't have to share, as I said. As Ben said. Whatever he wrote is for you alone and to provoke thought." Autumn hesitates, uncertain herself. "Or maybe cause action. Maybe both."

I nod in acceptance, then turn to gaze out the window and notice Mason has gone down the stairs. "I think I'll go check on him."

I won't need to grab a bottle from the bar. I'll simply share with Mason as I did last year when I told him about my cheating wife and my plans to divorce Jeanine. Mason was surprisingly supportive. He got me drunk.

Descending the stairs, I quickly spot Mason sitting in a chair on the beach. It's a wonder these things haven't ever been stolen. However, they are solid, and you'd need to be strong to hike them away. That's one thing I love about this area. People are rather trusting compared to where I live. The suburbs of Detroit aren't nearly as bad as downtown, but you acquire a level of caution working in a large metropolis that you don't need in a sleepy beach town.

"You okay?" I ask, falling into a chair next to Mason as a sliver of the descending sunlight reflects across the lake. I'm not relaxed enough to enjoy it quite yet, but it is beautiful, peaceful even. Unfortunately, this letter business from Ben has put people on edge.

"I will be," Mason mutters, tilting his head back on the chair and closing his eyes. He tips up the bottle of tequila, reminding me of all kinds of trouble from last summer.

"Going for the hard stuff on the first night? That bad, huh?"

"What's yours say?" Mason huffs. Lifting his head, he nods at me while ignoring my question.

"I didn't open it yet."

L.B. Dunbar

"Coward." He's teasing me, but he isn't wrong. I don't know what Ben could possibly say to me that he didn't say while he was still alive. We discussed business and fatherhood. My divorce and his marriage. We even talked about my boys and how lost I felt with them. Ben wasn't the type to hold back. If he had something to say, he said it, especially at the end when he willingly told everyone how much he loved them. And I was never strong enough to say the words in return.

The thought gives me pause, and a deep ache presses at my ribs.

"Fuck it." I rip open the seal of my envelope and pull out a notecard similar in size to the envelope just like Mason's. Also like Mason's, mine has one line, and I curse Ben as Mason did at the cryptic words given to me.

Fly in love.

Just what the fuck does that mean?

$$+ + +$$

Later that night, I'm staring up at the ceiling, wondering what Ben could possibly mean in his message to me. He must have meant *fall in love* and simply misprinted his words. Still, the statement feels damning as he knew my relationship with my ex-wife was not inspired by love. It wasn't even close.

Ben and Anna were in love, though.

The love of my wife is the greatest gift I ever received, Ben once said to me. *It means more to me than birthdays and Christmas, and even this disease cannot take that blessing from me.*

They were the very definition of the term. Under love in the dictionary, it reads: tender kisses, meaningful stares, and happily ever after. For an example, see Ben and Anna Kulis. Only, even their happily ever after has been ruined.

Suddenly, laughter filters up to my room. The window is open, the distant sound of the lake waves a melancholy harmony to my mood. The pleasant echo of giggles feels invasive. I want to lie here angry with Jeanine for cheating on me, marring my hopes of marriage and family. I want to lie here upset with Ben for dying and leaving cryptic notes I have no hope of fulfilling or understanding. I just want to lie here in peace.

Another trilling laugh flies up to my window, and I hastily hoist myself off my bed before rushing for the window. Gazing outward, I see who I assume is River dancing in her yard. Her hips sway. Her arms rise. Her head tilts backward once again. She spins in a circle, giggling to herself as if soaking up the darkness while relishing the moonlight. She's wearing another one of those nearly see-through dresses. The wide collar topples over one shoulder and down her arm.

Her twirling brings her closer to a large chaise lounge in the grassy portion of her yard, and she knocks into the wood base, tumbling down to the cushion. Her laughter grows louder.

Is she drunk?

For some reason, my lips curl at the possibility. Awkwardly, she scoots upward on the chaise, resting her back against the angled portion. Her arms stretch over her head. Her legs straighten a second before her knees bend. As her head lolls to the side, one arm lowers, lifting the hem of her dress.

In my head, I'm the one lifting that sheer fabric. I'm the one sliding my hands over her summer warm skin. It's me slipping between her legs. Kissing her inner thighs.

I should turn away from the window. I should stop watching, but everything about her mesmerizes me. Her hair glows once again in the dim light cast into the yard from the house. Her bare legs are exposed in the dark. Her hand disappears between her thighs.

Apparently, I'm a voyeur because watching her please herself pleases me.

Leaning a hand against the window trim, I lower my other hand to the stiff length tenting my shorts. The heel of my hand presses along my hard dick, and I groan as I observe her head roll against the cushion. Her knees spread wider. Her now-lifted dress pools around her hips, but I'm too far away to see anything sacred. There's no mistaking where her fingers touch, though.

My imagination takes over again as I envision her with pretty pink lower lips, swollen and dripping with anticipation. I intend to French kiss her there, curving through those folds and lapping at her sticky sweetness. She'd taste delicious, like a summer peach.

A sharp hiccup travels to my open window, and her head tips back on the chaise.

That's it, honey. Let me have a lick.

My mouth salivates. My hand hastily slips under the elastic of my loose shorts. Within seconds, my palm wraps around my rock-hard shaft while I fist my other hand on the window casing. I should stop looking at her, but I can't. I continue to imagine it's me between those bent knees and spread thighs. It's me sipping and nipping at her, and she's losing her mind. She's soaked and dripping, leaking down her inner thighs as she clenches against my tongue. Her legs quiver, and her breath catches. She's on the edge, and I work myself—squeezing, tugging, jerking my dick harder than I've done before. She's effervescent, and I want that glow to spill over me. I want her otherworldly essence to coat my tongue.

Then she opens her eyes, sits upright, and looks directly at my window.

Shit.

Did she hear me? Did I say something out loud? Did my ragged breathing travel down to the yard?

Good God, I can't seem to quit working my dick with my fist. I can't see her eyes, but I'm certain they are looking up at me, knowing I'm here at the window, watching her get off. The thought tips the cup, and I spill over, pouring into my fist and covering my fingers in a liquid mess. My chest heaves and swells. I can hardly breathe. Though I work out religiously, I feel like I've never spent a day in the gym. My knees shake. My heart races, and I close my eyes for only a second.

When I open them, she's gone. Her yard is dark, and my breath hitches.

Did I imagine it? Was she not out there? Had I seen a ghost in my head?

What have I done?

Quickly, I turn away from the window and press my back against the wall just to the side of the casing. Tipping my head back, I bang it ever so slightly against the plaster. My hand is a sticky mess, and I'm breathing so loud, it's like I'm announcing I've run a 5K in under ten minutes.

Rolling my shoulder against the wall, I tilt my head only enough to peer back into the yard once again.

Did that really happen?

Unfortunately, there's no mistaking what I hold in my hand and what covers my fingers. I'm guilty regardless, and then I see a form just outside the sliding glass doors next door. The whiteness of the dress gives her away despite the dark night, and for the briefest second, I wonder if Ben sent her to me again on the night his cryptic message was given to me.

Just as quickly, I dismiss the thought, not believing in such voodoo or diddle-le-do or love—flying, falling, or otherwise.

3

[Zack]

The following day, I'm in a mood and determined not to think about my mysterious, sexy neighbor or Ben's message as I stare out the window of my bedroom in the early morning hours. *Was he kidding me?* Ben knew Jeanine and I were never lovers but a moment of insta-lust. A one-night stand led to two babies nine months later. We hardly even liked one another after we were married, and sex was a rarity of treating one another as an available vessel more than a passionate partner. I'm too busy to fall in love—*or fly in it*—and now I'm even busier with two rambunctious boys.

Today, the guys—three of the four points in our compass—have plans to go golfing. We invited Calvin and Bryce to join us even though it won't be the same with the younger set instead of their father. Mason will need to be on his best behavior, but he's been living here for a year, so I'm hoping that means either he's tampered his inappropriate comments around the teens, or they've come to accept his reckless behavior.

Either way, I'm looking into the yard next door once more. I can't seem to pull my eyes away from the house at this angle where I can see the old tree fort and recall all the games played back there. Images fill my head of being chased by my brother, hitting golf balls off the cliff with my father, and helping my mother in her garden.

Movement in the yard catches my eye.

It's her. River. Or at least the woman who has haunted my thoughts since the night of Ben's funeral. Is she an angel or a demon sent to torture me like she did last night? Then again, who can I blame but myself? I didn't look away. I didn't stop myself, and I'm actually angry when it isn't exactly her fault.

With bright golden hair that glistens in the sunlight, whoever she is, she's the woman I feel a strange magnetism toward. Once again, she's covered from her neck to her feet in a long, flowing dress. Then she does the damnedest thing. She removes the dress and lays on the chaise lounge in nothing but her skimpy panties. She might as well be naked. With her hair spread out around her head, her toned body and ample breasts are on display, and I'm instantly hard as a fucking rock.

My hand grips the window casing like I did last night. My fingers dig into the wood as I take a shaky breath. I'm paralyzed by the sight of her, or maybe I'm just desperately horny.

"What are we looking at?" Logan's voice at my ear should startle me, and it does, but I still can't pull my eyes from the glorious sight.

"Her," I croak like a pre-pubescent teen.

"Dude," Logan mutters beside me. Reaching into his shorts, he pulls out his phone.

"Don't take a picture," I snap, turning my head to him.

"I'm not taking a picture. I'm not even looking, but Mason has to see this. He's missing out." Logan's fingers move fast over the screen, and I can almost here him telling Mason to haul ass up here.

"Don't call Mason," I snap, reaching for Logan's phone. Swiping it quickly out of his hand, I glare down at the device, but the message has already been sent. Within seconds, we hear Mason thundering up the staircase.

"Fuck," I hiss, not wanting Mason to see the naked beauty in the neighbor's yard. Angel or demon, she's *my* angel or demon, and I don't want to share her with them. For the briefest second, I have that strange thought again that Ben sent her to me. Quickly, I shake the notion and turn toward the door, prepared to intervene when Mason enters the room.

He hardly crosses the threshold when Logan announces, "Dude, you need to see this."

Body primed with legs spread and hands on my hips, I'm determined to block Mason's view, and I twist my head in Logan's direction where he's staring out the window. "I thought you said you weren't going to look."

"I'm not. I'm just checking out the shrubbery." He chuckles as Mason passes me.

"Fuck," Mason groans. "Nice shrubbery."

L.B. Dunbar

"Don't fucking look at her shrubbery," I snap, racing up behind my friends and squeezing myself between them, equally ensnared by the *shrubbery* of the neighbor.

"But she has nice bushes," Mason states, his eyes glued to the yard next door. Logan snorts.

"Quit looking at her bush," I demand, and Logan starts to lose it, his laughter loud and vibrating.

Mason keeps a straight face as he says, "Her trimming is exceptional."

"You can't even—" I stop. The heat in my face counteracts the chill up my spine. She's removed her skimpy panties, leaving nothing to the imagination. So Mason and Logan *can* fully inspect her landscaping technique.

A hand of mine shoots out in front of each of them, covering their eyes as if they were my seven-year-olds.

"Daddy, why can't I looky?" Mason pouts while Logan continues to guffaw next to me.

"We are not looking," I state as my eyes return to the naked vision, glistening in all her glory in the sunshine.

"What aren't we looking at?" Calvin's teenage voice comes from behind us, and all three of us turn in unison.

"Nothing," we choke out in various pitches.

"Is River naked again?" Calvin questions without a hint of chagrin.

"How do you know the neighbor is naked?" Mason questions. His tone sobers a bit.

"We're only allowed to landscape her on certain days."

Logan coughs into his fist, unable to contain himself while Mason slowly grins.

"What do you mean you have certain days you can landscape her?" I bark, my voice cracking as though I'm the teenager in the room.

Calvin shrugs. "We trim her bushes." Logan completely loses it, bending forward at the waist and choking on laughter while Mason chuckles, shaking his head. A moment of pride crosses his face, and then his expression straightens.

The clarification reminds me that Calvin works for his late father's local landscaping company. Ben inherited this one from his father while he had his own in Chicago, where he and Anna had lived since they married.

"And you know she's naked how?" Mason states, his voice sounding a bit authoritative, which surprises me. Looking over at him, I'm dumbfounded at his demeanor. He looks upset, but he can't be serious. He was just gawking out the window at her like the rest of us.

"She told us." Calvin speaks in the *well, duh* manner only teens have mastered, ranking right up there with the word *whatever*. Thankfully, I don't have direct experience with this attitude as my boys are young, but I'm certain they'll be perfecting that tone and enunciation before they reach ten. Such overachievers.

"She didn't want us to accidentally show up when she was sunbathing," Calvin clarifies.

"Sunbathing?" I choke. She certainly looks like she's bathing, all glistened up and in the nude while soaking up the sun's rays and absorbing the heat on her skin. My skin feels equally hot, and I want to slippery slide all over hers. A shaky hand comes to the bridge of my nose, pinching it. I close my eyes a second.

"Okay. Are we golfing or what?" I demand, my voice sharper than normal.

"Golfing," Calvin mutters, spinning on his heels and leaving my room.

"I wonder what kind of landscaping they have on the course," Logan begins, placing a hand on my shoulder and squeezing it. "Because you, my friend, are in a serious need of a hole in one."

It's Mason's turn to laugh out loud, and he high-fives Logan over my head.

Sometimes, I hate these two.

4

[River]

"What's going on here?" The rough masculine voice startles me from my position kneeling beside the flower beds along the side of my yard. When I moved in, the run-down house was in need of a good cleaning, but the yard was worse. It's been a labor of love to get the outside under control. My goal is to restore these gardens to their original glory.

My hands are covered in dirt as I twist at the waist and face a grumpy, growly gorgeous man. Dressed in khaki shorts and an untucked pink dress shirt, he looks uptight for someone wearing such semi-casual attire.

"Hello," I say, ignoring his rude tone and offering a bright smile. *Kindness soothes the toughest moods*, my grandfather would say. Standing, I brush at the mix of grass and soil caked on my knees. My hands are hopelessly dirty, nearly black. Holding them up palm out suggests I'd reach out to shake his hand, but it's probably not a good idea. What's also not good is how this yummy man is glaring at me. His eyes roam my body before drifting to the two boys up in the tree fort, and it gives me a moment to observe him.

His hair is dirty blond and a bit longer on the top than the sides. His cheekbones are edgy cliffs, and his light eyes are hard. A bit of shadow covers his jaw, accentuating a lush mouth that could dazzle if he smiled. He's not dazzling at the moment, though. He's scowling.

"I assume these two belong to you." Keeping my voice light, cheery even, I nod toward the tree fort. I offer another smile before turning to face the boys who have climbed the rickety wood ladder and found their way into the tree fort in one of the solid old maples. Uncertain who they were at first, how they wandered into the yard, or where they belonged, I decided to hang outside to keep an eye on them. They weren't easily deterred from leaving the tree fort that didn't belong to them, but they eventually told me their names. They said they were on vacation next door, and their dad knew where they were. If I thought it strange that a man would let his two boys wander uninvited into my yard, I let it pass. They weren't causing any harm, and it was nice to see little ones enjoying that ancient platform in the tree.

"Get down from there," the man snaps at the boys, causing me to flinch before he turns back to me. Another scowl instantly forms on his sculpted cheeks. "They shouldn't be up there. It isn't safe."

He's probably right, but I've been up there myself in the past year, and it held me. Those boys can't weigh more than a hundred pounds collectively. Plus, I don't know why he's angry with me. His boys wandered into *my* yard.

"They haven't been a bother," I remark, still keeping a smile plastered on my face.

"That's not the point." His sharp retort startles me, and my kindness meter wavers. I'm used to grumps, those who overreact, and overall grouchy people, but I normally have a handle on *why* someone is this way before they give me attitude like this stranger is giving me. Have we met before? What am I missing here?

"What *is* your point?" I teasingly demand, placing my hands on my hips and cocking one to the side. I do not like his tone, nor do I appreciate the way he's glaring at me as if I did something wrong. Still, my smile only falters a little bit. "Are those your boys or not?"

"They aren't yours," he barks with an implication I'm not liking. His eyes are fixated on me for the blink of an eye. Literally, he blinks and looks away, scowling even harder as he growls again. "Trevor. Oliver. Get down here."

"What's the problem?" His surly tone toward his boys concerns me, and so does the glare he returns to me. Is there something on my face? Dirt smudged everywhere shouldn't be enough to disgust him. It's obvious I'm gardening. Then I take another sweep of his body. His impeccably pressed shirt suggests he's never done a day of hard work in his life. A little dirt on his face might do him wonders. He might even smile.

"The problem?" Hothead snaps. "Do you always let little boys play in your yard?"

L.B. Dunbar

I realize it might seem strange to let two little boys play in my backyard when I don't know them, but *they* wandered here. It's not like I lured them in. They were enjoying themselves, and I rarely hear such easy banter and innocent laughter from children. Normally, it's hard-pressed and not easily earned in my line of work. The sound of children laughing has a priceless value. Staring at his spiffy clothing, I'm not certain this dad appreciates the gift he has in two healthy children scampering in a tree fort. Plus, if these are his boys, he's the one who lost them.

"Just what are you suggesting? I thought I was being nice, helpful even. It's only next door. It's not like they wandered out to the street or down to the lake. It's not like I've told them to get lost. I kept them safely within eyesight."

Admittedly, other than friendly waves and brief words, I don't *know* my neighbors. I'm aware someone recently died as I saw the black attire and endless visitors. I hate how familiar I've become with such clothing and gatherings. The only person I've officially met next door is Mason, who lives over the garage. One day, he felt the need to introduce himself. His words, not mine. *Just being a friendly neighbor*, he flirted with a blinding smile. He's too good-looking for his own good and has player written all over him, but he was harmless enough.

Hot Daddy swipes a hand through his hair in frustration and glances away from me for a moment.

"I'm sorry." He blows out a breath in exasperation and lowers his voice. "They're . . . a handful."

My brows lift, surprised at his assessment. The boys have been a joy. When I first heard small voices in the yard, I thought I was losing my mind because I didn't see them right away. I hadn't thought to look up, but instead gazed out across the lawn leading to the cliff's edge. When I finally glanced toward the tree, my first concern equaled their father's. It wasn't safe up there, but I'd been on the platform myself, and the second I heard their laughter, my worry eased. I came outside to introduce myself and learn who they were. Admittedly, I did hesitate, wondering how they'd entered the yard and if a parent really did know where they were. While I wasn't opposed to bribing, I wasn't about to give candy to a stranger's children to coax them out of the fort. Plus, they were playing, using their imagination, enjoying the outdoors. It was a marvel and a rare commodity among the children I knew.

Eventually, curiosity must have gotten the best of them because the slightly smaller of the two wandered down to me, asking if he could help. Pulling weeds can be tricky business, but I love the satisfaction of a clean flower bed and didn't mind getting my hands dirty. Oliver was a little thinner than his brother, and between that and his eye color, it was the only way to tell the two apart. He was so sweet in the way he hesitated as he asked me, almost as if he was afraid to offer or suggest *he* might help *me*. Quickly, the boys got carried away, tugging anything and everything green, so I suggested they return to the fort, calling it a ship— a pirate ship. I told them the weeds were treasures I was handpicking, and I needed them to look out for potential invaders who might want my bounty.

"They've been very helpful." I smile at the boys who have stopped playing to watch us from their perch in the tree. Their father immediately snorts in disbelief. His forehead furrows, and he breaks into a strangled laugh while he scrubs at his head. His entire face shifts, hinting at the potential to dazzle. My lips slowly grin at him.

"I'm River, by the way."

"I know." His tone lowers, and the sudden shock in me cannot be masked. While my shoulders fall a little, I keep a smile plastered on my face. I don't want to ask how he knows my name. The rumors don't bother me. I know the truth, and it's nobody else's business.

Straightening my back, I continue the forced grin. "Well. Trevor and Oliver are welcome over here anytime I'm in the yard. It's a treat to have little people use that fort." I don't have children, and I don't consider Quincy's grandchildren mine either, so having little ones around to use what might have once been a beloved play space warms my heart.

"Just keep your clothes on." His direct tone and abrupt words startle me.

"Pardon me?" I blink in surprise, wondering why he's returned to such a sharp tone.

L.B. Dunbar

"Your clothes. Keep them on."

My mouth falls open, but he points up at the second-floor window facing my yard from the side of the house next door, and I instantly understand his meaning. I've never seen the light on in that room, and most of the time, the blinds are lowered, so I didn't think the space was used.

"Have you been spying on me?" My voice drops all pretense of friendliness, my tone incredulous. My hands fist at my side.

"It was an accident." Not a drop of contrition marks his voice.

"You *accidentally* saw me in my own yard?" *Naked*, I don't add.

"Well, it's not like the room faces another direction." His answer is doubtful. The position of that corner room suggests it most likely has a window facing the lake. *Look in that direction, pervert.* Not to mention, if he's a father, there must be a mother somewhere, which means he shouldn't be checking me out. I cross my arms as if it hides what he's already seen. His gaze drops to my breasts. Wearing a tank top, I'm certain the thin cotton is streaked with perspiration and dirt. Folding my arms only seems to accentuate my chest, and his glare intensifies for a second before he quickly shifts his gaze to the left and growls out the boys' names once more.

"Trevor. Oliver. Now."

It isn't my place to question how people parent their children, and I've heard tones of frustration, anger, and grief, but this man's growl doesn't sound like any of those emotions. He sounds like he's being strangled or tortured, and once again, I can't imagine what I've done to him. Our exchange has only been a few minutes at the most.

"Are they really yours?" The juxtaposition between those squirrelly, active boys and the man digging fists into his pockets as though he's trying to hold back from I don't know what isn't meshing in my head. Then again, I'm not a stranger to parents and children who appear in opposition. Appearances can be deceiving. I know firsthand about passing judgment without explanation. It's happened to me.

"Yes," he hisses. His jaw clenches. His eyes narrow. It's time for him to leave my yard.

As the boys haven't responded to their father's demanding call, I address them. "Trevor. Oliver. Sweets, come down please. Your daddy says it's time to go."

"Do we have to?" Trevor whines. He's been the alpha of the two, encouraging his brother to take risks and follow his lead. His whining is addressed to his father, but I interject.

"Remember what I said." My voice remains softer with the boy as I remind him of the promise I made his brother and him. "You can visit the tree fort anytime, but when time is up, it's up. No complaining." Trevor's little shoulders fall in defeat. It's hard to face disappointment in a child. I've seen it too often lately. It's been nice to see the tree fort get some use.

"Okay, Miss River," Oliver offers, scooting himself off the platform to the ladder. "How did you do that?" Their father's voice isn't more than a whisper. He's completely baffled by how easily the boys acquiesced, and I'm puzzled by his reaction. I watch as the twins sullenly stalk toward their father, whose gaze remains on me before his irritation zeroes in on them. "I wish they'd listen to me like that."

The words are so quiet I'm not certain I've heard him correctly.

"Back to the house," he suddenly demands with a gentle nudge in the direction of next door. As soon as they take a step away, he stops them each with a hand on their shoulders and pivots their little bodies toward me. The poor boys are so confused. "What do you say?"

"Thank you for having us," Oliver says.

"Thank you, Miss River," Trevor adds.

"Or Mrs. . . ." Hot Dad pauses. His expression shifts, returning to that puzzled glare.

"Miss River will do." Squatting so I'm at the boys' level, I continue to speak to them. "And it was my pleasure having both of you here. Remember, anytime as long as Dad here approves." I wink at them, hoping they know I'm not upset with them when clearly Grumpy Daddy is. To my surprise, he strokes a hand down Oliver's hair and squeezes the back of his neck, softening his expression as well as his touch. The boys then turn on their own, and with slumped shoulders, they walk to the side of my house and disappear around the corner.

L.B. Dunbar

I stand, crossing my arms while I watch the boys exit my yard. "I'm sorry, I still didn't get your name." I point at their father before tapping my chin.

"Mr. Weller will do." His formal retort is another strike against him. He's so uptight and a shit dad judging by first impressions, and while I shouldn't be judging, I am.

"When did the fence go in?" The question surprises me, and I gaze at the fence behind him. I'm assuming he means the metal chain link dividing this property from the one next door. As I haven't lived here for very long, I have no idea.

"I don't know."

He nods once as if he doesn't like my answer. "How did they get over here?" He questions next as if I know that answer any more than I can answer about the fence. One minute, I'm in the kitchen cleaning up after my breakfast, and the next, I look out the window to see two little beings in the tree fort.

"Shouldn't that be my question?" I pause, taking him in once more. Too bad he's hot and a dad. "Maybe, just maybe, rather than casting a stone at me for allowing them into my yard, you should examine how they got away from you in the first place." *Or why?*

His expression is more than shock. He looks like I punched him in the stomach. Slowly, his face morphs, cheeks drawing edgier, eyes shifting darker.

"They're my children. I'll worry about them, thank you." Sarcasm does not suit his pretty face.

"You do that," I remark.

"I will." His hands slip into his khaki shorts.

"Fine," I hiss.

"Fine," he snaps. We remain at this impasse. He should be leaving, yet he isn't moving. His eyes spear mine, digging deep into them. The stare is a bit unnerving, but I don't try to evaluate it as I just want him out of my yard.

"Well?" I question, arching a brow and wondering what he's still doing here.

"Right," he mumbles, swiping a hand through that sandy hair. He shakes his head, tugging his gaze from me. Turning, he gives me his back, and I note the snug fit of his dress shirt across his shoulders and the firm muscles of his calves as he stalks to the side of my house.

"And it's my yard, so I'll worry about keeping my clothes on or not."

He stops in his tracks. Somehow, that sounded better in my head. I should be warning him to keep his eyes to himself. He shouldn't be watching me in my yard. That's just creepy. However, I'm a little bit flattered. Did he like what he saw? Quickly, I dismiss the thought. He shouldn't be looking over here, especially if he's married *and* has children.

He spins to face me and takes two steps back toward me. "Keep your clothes on," he hisses, his voice dropping to the harsh tone he used with his children. Jeez, *chillax*.

"Keep your eyes off me." I take two steps toward him and don't miss his gaze sweeping down my body. It's the kind of glance that suggests he likes what he sees. He bites his lower lip and holds the pose, and a shiver ripples up my middle. A good kind of shiver that hints I might like his eyes on me. Then I want to kick myself for such thoughts.

He's probably married, I warn myself.

"The window faces this direction," he reminds me, his voice dropping, released from the growl but definitely an exasperated groan.

"Whatever makes you feel better," I snark, but I've lost a little of my own bite. Suddenly, I'm feeling a bit defenseless against this man when I'm typically good at holding my own with disgruntled parents.

"You . . ." He stops, clenches his jaw, and fights against whatever he planned to say. He turns away from me, fists at his sides, and stalks around the side of my house.

Good riddance, Grumpy Dad. But suddenly, without explanation, I'm a little disappointed to see him leave.

5

[River]

That night, I enjoy a glass of wine in the summer breeze of my backyard. Other than the low glow of light streaming through the kitchen window, the yard is submerged in darkness. I don't need a nosy neighbor spying on me, even if I have my clothes on.

Unfortunately, I can't seem to shake this morning's altercation with said neighbor. Arrogant. Insufferable. Uptight. He's everything I'd never want in a man. In my profession, I've encountered quite a few like him. The doctors I work with can be jerks. Even patients can act uppity, but when people are sick and vulnerable, their attitudes shift. Eventually, they become apologetic and forgivable.

Quincy had been like that. He'd been such a beast with everyone but me.

Lifting the glass to my lips, I sip the sweet flavor of a Michigan favorite. As I drink, my eyes drift upward to the second-floor window facing my yard from the house next door. I haven't given much thought to that home, as I mainly keep to myself. There are a couple teenage boys over there and a little girl. A couple plus Mason. I don't understand the dynamic, but I don't need to. I've seen people come and go over there in the year I've lived here, and what a year it's been.

Slowly, I take another sip of wine, swallowing the rich berry flavor as I stare at the dark window. *Is he up there? Is he watching me?* I'm confident he can't see me as the yard is dark. I don't have the outside lamps on, but a single light inside illuminates the kitchen. The gleam through the window highlights only the patio.

As I sit in the chaise lounge in the center of the dark yard, I'm wearing a summer maxi dress that falls to my ankles, but it's wrapped over my legs like a blanket this evening. *Perfectly covered*, I snark in my head. With my eyes lifted, the bushes rustle, and I turn in the direction of the lake, assuming the noise is a nocturnal animal. I close my lids and allow the breeze off the water to caress my face. I love this location, and I love this house even though it needs so much work.

Quincy had let aspects of the house fall into disrepair. He'd hardly visited the place because he'd used it as a rental property. Most of the inside is outdated, but the yard has been my first priority.

When I turn away from the lake, a figure stands near the corner of my house. My breath hitches, and I nearly drop my glass of wine. Sitting upright, I stare at the outline of someone lingering just beyond the glow of the kitchen light.

"It's only me."

"Mr. Weller?" I question, although I'm already certain it's him. The masculine tenor shouldn't be recognizable after only one meeting, but it is. My heart races, and I chalk it up to being startled and not the fact he's such an attractive man. As he steps into the light, he wears another button-up in white, this time along with dark jeans. Flip-flops are on his feet, and it dismantles the stick-up-his-ass appearance of him just a little bit.

"It's Zack, actually," he corrects.

"Are you lost?" Balancing the glass of wine on top of my bent knees, I sit on the chaise lounge, recalling the question I asked his boys earlier. Their immediate response was to ask me if I was.

All who wander are not lost. Sometimes those who stand still are.

"I just . . . I wanted to apologize for earlier." He scratches the back of his neck as he speaks. The apology comes as a surprise. Leaning back on the lounger, I take another sip of my wine, eyeing him over the rim. Zack doesn't move.

"And what exactly are you apologizing for?"

He swipes a hand through his hair while the other slips into his pocket.

"A few things." When he still doesn't move, I wave a hand, suggesting he take a seat. Two upright outdoor chairs sit near the foot of the lounger.

"That's an interesting seat." He nods at the chaise as he approaches. Running a hand over the cushion, I smile to myself. The old chaise lounge cushion is one of the first things I replaced in this yard. New fabric and a quick stain job to the wood base brightened up this little slice of heaven. Made for more than one person, it's not quite big enough for two.

"I call it a person-and-a-half lounger." Tipping my head back, I look up at the star-filled sky and close my eyes, luxuriating in the space on this thing. When I open my eyes, Zack has moved to the foot of the expanded seat.

"Want to try it?" I pat the space next to me before realizing what I've said. I don't know this man. He insulted me in more ways than one this morning, and he's probably married. Yet as he climbs onto the seat beside me, he looks as vulnerable as his children. Tension rolls off him in waves so strong I'm surprised I'm not forced off the chaise. And I'm reconsidering the invitation as our arms press against one another.

"Would you like a glass of wine?" I offer, holding up mine. The bottle sits beside me on the grass, and I'll need to retrieve a glass for him from the house. Without a word, Zack boldly takes my glass from me and sips. *I see where his children have learned their sense of propriety and manners.*

He tips his head back and closes his eyes to the dark sky overhead. Releasing a deep sigh, he relaxes only slightly.

"That was my glass," I mutter, directing my gaze forward toward the dark yard.

"Oh, I thought we were sharing." A tease that wasn't present in our first meeting laces his tone.

"Wine stealer," I mumble, and his head sharply turns in my direction. Side-eyeing him, I notice his eyes narrow at the side of my face.

"So, what are you apologizing for again?" I need to understand better what he's doing here, and I give in to the pull to look at him.

"I came off a little strong earlier, and I'm sorry. The boys . . . they elude me sometimes. I'm a terrible father."

The words almost break me as they're said with such honesty and regret. Perhaps he needs to apologize to them for being so harsh.

"Why would you say such a thing?"

"So many reasons." He gazes forward, staring off toward the house next door.

"You're full of vagueness," I tease, bumping his shoulder with mine as we remain so close to one another.

"I'm just not a very involved dad, I guess, and now, I have them full time."

The wording surprises me. "Are you divorced?" *Please be divorced and not a widower.* I can't handle if both of us are struggling with the eternal loss of someone.

"Recently divorced. Does it show?" He turns his attention back to me, and we gaze at one another. Our faces are close. Our noses could touch. His eyes are more of a silver color than the dark molten appearance of earlier. It's a strange combination with his lighter hair but striking like the rest of him.

"Divorce looks good on you," I flirt. Although I shouldn't be flirting. *You're so forward*, my mother would say. *Honesty never hurt anyone*, my grandfather would correct. Zack's eyes sparkle a bit in the dim light cloaking our dark location.

"I wasn't a very good husband either." His eyes shift away from me, and I clear my throat. Not flirting. *No to flirting.*

"I'm sorry. You loved her?" A question lingers with my desire for clarification.

"I didn't." He tips his head forward, swirling the glass of wine in his hand.

"Ah." I nod to accept his answer. While it stings to think he didn't love his wife, maybe she didn't love him either, and that was the reason for his melancholy tone. There's always more to the story.

"I also wanted to apologize for noticing you sitting in the sun . . . you know." He side-eyes me without turning his head.

"Naked?" I teasingly clarify for him, and he closes his lids.

"I really didn't mean to look."

"Your eyes just accidentally wandered," I jest, tipping up a brow while keeping my tone light.

He huffs in answer, and I consider he's sincere enough. I actually blush as though he'd caught me in a compromising position, which he did in a sense, but I'm not ashamed of my body. Also, it's my yard. Assuming I am well protected by the overgrown shrubbery around the place, I have the liberty to do as I please over here. A solid wall of arborvitae lines the south side of the property, marking the boundary between where he's staying and where I live. An ugly metal fence is on my side of the trees. Behind us is a solid six-foot wooden barrier built by my other neighbor. It clearly says to stay out.

"I accept your apology," I say, reaching out to pat his thigh. Instantly, I realize what I'm doing and withdraw my hand, but he catches it and crushes my fingers a moment. Then he flattens his palm over the back of my hand and presses it to his thigh. A magnetic tension crackles between us, but I can't seem to pull away. Heat seeps through his jeans and warms my skin. His fingers wrap around my hand, which is high on his leg, just to the side of his zipper region. My pinky twitches, and I faintly brush a sensitive area, feeling something I shouldn't beneath the denim. I jerk my hand underneath his, but Zack tightens his hold and takes another sip from my wineglass.

It's all rather forward, considering his earlier demeanor, but I can't find the warning that should be in my head, telling me to pull away from him.

We relax in silence a while, soaking up the quietness of the dark evening. The breeze from the lake rustling the leaves on the trees is a natural soundtrack that soothes the soul. I reach for the bottle of wine on the grass and take a pull directly from it. Then I refill the glass Zack still holds.

"Thanks." He doesn't bat an eye at my drinking from the bottle but takes another sip from the wineglass he stole from me. "How long have you lived here?" His eyes focus on the back of my house.

"Not long. I inherited the place."

"Really?" His attention shifts from the house to me. Our shoulders touch. Our forearms cross. Our hands are still together against his thigh. It's an intimate position, considering he's a stranger, but he isn't flinching. "Care to clarify."

It's a strange request from a man who baffles me. "My husband died." It wasn't entirely the truth, but it's the best explanation I'm willing to give a man I don't know. His eyes lower for my left hand, finding it absent of a ring.

"Oh," Zack whispers, pausing on the sound. "I'm sorry for your loss." He waits another beat before repeating my words. "You loved him."

My shoulders sag. "In my own way, yes. I'll always be grateful to him, but I suppose gratitude and love are not the same things." I glance back at the house. A year ago, I felt selfish for accepting the offer left to me. It didn't seem right. Being a decent human being didn't warrant this kind of gift. But Quincy's children are assholes. They never came to visit him and didn't communicate with their father. They didn't want to listen. Then they showed up like vultures ready to devour his estate once he passed.

"One of my best friends died a month ago."

Quickly, I turn back to Zack. This loss is different than losing his wife. Heartbreak fills his tone. My grandfather had been one of my best friends, and I lost him, so I understood the tear through Zack's heart.

He juts his head in the direction of the house next door.

"I haven't met them yet," I say, speaking of my neighbors. We wave or smile, but we haven't officially introduced ourselves. I stare at the side of the house, cloaked in darkness. "I'm so sorry." Assuming his friend was his age, his friend's young death feels even sadder. At least, Quincy had lived a long life.

Zack's gaze returns to the side of my face, but I don't look back at him. Instead, I lift the bottle of wine I've been holding on my lap and take another hearty drink.

"What's it like inside?" Assuming the direction of his question, I glance back at my house.

"In need of TLC, like a lot of things." The comment turns my head toward him. He could potentially use a little rebuilding, though it's not his body but his spirit that needs restoration. Or is it rejuvenation? His voice hints at the disappointment in himself in both fatherhood and marriage. It explains a lot about his behavior earlier in the day.

As we face one another, his attention drops to my lips.

"I have another confession to make." His gaze remains on my mouth, and I lick my lips, watching those silvery eyes flicker. "I saw you in this yard another time."

"Really?" My voice rises in wonder. What could he have possibly seen? Thankfully, he doesn't have creeper written all over him, but isn't that the way serial killers attract their victims? Charisma and good looks are a smokescreen for bad men.

"I saw another *something* I probably shouldn't have seen."

My heart skips a beat, and a nervous sweat breaks out on my palms, although I'm not fully comprehending what he suggests. My mind races through a mental calendar, counting back the days, wondering what I could have been doing in my yard to cause his voice to drop in both confession and contrition.

"You were out here. Alone on this person-and-a-half lounger. Alone," he repeats as his brow arches, hinting further at what he saw. It takes me a moment to catch his meaning. Oh. *Oh.* My cheeks flame, and I'm thankful for the dark night around us. That was a few nights ago, and I'd had the evening off. It was just one of those nights. I might have had a bit too much wine, watched an exhilarating movie, and the breeze just felt too good against my warm skin. I never expected someone to see me, but I remember sensing something watching me—which I now know was someone—and stopped what I'd started. Later, I'd been unable to pick back up where I'd left off in the yard.

I tug at my hand under Zack's firm grip, embarrassed that he saw me, but he isn't releasing me.

"You don't need to be embarrassed," he suggests, dropping his tone even further. His gaze doesn't leave my lips.

I don't have a good explanation for doing what I was doing in the yard, so I blurt out a different thought. "It was better than having a one-night stand." I have no idea why I say such a thing. It sounded better in my head. It's the truth, though. I'm not really a one-night stand kind of woman, and despite my occasional horniness, I'm not one to pick up a random man in a bar to get myself off. I'm well past those days.

Zack huffs before stating, "I had one of those and ended up with a wife and twins." I want to know more about this story, but he asks me something instead.

"Why?" His expression has lost some of the edginess from earlier. His curiosity softens his features. He's on the verge of dazzling.

"Why what?"

"Why alone?" His gaze roams my face. "You're a beautiful woman. Why wasn't a man out here pleasing you?" He's so forward. Just like his boys. Just like him stealing my wine.

I shrug, and my shoulder brushes his. How do I explain that I haven't dated in so long I can't remember when my last date was? How do I describe the relationship I had with Quincy or, rather, didn't have? How do I tell him it's better to be alone?

"I wanted to join you," Zack admits, and my mouth falls open.

"What?" I croak, my throat suddenly dry.

"Never mind." Zack glances down at our hands, where his thumb caresses my knuckles. When he lifts his gaze, our eyes lock, and the magnetic sensation returns. Warning bells go off as I'm drawn to him when I should pull away. Licking my lower lip, I watch as his gaze drops to the movement of my tongue. He mimics the motion with his own against the lower swell of his mouth, and then he bites his lip hard, holding his teeth against the sensitive flesh. The smirk sends a thrill down my middle, and I squeeze my thighs. The responding tingle feels similar to the rush before . . .

"You should really stop spying on my yard," I whisper, my voice raspy and rough.

"I don't think I could stop if I tried," he admits, still focusing on my mouth. I lick my lips again. The silence between us grows heavy, like a warm blanket around us. A light breeze whispers through the air. The trees seem to echo my thoughts. *Kiss me.*

Suddenly, Zack shifts. He slips my hand off his thigh, resting it in the barely-there space between us, and releases it. He lifts the wineglass and finishes the remainder in one long swallow. I roll to my back, not having noticed I'd shifted to my shoulder, mirroring his position of facing me.

"Thanks for the wine." He holds out the glass like I'm waitstaff sent to do his bidding. Then he surprises me by pressing a kiss to my shoulder.

"Keep your clothes on," he teasingly warns while a touch of that edgy tone from earlier returns.

"Close your blinds," I advise, coyly narrowing my eyes at him.

"Not a chance." He presses off the chaise and stands. Without a glance back from him, I shamelessly check out his ass while he retreats, and my girly parts dance with thoughts of him seeing me naked in other places than my backyard.

6

[Zack]

I'm a man who hardly sleeps. Every minute is money to me when it comes to my attorney practice and the development of Four Points. Money hadn't always been a concern until I was a teen. Then every dime mattered. So, I'm up until three in the morning or waking at that time to get in a day's worth of work before a day of play, even when I'm on vacation.

It's only been twelve minutes since my boys snuck into River's backyard again, and I had to retrieve them as she wasn't home. They've just finished telling me how they found a loose piece of fencing behind Anna's garage and slipped through the metal chain link to enter the neighbor's yard.

"We were searching for Narnia," Trevor states.

I don't even know what that means until Mila clarifies. "Those kids went through a wardrobe, not a fence."

What are we talking about? "Who went through a wardrobe?" I ask. Anna made breakfast for our crew, and we linger around the kitchen island and the small dining table in front of a large bay window near the sitting area. Pancakes on a Monday morning feel like heaven.

"The kids searching for Narnia," Mila explains. Swiping a hand through my hair, I look at Anna for help. She's putting away dishes that Mason has washed.

"It's a book. *The Lion, the Witch, and the Wardrobe.*" Anna tips a brow at me as if I should know this story. I vaguely remember a movie about such a thing when I was in my twenties.

"How do you know about Narnia?" I ask Trevor.

"Alexa read us the book."

"Does he mean a nanny or the machine?" Mason asks, tipping up a brow, and sadly, I have no idea. The guilt of my ability as a father is layered thicker and thicker.

"So what's today's plan?" I interject, wondering if Anna would like some solitude instead of our crew's constant chaos. Mason's been surprisingly quiet while a shadow to Anna's every movement. He does the dishes. He picks up things. He acts before being asked.

Our friend is a manwhore to the extreme, but his domestic support has been interesting to watch. He was here when Ben needed to be driven to appointments and eventually bathed or positioned. I honestly don't know how Mason did it.

When I'd met Ben, he was the lawn boy. His father owned the local landscaping company, and Mr. Kulis worked on our yard as well as Anna's next door. That's how Anna eventually met Ben, and the rest is history even though it wasn't that simple. Think princess and servant, and that's the way I judged him until I had my own fall from grace. Ben was one of the first to accept me when others didn't know how to react to what happened to my family. When most people shunned us. As Anna was my friend first, Ben became my friend by default until true friendship took over, and I've always regretted thinking less of Ben before getting to know him.

He never judged me, and I deserved judgment, especially when it came to River.

I can't believe I admitted to watching her and swipe a hand down my face to calm thoughts of her touching herself, pleasing herself in that damn person-and-a-half lounger. I haven't been able to stop thinking about her—again—and when I sat beside her on that same chaise lounge, rubbing arms, holding her hand . . . I am a mess of unfamiliar desire.

"Hot flash?" Mason teases when he sees the sudden dull red flush heating my face.

"Something like that," I snap, harsher than necessary. "What's on the agenda again?"

Mason tips his head, but he can't read me. I'm an enigma to him as I married my one-night stand when I got her pregnant. Even Mason didn't offer to marry Samantha when he got her pregnant, and they'd been friends with benefits for a year before it happened. I'd made a promise to myself, though. I'd always be present for my children, even if it meant taking a wife I didn't love. I'd been loyal to her as well.

"Beach day," Mason comments.

"We don't want to go to the beach. We want to go to Miss River's," Trevor interjects. My boys have been on the floor playing with Legos.

"Miss River?" Anna asks, her head popping up from something she's reading set on the countertop.

"Your neighbor."

"Oh. I feel so bad I haven't had a chance to really meet her." Hearing her reminder recalls something River said last night. She's lost her husband. Anna and River have something in common, and Anna could use a friend outside of our group. Someone who relates to her loss on a different level than we do as Ben's guy friends.

"You should introduce yourself. I think you'd have a lot in common." The moment I suggest it, Mason glares at me, and I realize my mistake.

"What do you mean?" Anna questions, tilting her head.

"Umm. . ." Mason shakes his head at me, and I'm wondering once more how much he knows about the naked neighbor. He said he doesn't have carnal knowledge of her body, but that doesn't mean he hasn't tried. Flirted with her. Attempted to charm her. "I just think you might be friends."

Anna gives me a quizzical look before Mason interjects, "Beach time."

Oliver groans.

"What did Miss River say about that tree fort," I remind my boys.

"The boys were in her tree fort?" For some reason, Mason made that sound sexual, and I want to throat punch him.

"She said we could come over anytime we wanted," Trevor states, but that isn't true.

"Really?" I say, finding myself on the verge of arguing with a seven-year-old.

"She said we could come over whenever she's in her yard," Trevor clarifies.

Mason coughs, and I catch his eye. He has the same thought as me—naked River in her backyard. "Maybe Daddy wants to play in

River's tree fort." Mason wiggles his brows, and I narrow my eyes at him.

"Yeah, Dad, you could play, too," Oliver says.

"I'm not playing in River's tree fort," I snap, glaring at Mason before turning to see my son crestfallen by my tone. *Fuck*. Swiping a hand through my hair, I address my slightly sensitive son.

"Ollie, we need to respect that the tree fort belongs to Miss River. We can't just go into her yard without an invitation."

"Yeah, Ollie, you can't just barge into her tree fort. You need to ease into it," Mason adds, and Anna's head pops up, narrowing her eyes at the man beside her. She hasn't missed the drop in his voice or the salacious addition. Glancing over at me, I shake my head, suggesting she ignore Mason.

"Plus, that old wood might be *old*." Mason chuckles as his eyes dance when he looks at me.

"Speak for yourself."

"Shriveled and splintering from disuse." His brow tips as he shivers.

"I think I'll change while you sling euphemisms at one another," Anna interrupts and exits the room.

"Right. No one wants to hear about inspecting old wood." Mason grins.

"Mason," I hiss, shifting my eyes from my annoying friend to my boys. "River will not be checking out my wood."

In mock horror, Mason lifts a hand to his chest. "Who said anything about *your* wood?"

"We damn well better not be talking about yours," I hiss, glancing sideways at my sons once more.

"Cut the defense, counsel. We both know mine isn't suffering from shrinkage and disuse."

I scrub two hands down my face with a visual of Mason and River on her chaise lounge, and I *seriously* want to throat punch my friend.

"Okay, beach time," I mutter. "Later, we can ask Miss River if there's a time you can play in her tree fort."

"Maybe she'll give Daddy a private tour of her tree fort." Mason chuckles as tree fort has taken on a new meaning. Pinning him with another warning glare, he laughs harder and thrusts his hips toward the counter, imitating what he thinks I should do with Miss River and her tree fort.

He's such a child.

+ + +

To my surprise, I don't need to find River because she comes down to the beach in the early afternoon. She's wearing another loose flowing dress, reminding me of a picture of hippies from an era of free love, racing through meadows, and passing peace signs to others. She's too young to be from that time, but she pulls off the hippie look with her long golden hair and lightly tanned skin.

When the twins see her, they race toward her, and I stand from my chair, knowing my boys are begging her to allow them to come over. As I approach, she's speaking to them collectively.

"Before you play in there again, I think we should inspect the wood." I nearly fall over at River's suggestion and hear Mason chuckling behind me when I didn't realize he'd followed me.

"Hey, River," Mason calls out, and she offers him a wide smile.

"Hi yourself, handsome."

Handsome? Fuck. No need to feed Mason's already enormous ego.

"I see you've met my little friends and their dad." Mason claps my shoulder like I'm a child myself, and I shake off his touch.

"We're well acquainted," River says, glancing at me with brilliant blue eyes. I noticed them last night as we sat on the lounger. They sparkled and danced while she spoke as if she was constantly on the verge of laughter. Even when they softened as she mentioned her husband or offered sympathy for Ben's passing, her eyes still sparked. *Crackle. Pop. Snap.* I could get lost in those eyes. I wanted to get lost in them. I also wanted to taste her lips and lick her everywhere.

"Interesting," Mason mumbles. "You should join us."

L.B. Dunbar

River hesitates, glancing over at our collection of Adirondack chairs and other shit—coolers, towels, bags, and toys.

"I don't—"

She doesn't have time to finish before Mason has his arm around River's shoulders, guiding her to our group. Logan has joined us again as we agreed we wouldn't work much during these two weeks, giving our attention to Anna and our memories to Ben. Autumn had to work today, so Logan holds his sleeping son while his daughter, Lorna, digs in the sand with Mila.

My boys hover behind River until I tell them to go play. Trevor groans, but Oliver pulls his brother away from our cluster.

Mason handles introductions while Logan offers River a beer, which she declines.

"So I heard the little hellions commandeered your tree fort," Logan states after River takes a seat next to me.

"Hellions?" River questions, lifting a brow in his direction.

"Zack's boys," he clarifies.

River peers over at Trevor and Oliver throwing sand at each other before turning back to Logan. "Do you want someone calling your boy a hellion?" Her mama-bear tone is teasing, but the offense is evident. Mason chokes on a swallow of beer, and Anna slowly smiles while my mouth falls open. No one ever defends my children. Hell, even I don't always stand up for them when I know I should. My gaze finds my boys still torturing one another with fists full of sand. I shift back to River, still shocked by her soft expression but protective words. I don't know what to say.

"Zack mentioned that you and I have a lot in common," Anna says, and I tip back my beer. *Shit.*

River glances at me before addressing Anna. "I think we might both like gardening." The comment is a decent save from an awkward topic, and for the second time in a minute, River covers for me. Anna looks in my direction.

"Maybe," Anna mutters. Ben was the gardener, but she occasionally helped in their yard.

"The tree fort," Mason interjects. "I'm in construction. I'd be happy to come inspect your wood."

Next, I'm choking. I don't want River anywhere near Mason's wood, or rather, Mason near River's wood, or Mason near her *tree fort*. River gazes at me, a questioning look on her face, before glancing back at Mason.

"I can handle my own tree fort, thank you." Her sly smile suggests she's on to him and his innuendos, and the comment has me choking once more. She's more than capable of taking care of herself, but I'd really love to be the one to take care of her. "I'm going to have the boys help me. It will be a fun project for them."

"What?" The word rushes out loud and sharp. I'm not certain seven-year-olds should be dismantling and rebuilding a tree fort. Suddenly, I recall my own father building the platform as I scrambled around the yard, probably offering to help while being more of a nuisance. River shouldn't be tackling such a project with my boys. Deep down, I know it should be me building a tree fort with my sons.

"Sounds like a wonderful idea. The boys could use something constructive to do," Anna interjects, smiling in agreement with River's plan. "I'm so sorry I haven't gotten over to your house to introduce myself."

River waves a dismissive hand. "Life gets in the way."

Anna's smile falters a bit. In her case, it's been death, and I swallow back the reminder.

"But we've met now, and I'd love for you to come over for wine some night. I could use some decorating advice on the interior of the house."

"Oh, I'm not a decorator. I'm a teacher."

"Even better," River adds with a wink. "I'm a nurse. I'm sure we have stories to share."

The reassuring smile River offers Anna puts my old friend at ease, and I could seriously kiss River for making our sad friend grin in return.

Then again, who am I kidding? I just want to kiss River, period.

7

[River]

After a barrage of questions with Zack's friends, I now understand the dynamic. Mason, Logan, and Zack were roommates in one form or another during college. Anna and Ben were high school sweethearts, and she went to college with the boys. Mason has been living at the house, and I can only imagine his bedside manner. To his credit, I've learned he's given up a year of his life to stay with them.

I hang with the friends for longer than I expected before excusing myself. Being with the group was fun but also a reminder of how alone I am. I wasn't someone who had many friends. My grandfather would say I could make friends with a stinkbug. My mother would say I had many, but none of them were close. Nothing like this group. I haven't broken out to make friends in the community. I've heard the rumors. I don't wish to propagate them, so I keep to myself other than a yoga class and my job at the local hospital.

Later, as I'm getting ready to turn off the lower-level lights in my house and head to bed because I'm on the early shift tomorrow, I hear a knock on the sliding glass door off my kitchen. A short, sharp rap hits the glass a second time. Wandering through the dark kitchen, I glance out the window over the sink to see what it was, assuming it could have been a wayward bird or a falling twig.

Instead, Zack stands outside the double doors. His head lowered. His stance hesitant. He's a puzzle to me. There's no doubt I find him physically attractive. He's not as vivacious as Mason or sweet like Logan, but there's still something about him. He has a serious edge to him, but he also looks like he's on the verge of snapping.

I head to the door and flip on the patio light, which causes him to look up at it first before noticing me opening the slider.

"And to what do I owe tonight's honor?" I tease, assuming there's no apology necessary this evening. "I kept my clothes on all day," I proudly jest.

Zack slowly smiles and then bites his lower lip like he did last night. That smirk. It's like a fire hydrant to my panties. He's so damn good-looking. Those silvery eyes sparkle like his son Oliver, and I recognize a hint of mischief behind them. A hint of where the boys might get their wild streak, other than being seven-year-olds, of course.

Holding up a bottle of wine, Zack says, "I thought I'd repay the wine from last night. I even brought two glasses." He shows me two goblets trapped between his long fingers. When I don't move at first, Zack adds, "You called me a wine stealer last night. I want to be clear. I've never stolen anything in my life." He turns serious, guarded even. "And I always repay my debts."

His somber tone puzzles me. Taking my wineglass and drinking my wine doesn't constitute a debt. Still, he seems eager to repay me.

"Noted," I state. "But I have an early shift," I tell him next, reminding him I'm a nurse. When the group asked what I did for a living, I stuck to the most basic answer.

"Just one glass." He pouts at me, jutting out those lush lips, and I laugh. It's the first funny expression he's made, and it's definitely dazzling.

"Okay." I give him a soft smile before stepping out into the yard. I should invite him inside, but I'm afraid that might send the wrong message, and I'm still uncertain what message I want to send this man.

"Where are your boys?" I ask, closing the sliding door behind me.

"I earned the night off. They're having a video game marathon with Anna's son Bryce."

We cross the lawn, and I wave a hand at the lounger. While Zack takes a seat on it, I choose to sit in one of the individual chairs near the foot instead of next to him. I don't trust myself. Last night, we sat so intimately close, but he didn't end up kissing me when I thought he might, and I don't need to put myself in that kind of position if he's only trying to be neighborly. *Repaying his debt* as he incorrectly thinks. Maybe he just wants a friend, and I can be one of those. Quincy had turned out to be one of my best friends.

Zack frowns as I sit, and he scoots to the end of the lounger. Hooking his foot around my chair, it doesn't slide easily through the grass, so he cups the base of the lounger with his hand and tugs it closer to me. When he sits again, his knees bracket mine. With our legs touching, I'm trapped within the space, and it's just as intimate as when we were rubbing arms and holding hands last night.

"You were too far away," he offers as an explanation. The wine bottle in his hand has already been uncorked, so he easily pours two glasses. After handing one to me, he then lifts his to tap the edge of mine. Silently, I make my own toast, hoping he won't be a disappointment. I follow his lead and drink but remain quiet.

"Tonight, I owe you gratitude," he says.

"You don't owe me anything," I murmur, slowly shaking my head.

"You defended my boys today. No one ever does that." He stares at me, firm in his statement while soft in the eyes. The tenderness and confusion in them stop my heart.

"You should be doing that," I gently suggest. Zack should be proud of his boys, and I worry he underappreciates what he has in his healthy, rambunctious sons. He should be thankful for what he has. I'm a single woman nearing forty with no prospect in sight of having children. Not to mention, the parents I've worked with would give anything for their children to be a little bit wild and a tad bit reckless like his boys.

"I know." He sighs heavily. "Like I said last night, I just don't know how to relate to them or even where to start. I mostly worry I'm too late."

My brows pinch at his self-deprecating words. He's not too late. He has potential. He's just . . . lost, but the fact he recognizes his faults and wants to improve is half the battle. Earlier today, I was able to watch him with his sons. It's like he's on the edge of interacting with them yet not certain how.

"You aren't too late." I smile to reassure him. I actually want to hug him. *A smile is as good as a hug sometimes,* my grandfather would say. "You just need to remember how to play."

"Play?" he questions.

"You know, remember what it was like to be a boy again." Isn't it that men never really grow up? The little boy is still inside them even when they're over twenty, forty, sixty.

He's silent a moment, pondering perhaps before he says, "I also want to thank you for making Anna smile." I'd learned earlier that Ben, the friend who passed away, was Anna's husband. Also, Anna and Zack's mothers were best friends, and it's another connection between the couples. In addition, Ben's younger sister recently married Logan, one of the friends. Their friendships interweave in so many ways, it could make a person envious.

"It was nothing, handsome," I say, uncomfortable with so much gratitude.

"You called Mason handsome earlier today." He pauses, directing those silvery eyes at me. "I didn't like it."

Oh. *Oh!* "Is that why you're really here?" He can't possibly be jealous of me giving his flirtatious friend a nickname. Mason's face might be handsome, but his ego is big enough to fill the lake.

"I'm *really* here because I'd like to make up the other night to you. The one when I watch—"

I hold up a hand to stop him. "Are we really going there again?"

Zack swipes a hand through his hair while the other dangles his wineglass outside his leg. He averts his eyes. "I'm a bit out of practice at this."

"Out of practice with what?" I tilt my head.

"Flirting." His eyes quickly shift to mine and away before he lifts his wineglass and takes a hasty drink.

"Oh, are you flirting with me?" I tease, arching a brow and fighting a grin. He's so flustered, and it's kind of cute although cute does not do him justice. With his finger-combed hair and shifting silver eyes, his frustration flatters me.

"See, I'm shit if you can't tell." He softly chuckles and turns his head in the direction of the lake. His eyes pinch. Vulnerability vibrates just beneath his overwhelming sense of confidence, and that hint plucks at my heartstrings.

"What exactly is it you think you need to make up to me from that night?" He has no idea I didn't complete my mission in the yard.

"You shouldn't have been alone." His eyes narrow in on mine. "You deserve to have someone between those thighs, worshipping you with fingers and lips and tongue."

Oh my. I pull at the collar of my dress. "You might be better at this than you think."

A gleam sparkles in his eyes as his hand lands on my thigh and strokes upward, massaging the top of my leg. Instantly, my skin hums. My center pulses.

"How long will you be in town?" I ask, surprising myself. Where am I going with this thought?

"Two weeks from last Sunday." He's already a few days into his stay. "I could offer a ten-day fling." His fingers squeeze tighter on my leg, but it's his voice that throws me off. He's too monotone to sound flirtatious.

"Are we negotiating something?" My voice rises before I bite the inside of my cheek and lean forward. His knees tap the outsides of my thighs, and he takes another sip of his wine. *Could I do this with him? Could I accept the terms of ten days?* I study him as he swallows. The roll of his Adam's apple. His sculpted cheekbones. The artful scruff on his jaw. Another question comes to mind.

"Don't you think you should kiss me before you decide you want a fling?" I'm teasing him. Maybe flirting with him. Definitely encouraging him to take the first step.

He stares at me, his gaze dropping to my mouth where I lick my lower lip, and he mimics the motion as if he can already taste the moisture from mine on his.

"My grandfather used to say if you want something, you should ask for it." My voice drops as I speak. I don't think Grandpa was implying kisses exactly.

"I thought I just did," he counters.

"Let's be specific."

"I don't like confrontation."

Are we arguing? "Aren't you a lawyer?" I learned earlier today he's a prominent attorney in Detroit as well as a business partner in a new venture with his friends. Tipping up my wineglass, I take a fortifying drink while I wait on his answer.

"I am, but I don't like to argue outside the courtroom."

"This is a negotiation then. Or a compromise, perhaps." My heart beats faster. *What am I doing?* I am not supposed to be flirting with him.

"I don't want to have to think." His directness doesn't surprise me. Blunt could almost be his middle name. He continues to stare at me. His gaze is hard while hesitant in one searing look.

"Kiss me," I whisper, leaning closer to him. Zack leans toward me as well, and his mouth touches mine. His lips are soft, cautious even, as he takes his time to explore. It's a front porch kiss after a first date that hasn't gone well. For a man who just spoke of fingers, lips, and tongue between my thighs, I'm underwhelmed. I don't want to hurt his feelings, but I didn't think he'd kiss like this. And I'd been thinking about his kisses since he showed up in my yard last night. Adding fuel to my desire for him was spending time on the beach with his friends. He was more relaxed around them, more carefree than closed off. He was starting to dazzle me.

Soon enough, he pulls back, and even he looks dissatisfied. Maybe it can only be friendship between us, and that's fine. We stare at one another for a few seconds, and that intense gaze of his speaks volumes.

"You were holding back," I whisper, reading it in the tight expression on his face. It's like watching him with his boys. He's on the cusp, on the verge of something, but he's holding it all back. He's a branch on a tree ready to snap in a fierce wind. He's too controlled, and for someone in want of not thinking, that kiss was not one to lose his mind in.

He lowers his wineglass to the side of the chaise and then reaches for mine, placing it next to his. He watches me for another moment, and I swallow under his searching gaze. The tension builds between us, and that magnetic sensation occurs, the pull like powerful steel in a room full of soft metal shavings. The intensity of his eyes has me anxious and questioning if I've underestimated him.

When my jaw is cupped by both his hands, his mouth crushes mine, and I have instant confirmation that I have strongly misjudged him. The force of this kiss pulls him upright, tipping over me until his tongue thrusts forward. I savor the intrusion and kiss him back with as much fervor. This kiss is firework explosions and crashing waves. It's summer heat, rushing water, and a touch of everything I'd ever want in a kiss.

With his hands still on my jaw, he sucks at the bottom swell of my lips. His tongue returns like another rush of sky-lighting flames and water slapping soft sand. It's as if he can't breathe without kissing me, and it's more than any kiss I've ever experienced.

Guiding me by his grasp on my face, he draws me toward him, and I slowly move without breaking our connection. He continues to lean backward, falling to his back and forcing me to straddle his lap to follow him down to the cushion. I'm in the cotton T-shirt dress I wear to bed, and the short length easily rides up my thighs as I cradle his lap. Our mouths are relentless, thirsty, and unquenchable. A hand shifts to fist my hair at the nape of my neck, and he lowers his lips to my jaw.

"You're so incredibly beautiful, angel," he murmurs with praise and awe. His mouth moves to my neck, slowly scraping his teeth along the column of my throat before sucking at the skin. His fist relaxes, and his fingers comb through the locks at the back of my head before tangling his grasp into my hair again. He returns his mouth to mine. His hunger has me wet and squirming over the hard length straining in his khaki shorts. Slowly, he twists us until I'm on my back, and he's partially over me. His leg slips between my thighs, and his hand lowers to the outside of my upper leg, stroking over my warm skin.

And my hand claps over his to stop him.

Breaking the kiss, he pulls back to look at me. His eyes search mine, and the vulnerable gaze returns. For a confident man, he almost appears frightened.

"Am I fucking this up?" he asks.

"I'm not really a one-night stand kind of girl," I admit. While I'm hot, pulsing, and greedy for him, I still don't want to sleep with him on our first night and know he's next door for nine more without a repeat.

"Ten-day fling," he whispers, eyes focused on my mouth.

"I think we should stick to one topic at a time."

"I'm out of practice," he whispers, biting hard at the bottom curve of his lip while his eyes scan mine. His hand leaves my thigh, and he swipes through my hair again, combing it back from the side of my face. My hair can be wild and slightly wavy after only a wash and air dry.

"Kissing is good. *Your* kissing is good." I bite my lip to fight the anxious giggle riding up my throat.

"Can I keep kissing you?" he asks sweetly. Sheepishly.

"I'd like that," I admit. I want his mouth back on mine. I want him, but one topic at a time, like I said.

He lowers but hovers over my lips. "What else would you like?"

So many things, I think, realizing he can't give them to me. *Only a ten-day fling.*

"Just kissing," I whisper. I'm not opposed to continuing if he keeps kissing me like he was, and his mouth crushes mine to prove he will. His leg remains between my thighs, and I hitch mine over his. We're as dangerously close to grinding against one another as we were when I was straddling him. My hips buck, and my core clenches. My underwear against his shorts is too much of a barrier yet not enough protection. He's going to catapult me over the edge if we keep this up.

My fingers delve into his hair, tugging gently at the nape, and his mouth widens, devouring mine while his tongue dances in an erotic twist. I squirm against his thigh and slip my leg farther up and over his hip, acting in opposition to halting him. His hand cups the back of my leg and slips upward to the edge of my backside.

"Christ, you're gonna make me come with only your mouth," he mutters before kissing me harder and surging his hips forward. His hard length rubs at my pelvis. *This is ridiculous.* I should just give in. I should just sleep with him. *What is one night compared to all the other nights?* The question douses the flame a bit. The odds are not in my favor. For another three hundred and sixty-four nights, I'll be exactly where I am— alone. Slowly, I pull back.

"Where did you go?" he says, lowering his mouth to my jaw then my neck, peppering softer kisses there.

"What do you mean? I'm right here." But I stare up at the dark sky overhead, pinpricked with stars.

"In your head. I'm losing you." He kisses the dip between my collarbone before leaning back. Logic is overruling my libido. My thoughts have taken over, and I find Zack's window next door just over his shoulder. *It isn't him; it's me.* In ten days, he'll leave, and I'll still be here. Alone. My eyes focus on the darkened glass, but Zack cups my jaw, forcing me to look at him.

"We don't have to do anything you don't want to do," he says to my lips before meeting my eyes and repeating my words. "Kissing is good. Kissing you is good."

Kissing, it's only kissing, but I already know it could be so much more than our mouths meeting. He could be so much more, and I can't allow that to happen.

Suddenly, his phone rings, and Zack groans, lowering his forehead for my sternum.

"Is that 'The Imperial March' from *Star Wars*?" I laugh at the sound.

"It's actually from *The Empire Strikes Back,* and it's my ring tone for the boys."

"Zack!" I choke around more laughter. "That's a terrible theme song for your boys." The laughter breaks all the tension filling my thoughts.

Zack shakes his head and kneels upright, straddling my right leg while my left slips from his hip. "I need to answer this."

"Of course." I softly smile at him.

"Hello." His short, clipped greeting reminds me of how he addresses his children. I shift to sit upright, but he places a hand on my stomach, willing me to stay in place. Instead, I balance on my elbows, glancing up at him. I should give him privacy, but the call is quick.

Zack's eyes close as he says, "Okay, I'll be right over."

When he clicks off the phone, he tosses it on the cushion and falls forward, bracing himself with extended arms over me.

"The stormtroopers are invading," I tease as I drop to my back again.

"Oliver says he has a stomachache."

"Poor baby," I whimper, pouting my lower lip.

"Poor daddy," he huffs. "I wasn't finished with you." He lowers his face, running his nose along my neck before nearing my ear.

"But you are a dad, and your boys should always come first," I whisper to him, shivering under the drag of his nose.

He traces the shell of my ear before whispering to me. "I like your laugh." His voice hints at a smile. He's sweet, and my lips curl as his nose retraces his path along my neck. My hands reach for his shoulders, coasting over them before sliding down his arms to his wrists.

"You need to go," I whisper, disguising my disappointment. I meant what I've said. His boys should always come first, and perhaps that phone call was what we needed to stop us from going further than we should in one night.

"Are we all good here, angel?" He pulls back, staring down at my mouth, and I have no idea what he means with that question. As I don't answer him, he places a final kiss to the side of my neck before pressing upward over me and removing himself from the chaise lounge. He stands with his back to me a second, adjusting the ache that matches mine.

Zack rounds the lounger for the bottle of wine and the half-filled glasses. He picks up the wineglasses by slipping his fingers inside the rim and curls a fist around the bottleneck as I sit upright, straightening my sleep dress. With his side to me, I open my mouth, but I'm uncertain what to say, until he speaks.

"Get some sleep. Have a good day at work tomorrow." Giving me a final look, I weakly wave with a single flip of my wrist. Once he disappears around the corner of my house, I toss myself backward and stare up at the blanket of stars, wondering just what the heck I'm doing with one hot single dad who can only promise me ten days.

8

[River]

It's been a particularly long day. After not sleeping well because I was too keyed up from Zack's kisses, one of my favorite patients is having a rough afternoon, and I'm emotionally exhausted. I knew things would be different when I took the position at the local hospital. The diagnosis of my patients is the same, but their age is at the opposite end of the spectrum from my previous experience. I love what I do, but some days are more difficult than others.

As I pull into my yard, I don't even have the energy for a run, which normally releases tension after a tough shift. I don't even have the brainpower to struggle through thoughts of Zack and kissing him last night. All I want is a quick, hot shower and a silent, comfy bed. Instead, the ruckus of power saws and hammers rattle nearby. So near that I realize the noise is coming from behind my house.

After I round the house for my backyard, I still in my tracks. My mouth falls open at the sight of two sweaty, shirtless men with jacked abs and intent focus on their faces—one cutting two-by-four boards and the other measuring the tree in my yard. Assisting these two wannabe lumberjacks with their loose hanging khaki shorts and construction boots are two little men, also without shirts but quite a bit skinnier, shorter, and younger by almost thirty years.

"What the hell is going on?"

The power saw drones to a stop as Oliver races up to me. He runs like he's ready to tackle-hug me, and I brace myself, but he halts a foot away. A coat of sawdust covers his brow. He's wearing child-sized workman gloves, and his excited expression falters when he glances up at me.

"We're rebuilding the tree fort." His small voice should melt my fury, but this is my yard. My head pops up, and I peer at Zack across the lawn. He's leaning over the sawhorses holding fresh-cut boards. Mason stands a few feet away, looking upward where he just finished measuring the height to the original platform from the ground.

Slowly, Zack approaches, tipping up safety goggles while he walks. "You mentioned yesterday it might be a good project for the boys. I thought we'd get a head start."

"You realize this is private property, right? *My* property. My yard," I snap. A shaky hand presses at my forehead, where I suddenly feel the pressure of a headache. Softer, I mutter, "You have no boundaries." Drinking out of my wineglass. Watching me in my yard. And now this, helping himself to build a fort in a tree when I don't even have children of my own to enjoy it. Hell, even his children will only be here for a limited number of days.

After barking at Zack, my eyes drop to Oliver, whose stricken face twists my insides. Lowering to a squat before him, I stare up at his dirty little face and brush back hair sticking to his forehead.

"Hey." I soften my tone by taking a calming breath. "I thought we were going to fix it together."

"Dad offered to help." *Dad offered to help*. My eyes leap up to Zack. Honestly, it's more important that this man does things with his boys. Their behavior is a desperate cry for attention, and once again, I wish Zack would appreciate what he has in them—healthy, generally happy, rambunctious seven-year-olds.

"I'm glad your dad wants to do this with you." Glancing back at Oliver, I reach for his thin wrist and give it a little squeeze while bolstering a smile on my face. "I'm sorry I yelled at him. I'm not mad at him. I've just had a tough day." I'm still wearing my purple scrubs and matching rubber clogs. All I want to do is remove this uniform and forget my shift for a little while, which feels like a betrayal to my patient. She deserves so much more.

My eyes shift to Oliver's father once more. Mason walks up to Zack, and the sight of both men with their low-slung shorts and sweaty abs screams August in a calendar of hot men over forty. Returning my gaze to Oliver, I tug at his delicate wrist, playfully swinging his arm.

"Ollie, do you think Miss River could have a hug?"

Without a thought, he opens his arms and wraps his skinny limbs around my neck, and I breathe in the scent of him—suntan lotion and sticky skin. My eyes close as I inhale for a second. *Ain't nothing a hug can't cure*, my grandfather would say. If only it were the antidote for cancer.

"Thank you," I whisper-choke before pressing him back by his bony shoulders. I kiss his sawdust forehead before standing upright again.

"Rough day at the office?" Mason teases.

"Something like that," I say, watching Oliver run back to his brother.

"What do you do again?" Mason asks, his eyes scanning my attire. If he envisions naughty nurse and playing patient, he can think again.

"I'm an oncology nurse. Pediatrics."

"Shit," Zack mutters and lowers his eyes. Mason drops the measuring tape he was holding.

"I'm sorry," Mason mumbles. I hadn't mentioned it yesterday because of Anna. When I learned Ben died of cancer.

Trevor walks around his dad next. His devilish face matches the hard edge of his father's, and the resemblance is striking. He's the tougher of the two boys, and he knows his position. He's the top dog to Oliver's puppy.

"We can take it down if you don't like it," the child offers of the start they've made on a new improved, definitely safer, tree platform. His suggestion sounds genuine and not like a ploy of opposites—saying one thing and hoping for another. At seven, he recognizes the error of what they've done.

Slowly, I exhale. "It's okay," I whisper, fighting the thickness suddenly clogging my throat at his heartfelt offer. Forcing another smile, I add, "I can't wait to see it finished."

I take another deep breath and point over my shoulder. "I'm just going to shower and nap." Zack's brows pinch as I make brief eye contact with him, and my vision blurs a bit. I tell myself exhaustion is the reason I'm on the verge of tears. Quickly, I turn around and take steps toward the sliding glass doors, but before I reach it, my wrist is circled.

"Hey," Zack's soft voice stops my retreat. Keeping my back to him, I close my eyes, letting one tear slip free. Brusquely, I brush at my cheek. *I will not let him see me cry.* Pediatric oncology is not for the faint of heart, and I'm typically stronger than this. I'm used to struggles and loss with the disease. Today's just been a difficult day.

"Won't you turn around?" he asks, his voice remaining low and encouraging, but I shake my head.

"I'm just tired." My voice cracks, giving away the sob I'm struggling to contain. He drops his hold on my wrist, but his presence becomes more apparent. The heat of his warm chest seeps through the clothing on my back. His scent overwhelms me. He matches his child with the fragrance of sunshine and exercise.

"We overstepped. I'm sorry."

I wave a hand at him over my shoulder. "It's fine."

His hands come to my shoulders and rub down my arms. "I don't like that you aren't looking at me, angel."

The endearment turns the lump in my throat to a boulder. "Please, Zack," I whisper. I can't deal with him right now. Sometimes in life, there are just bigger things than kisses and wishes.

"I should have asked permission. We'll stop for today and let you rest."

"Thank you," I choke, stepping free of his touch when what I really want is to collapse against him and absorb his strength. Visions of his naked chest and the hint of hair leading lower in those shorts will haunt my dreams. It's just the distraction I need after I nap.

+ + +

Later that evening, I'm sitting in my yard once more. It's my favorite thing about this place. Off in the distance, the sun is lowering to a golden yolk while streams of yellow and orange filter through the darkening sky. I sip a glass of wine in hopes of continuing the calm I mustered after a hot shower and a decent nap.

The late afternoon rest will screw up my sleep pattern, but I'm also used to a flip-flopping schedule. Two days on. One day off. Morning,

morning, and then night, night . It's a cycle I don't mind. I typically pick up additional shifts as I'm a single woman without much more going on in my life. Still, I appreciate what I have—a steady job and a decent home that I own outright.

My thoughts drift to Quincy. After years of adult patients, I needed a change. Labor and delivery would have been a happier position. Life versus death should have been the option, but with decades of oncology practice, I stayed within the field and just moved from elderly patients to a younger set.

Slowly, I sip my wine and think of little Jessica. She's a spitfire, so to see her defeated earlier today threw me off. She'd had some disturbing news after months of treatments. Her parents were understandably wrecked. Life is so unfair sometimes; death is even more unjust.

Briefly, I think of all the people I've lost. Quincy. Grandfather.

Pity parties don't serve cake, my grandfather would say in times of self-sorrow. He didn't live long enough for my sarcastic streak to hit, where I would have replied that those kinds of parties should serve cake along with ice cream and alcohol.

I close my eyes, but images of Jessica's parents' tear-stained faces flutter behind my lids. Quickly, I open them to focus on the setting sun. Taking a deep breath, I concentrate, nearly meditate, on the lowering orb and the reflective light skittering across the momentarily calm water. I sit long enough that the evening turns black around me, and stars fill the sky like a pop of polka dots—one here, one there. My eyes drift to the beginnings of a new platform in my tree. It will be the perfect spot for stargazing.

"Hello." The masculine voice has me spinning in the chaise lounge. I moved its position, so it faces the dark lake and descending sun.

"Hi," I choke around the panic in my throat. I need to invest in a gate as these Weller boys have no boundaries.

Sheepishly, Zack approaches me, hands buried in the pockets of a fresh pair of shorts. His hard abs are covered by another dress shirt. This one is bright blue, sleeves rolled above his elbows. He could still make a "hot men over forty" calendar, only this look might land him under September. He stops at the end of the lounger, standing near my feet.

"I wanted to see how you were doing. You were upset earlier." It's an understatement and an opening to discuss my day, but I don't really want to talk about it.

"I'm better, thank you." I lift my glass of wine to salute him before taking a sip. Zack glances toward the disappearing sun before looking back at me.

"Seems I'm always entering this yard to either apologize or thank you."

"Or to steal wine or deface my tree." The sarcasm is harsher than it needs to be.

"I told you I don't steal." With his tone defensive, Zack scratches at the back of his neck. He exhales before continuing. "But my boys and I had a chat about that, where I admitted I'd done wrong by assuming it was okay to build a new fort. You suggested fixing the old one, and I got carried away."

Weakly, I grin. "You should get carried away with your boys. They just want your time and attention." My thoughts leap to little Jessica and her parents. Time is all they have with her.

"I know," he softly huffs. His lids lower a second before those silver beams look back at me. "What about you? Do you want my time and attention?"

I don't think it really matters what I want. He seems to take charge whether I like it or not which might be a big reason I didn't give in to him last night. I don't need the likes of Zack Weller bulldozing my life. I don't want to be dazzled by him. However, as he stands at the end of the lounger looking flustered and contrite, I want nothing more than to lose myself in him.

Maybe I could have a one-night stand if the right kind of man offered.

"I'd like to make it up to you," he states when I haven't answered about his time or attention. His voice drops low and seductive as he bites the edge of his lip. "The imposition of the tree fort. Sharing your wine. Watching you in your yard."

He isn't indebted to me like he suggested last night, but *Jesus*, his voice is like a slow caress up my legs and between my thighs. "What do you have in mind?"

"Negotiation." My breath hitches as I meet his hungry gaze. "Lift your dress. Slowly."

A thrill runs through me at the soft command. On a million levels, I should not satisfy his request. *This is so wrong*. Yet I set my wineglass aside and scrunch up the gauzy material, exposing more and more leg as the fabric rises. When the dress reaches the apex of my thighs, Zack makes another demand. "Take off your underwear."

Keeping myself covered, I reach under my dress and slip my underwear down my hips and over my knees until I can kick them free. Zack catches the flimsy lace and squeezes it into a fist before slipping it into his pocket.

"Touch yourself." *Holy shit*. He can't mean it, but as I hold his gaze, I slip a hand over my upper thigh and between my legs. Brushing against my clit, I keep my eyes on him and hiss at the sensation. The featherlight tease is only the beginning, but I'm already so turned on by his seductive voice and smoldering gaze that I'm not going to last long.

Stroking over damp folds, I lick my lower lip, and Zack pops the button on his shorts. The sharp sound of his zipper rips through the magnetic tension between us. He isn't watching me touch myself but focused on my face, looking at my lip which I bite in response to his pleased smirk. The scent of my sex fills the air around me. His hand disappears into his shorts, and my lids lazily lower.

"This is what I did that night while I watched you."

My eyes snap open and widen. *He got off while watching me*. The possibility has me stroking faster, rubbing harder. The intensity with which he presently observes me could incinerate me. My skin sizzles with desire. My mouth dries.

Zack places a knee on the edge of the chaise as his arm moves, the jerking motion clear although the tails of his shirt cover everything from sight.

"I wanted it to be me," he says in a raspy, rugged voice. "I wanted to glide between those thighs and nip at your sweet skin. I wanted to smell your pussy and press my tongue against it."

"Oh God," I groan. For a man who doesn't want to think, he's thought an awful lot about that night. And with his soothing voice and commanding instructions, I'm falling under his spell. My mind clears of everything but what his tongue might feel like against me. What his tongue could do to that spot where I need him most. He'd devour me like his mouth did mine last night, and I moan with the thought.

"Do it," I demand, not recognizing my own voice. I spread my legs just the slightest amount, hinting at what I want.

"Angel," he hisses.

"Make me come," I softly strain, recognizing I'm close but knowing his mouth will get me over the edge. He releases himself and places both knees on the end of the lounger. His warm hands grip my ankles and tug my legs wider. Lowering his body between my legs, he slips his hands under my knees as he bites the tender skin of my inner thighs. He scoots upward, running his nose over my clit before his tongue strikes. He doesn't hesitate as he did with that first kiss last night. He dives in, kissing me like he had my mouth. Tongue. Teeth. Lips against lips. He sucks at the sensitive folds, causing my hips to buck. He laps across my slit, and my back arches. His tongue thrusts forward, flicking my clit, and I'm ready to break. I'm outside my head with thoughts only of Zack and what he's doing to me, what no man has done to me in years.

"I'm going to come," I state in both warning and wonder. I'm going to come, and it's going to be big, like tree-fort-shaking, tectonic-plates-shifting big. My legs stiffen, and my thighs squeeze the sides of his head as I erupt from his relentless tongue. His fingertips press into my skin as his tongue licks up my release and immediately pushes me toward another.

"Oh God," I whimper, uncertain what's happening to me. I rarely come twice and never this fast on the heels of the first.

"Yes," he mutters as if he's the man himself. The vibration stimulates my already sensitive folds.

"I can't," I softly mewl.

"You will," he commands again. His tongue against me says *no more negotiation*. This is torture—quick, slick, and delicious. I crash within seconds, calling out his name in the dark night. Jackknifing upward, I cup his ears, staring down at his head buried between my thighs. He releases me, and I tug him by those ears up to my mouth, sucking at my essence on his lips.

"Fuck me," I whisper, my voice desperate with need. He's opened the hydrant. It can't be closed until the fire burning inside me is out.

"Not tonight," he says, ravenous for my lips. His tongue licks upward, lapping from the lower to the upper swells.

"What?" I choke, misunderstanding him and feeling his rejection. He just gave me two incredible orgasms, one on top of another. I need to feel him inside me.

"That was all for you." He was certainly generous, but I'm not done with him. My hands roam down his body, forcing his shorts to his hips.

"River," he warns against my mouth, but I break away. His hands land on either side of my hips, balancing him upright, and slowly I lower under him, scooting myself beneath his body.

"Angel," he chokes when I slip my hand inside his shorts, wrapping around a shaft that's velvet over steel. He's so hard and hot. He needs to lose control like I did. Releasing him for only a moment, I wrestle his shorts and briefs farther down his body to free his impressive length, then lick the seeping tip.

"Fuck," he groans, balancing on those arms like columns holding up a building. I swirl my tongue around the crown before opening and drawing him to the back of my throat, swallowing around him. My tongue dances around the head before sucking the firm shaft. His hips lazily rock. Reaching deeper inside his shorts, my hands squeeze the firm globes of his ass and he tightens.

"River," he pants once more, swiping a hand into my hair, fisting it as if he wants to remove me, but I'm not letting up. I want him to break for me. His backside clenches, and his hips surge forward once more. I gag around him. Quickly, he forces himself free, and I whimper, opening my eyes to watch him fist himself and jerk once before releasing against my pubic bone. My head falls back. My chest heaves.

"Jesus." Zack chuckles before collapsing beside me. Despite the heavy weight of my head, I roll it in his direction. "That was not supposed to happen."

His breathing is just as ragged as mine, but the grin on his face lets me know he's pleased by what we just did.

"You didn't like that?" I tease, rolling my body to face his.

"Don't be stupid. I loved it, but that's not what I intended tonight."

"It's called compromise," I state.

"Well, I like how you compromise." He smiles wider, and the full potential to dazzle graces his face.

"I like how you negotiate," I whisper, reaching out to run my fingertip down his nose. He shifts his body to mirror mine before kissing me tenderly.

"I'll negotiate with you anytime." His silvery eyes soften. I'd like to believe those words mean more, but I know better.

9

[Zack]

Within days of knowing her, the warmth my boys express for River's feelings surprises me. Oliver worried we'd upset Miss River and she wouldn't want to see us again, while Trevor genuinely meant his suggestion to remove the entire structure if she didn't like it. I was truly baffled by how easily the boys behaved for this woman, but I wasn't puzzled at their attraction to her. While not the same as the level of attraction I felt, of course, something about her drew all the Weller boys in her direction.

Thinking of attraction, I loved how she responded to my commands. It could have all blown up in my face—demanding she remove her underwear, telling her to touch herself, allowing me to watch—and then she flipped the tables like she has at every turn. She told me to do it. She told me to act out what I wanted to do to her on that outdoor chaise, and when I did . . . *holy shit*. In her terms of compromise, she returned the favor, which I never *ever* expected.

I blame it on that kiss she demanded the previous night, striking a match and setting the flame. My game was seriously off, and I knew I was fucking it all up with her. Even when she told me to kiss her, I hadn't known how. It isn't that I'd forgotten, but I was out of practice. Six years married to a woman I hadn't loved, and I no longer knew how to kiss a woman I might.

You were holding back. She was right. I was holding back. I didn't want to scare her away, but can you scare a woman brave enough to sunbathe nude in her backyard? Can you frighten a woman who is bold enough to touch herself before a man? River has a wild streak, and I want her to help me reclaim mine.

Before I left her last night, I apologized again for overstepping boundaries in building a new tree house in her tree.

"You seem to have a habit of it," she teased about my trespassing. Although I knew what she meant, I didn't want to come across as taking things that didn't belong to me. I'd been the product of a man who'd done such a thing, and I swore I would never beg, borrow, or steal anything that wasn't mine. Most of all, I didn't want her to think I'd taken advantage of her.

The next day, we return to her yard to continue our building project. The boys have had a blast making demands and following directions like little subcontractors. They've done Mason proud. Thankfully, River works during the day again, so we aren't disturbing her.

When our smoking hot neighbor finally does enter her yard in the late afternoon, Logan and Mason are arguing about finishing touches. You wouldn't think building a simple tree house would take more than two days, but with these two, it's out of control.

"I'm the architect," Logan states with authority, pointing at himself as he speaks to Mason.

"But I'm the builder. This will work best."

I chuckle at the two who have always had a competitive relationship despite being roommates and best friends since freshman year of college.

"Everybody getting along?" River teases as she approaches me. She's wearing her scrubs again today, and I'm certain Mason had the same thoughts as me yesterday. I'd like her to be my naughty nurse. The reality of her job, though, sets me back. Pediatric oncology must be a difficult position, and it explains why my children so easily react to her. She knows how to talk to kids. I'm clueless even though I always swore I'd be a better father than my own. I'd provide for them. I'd be present for them. I'd be supportive of them. However, since their birth, we've had countless nannies. Jeanine was just as busy as I was in her career, and our twins came second. I'm not proud of that fact.

"Architect and builder clash. I'm getting used to it in our new venture."

"And what's your role again?" She eyes me in my sweaty tee and dirty day-old shorts.

"I'm normally the paper pusher, but I wanted to be more hands-on with the boys on this project." If I had known activities with my boys would make her smile like she is, I'd find more projects with those two hellions. *Forgive me—children*. Then again, I've seen her mouth curl in reaction to other pleasant things, and I'm eager to repeat those actions.

"How was your day?" I ask, still focused on her mouth. Her eyes widen in surprise at my asking, and she bites her lower lip.

"Today was better. Thank you."

"Patient doing better?" When she didn't look at me yesterday, it stung. She was hurting and I felt a little helpless. I didn't miss the brush of her hand to dismiss the tears on her cheek, but I didn't want to draw attention to them when she clearly didn't want me to see them. Still, my chest ached, and everything in me wanted to pull her to me to comfort her. Last night, she dismissed my concern just as easily, and I distracted her the only way I thought might work.

I bite my lower lip, wondering if she's thought about what we did last night as much as I have all day.

"She's as good as she's going to get," River replies with a smile that doesn't reach her eyes. She's putting on a brave face again, and I imagine it often takes one to work with such sensitive cases.

"So, how're we doing today?" She nods at the progress. What was intended to be a new ladder up the trunk and rebuilt platform among the branches has turned into a real structure in her tree.

"It might be getting out of hand, but we'll be done today." *I hope.* We should have consulted River on what she'd want. It's her yard, as she said yesterday. It's her tree, and it's been a struggle to remember such things as I dismantle my old fort and build a new one in a backyard that is no longer mine. Still, she's smiling at the construction which has low walls and cut-outs for windows.

"Where are the boys?" As if they hear her asking, they appear from behind the tree. They've had some good swings with little hammers and come up with lots of plans for their temporary house, but they've been losing interest due to the lengthiness of the project. It takes time to measure, cut, and build.

We'll need to build a tree house in our own backyard, I've decided. I'm only saddened Logan and Mason won't be around to help. Neither will River, but I dismiss the thought for now.

"Miss River," my sons say almost in unison like she's their favorite teacher. She's definitely becoming mine.

"Hey, guys. I have something for you." Reaching down for a bag I hadn't noticed at her feet, River lowers to their level, kneeling on the ground to remove items from the large sack.

Object after object is revealed. Pirate hats. Eye patches. Dark bandanas. And a telescope.

"You need to share this," she tells them, and I huff. *Good luck with that.*

Mason responds instead. "You're making monsters by spoiling them."

"I'm making pirates of them, searching for adventure. Argh," she groans, and my dick unfurls at the throaty sound. Forget naughty nurse. I want her to wear a short dress with a lowcut bodice to swashbuckle me. I have buried treasure for her to discover.

"As long as they aren't stealing maidenhead. Or discovering a maiden giving head," Mason interjects, and I narrow my eyes at him.

"Really?" I mutter. Speaking of a man with no boundaries.

"I want to steal a maidenhead," Trevor says with enthusiasm.

"I want a maiden giving head," Oliver adds.

My eyes sliver into piercing slits. If I had a sword, I'd impale Mason with it. However, River laughs, and I recall the sound from the other night.

"How about searching for buried treasure instead? That's better than any girl," River teases, scrunching up her face in an adorable mocking of her own sex.

"A maiden is a girl?" Trevor questions, his face falling in exasperation. "Ugh. No, thank you."

"I like girls." Oliver shrugs like they aren't that bad.

"Thank you," River states with pride, smiling at my boys as she stands.

"You're not a girl," Trevor says, objecting to the thought.

"I'm not? What am I then?" River teases, and Oliver blinks up at her.

"You're a mom." His innocent statement floats around us. My mouth falls open, ready to correct him, hoping River isn't offended. However, graceful as she is, River gently reacts.

"Moms are just girls who grow into women and have children. I don't have any children, so I'm not a mom." Her voice is calm. Her explanation clear. She isn't offended.

Without a thought, Oliver replies, "You should be."

"Oliver!" I shriek, mortified on his behalf.

"Dude," Mason mumbles a few feet away.

"You can be our mom," Trevor says, shrugging like it's that easy. Then he adds, "Ours left."

"Trev." With the nickname softly on my tongue, I feel like the nail gun got loose and just hammered my chest. I glance up to find Logan watching me. He's the other divorced guy in our group. He pulled off the single dad thing for years, doing a great job with his only daughter. He knows I'm concerned I won't get my shit together. Jeanine has screwed up our boys with her absence, but I'm not without fault.

I swore I wouldn't be a bad dad. I'd had the best of fathers until he wasn't. We hadn't a hint to the things he'd been doing, or maybe I hadn't noticed because I was only a kid. He was my hero then. I never knew how far off-balance things had gotten. When everything fell apart, my mother was devastated, and I was left to pick up the pieces.

I glance at River, whose eyes fill with compassion. She doesn't know what to say in response to Trevor.

"Little guys, how about we ask River to join us tonight for the barbecue?" Logan asks, dissolving the awkward tension. My head twists from River to Logan, kicking myself that I hadn't thought of it or been the one to invite her. Logan and Autumn offered to host our crew at their new home tonight, hoping to remove us from the house. Anna's been holding her own, but she disappears in her head at times and needs a break.

The boys cheer, and Oliver doesn't hold back. He wraps his arms around River's waist and looks up at her with large pleading eyes.

"Please come. Please, please, please." He pouts, and River glances over at me.

"Did he learn this expression from you, or did he teach it to you?" I have no idea what she's talking about, but I watch as she blindly rubs her hand over my son's head. "I don't really want to intrude on your *friends*-cation."

"Why not? We've invaded your yard," I reply.

"Don't act like that's a hardship," Mason mutters, and I pierce him with another hard glare.

"Clothing is optional," Logan states, and River stiffens in Oliver's arms. "I mean, it might be best to wear something, but you know, you do you. Whatever makes you comfortable. My wife likes to be naked, too. Typically, it's only with me, but I'm not gonna judge."

River's head slowly turns in my direction, and her eyes narrow. "You told them."

My mouth falls open, ready to explain. Then I snap my lips shut, thinking it best not to speak. I lower my eyes, and her breath catches.

"You weren't alone," she growls under her breath. I kick at the ground, slipping my hands into my pockets. Biting the corner of my lip, I sheepishly lift my lids half-mast to glance up at her.

"Dammit," she mutters and closes her eyes.

Mason laughs, and River turns her attention to him.

"All three of you." It wasn't even a question. Logan turns his head and whistles a distracting tune. Mason salaciously grins.

"Don't be embarrassed," I whisper.

"You should be embarrassed," she says, eyeing each of us like errant children. Her voice rises while she continues stroking Oliver's hair, and his head relaxes against her waist.

"Dad, don't make her mad again," Oliver warns, and my mouth falls open.

How am I the bad guy? Then again, I've just been schooled by River. We should be embarrassed. We shouldn't have been looking, but dammit, it's her fault for being so distractingly beautiful.

"Yeah, *Dad*," Mason groans, but it's Trevor who hammers the nail into my chest again.

"Dad, we don't want Miss River to leave us, too."

"Oh, baby," River whispers, and she crouches once more, still holding Oliver at her side. "Trevor, come here." She stretches out an arm, but Trevor isn't as affection-desperate as his brother, nor does he seem to want River's embrace. He remains where he's planted, suspiciously eyeing River until she lowers her arm.

"I'm not going anywhere," she says to him, confident and convincing. "I'll be right here, guarding your tree fort for you."

Trevor stares at her, and I can almost see the fight in him. He wants her touch. He wants to believe her soothing words. Jeanine wasn't a loving mother, but then again, I'm just as guilty as a less-than-stellar father. Time was my excuse. Jeanine was just cold. I'm ready to grab my child and pull him to my chest. I don't want him to feel abandoned. He's too young to feel so rejected. I know the sensation, and it sucks.

When Trevor doesn't move toward River, she stands again chewing at her lower lip. She doesn't look at me, and I worry she's offended by his standoffishness.

"It's not you," I offer, reaching out for her arm, stroking from bicep to wrist. She doesn't flinch, but she's still stiff from his rebuff. Or maybe she's still upset three grown men saw her naked in her backyard.

Sensing new tension, Logan interjects with another invitation to dinner, and with another questioning glance from River, I confirm the invite.

"I'd love for you to be there."

She can't say I treated her like a one-night stand. We've had two nights together, and I'm looking forward to a third. And then, a few more after that.

10

[River]

Although I've lived here for a year, I haven't made the effort to meet people. I'd heard the murmurs and speculation. I didn't feel the need to explain myself to strangers, but I wanted to make a good impression with Zack's friends. So, I was nervous.

Plus, I was still struggling with Trevor's words and Oliver's embrace. Cloaked under their wild streak, those little boys are sad. In the short time I'd known them, I haven't heard them mention their mom once until today, and it was obvious Trevor misunderstood. His mother didn't leave him; she left their father. Or maybe Zack left her. I didn't know the details, and as I didn't want to share my own experience, I hadn't asked. However, I don't want to believe their mother abandoned them.

Children are a blessing, my grandfather would say. *But that doesn't mean we don't want to curse at them sometimes.* Somehow, I think Grandfather intended those words to mean exasperation and frustration with children, not abandoning them. He refused to see children as anything other than a gift, and he certainly cherished my mother and me.

Sadly, Quincy had abandoned his children, and at his advanced age, he was full of regret. His children were full of bitterness and eventually revenge. Just like with Quincy, it wasn't my place to judge Zack as a father. However, Oliver and Trevor were only seven. Zack had more time to make good on his position as their dad. In Zack's defense, he *wanted* to be better. It was written on his face when Trevor said what he said about their mother and when Oliver hugged me. *On the cusp again.* Zack didn't understand his children, but he *wanted* to know them.

A hard knock on my front door brings me out of my thoughts, and my hands smooth down my summer dress. The lightweight material is flouncy and flows almost to my ankles. I've paired it with strappy, flat sandals, but I'm worried I won't match Zack. His polished look isn't lost on me, even in his standard chino shorts and dress shirts. The emblem on his clothing hints at their expense, and when I open the door to find him wearing a silver watch worth more than fifteen-hundred dollars complementing his ensemble, I'm feeling very underdressed. I might as well be naked, as Logan joked.

"You look pretty," Oliver sweetly says, and immediately, all my worries vanish. Zack shakes his head and swipes a hand over his boy's freshly washed hair. It's been another day of sunscreen, sawdust, and overall dirt.

"Ready?" Zack asks. He suggested earlier we walk as the boys could use the energy release and Logan's home is less than half a mile away.

"I'm good to go," I say, noticing a tremble in my voice. I'm so nervous and I'm never like this.

"Are those brownies?" Trevor asks. I'm holding a tray of brownies. Thankfully, I had a box of mix in the cupboard. He beams at me while Oliver exaggerates licking his lips.

"Want to carry it for me?" I ask but realize too late that I have one tray and four eager hands when the boys collectively holler, "I do!"

"How about I carry the brownies?" Zack offers and tips his head to suggest we begin our walk. The boys scamper ahead of us while Zack stays beside me.

"My son beat me to compliment you," Zack says, almost pouting like he did the other night. He definitely taught his son this look. "He got it wrong, though. You look beautiful, angel." His eyes roam over my hair and down to my neck. A smile accentuates his praise. It's nice to be considered pretty.

"Why do you call me that?" Angel isn't the most common of endearments.

The corner of Zack's mouth quirks upward as though he has a secret, but he isn't offering it up. "It fits." *That's it*. He doesn't say anything further.

"Well, you don't look so bad yourself, handsome." I grin, and he does that dazzling thing by smiling wider, happy with my compliment. "Oh, come on. I'm certain you've heard that a million or two times in your life."

Zack laughs. "It's still nice to hear that a beautiful woman thinks I'm decent looking." That vulnerability hits. He's wearing another dress shirt, rolled to his elbows, and dark shorts. My eyes lower to his expensive watch, and he follows my gaze.

"It was a present to myself when I graduated from law school. I'd worked hard, and when I got my first job, I blew my whole paycheck on it." He shakes out his arm and bends his elbow in a sexy manner, acting as if he's checking the time on a *fifteen-hundred-dollar* watch. "It's the most frivolous thing I've ever bought."

I chuckle as well. "Last night was the most frivolous thing I've ever done."

Zack stumbles. "What?"

I shrug, dismissing my comment.

"Oh, no, you cannot just say something like that and expect me to let it go." His voice drops. "So, you liked it?" For a confident man, the question startles me and reminds me how uncertain he is under that hard exterior. The question is, why?

"Liked what?" I tease innocently as I smile back at him. He checks on his boys ahead of us before wrapping an arm around me, placing his hand on my hip and tugging me closer to him.

"Liked my tongue on you." He leans in to kiss my neck. "Liked my lips on yours." He nips my earlobe. "Next time, I'm going to use my fingers."

"Next time?" I flirt, turning to face him after a quick glance at his boys. My gaze drops to his mouth. "Think you'll have a next time?"

"Absolutely," he promises. "This is not a one-night stand."

"Ten-day fling?"

His eyes lower to my mouth, and his voice drops when he says, "I don't think ten days is going to be enough." He gives me a kiss that's too short, too quick.

"Dad," one of the boys cries out, and we both glance down the road toward them. I expect Zack to remove his arm, but to my surprise, he doesn't release me. His arm stays around my lower back with his hand on my hip, and I smile to myself with how right he feels next to me.

11

[Zack]

The barbecue is craziness and chaos as the younger set of kids run around the yard and the older set suddenly has friends lingering near the house. Logan has fallen into domestic bliss for the second time, and it gives me some hope it might happen to me someday. It would be the first time, though. Jeanine and I had a strained relationship. As another attorney, we met at a conference. One night with too much scotch led to a phone call from her two months later. She didn't want to keep the babies, but I did. We married to protect her reputation. She didn't want to be a single mom in a tough industry. However, she was never a mother figure. We had nanny after nanny, and as I buried myself in work, I hadn't paid attention. I let her run our home until she started having affairs.

Fly in love.

Ben must have been on some serious meds when he wrote that suggestion. He knew I didn't love my ex-wife. God forgive me, but Jeanine hadn't loved me either. We married for the children, which everyone knows is the worst reason. My boys hardly knew their mother or me, and I recall what Trevor said earlier.

Our mother left us.

River's response startled me even more. She assured him she would be here for him. Well, at least as guardian of the tree fort. Either way, that commitment would take more than ten days. It would take a lifetime. I glance over at her talking with Autumn, wondering if she meant it. Would she want a second chance at . . . *what?* Love? I didn't believe in love for myself. Would she be interested in marrying again? Could she love someone else's children? Of course, these were hypothetical questions. Autumn loves Lorna, Logan's daughter, but that's different. She's known the girl her entire life, and Autumn has loved Logan since she was a teenager.

You can't fall in love in ten days, can you?

You can't really fly in love, whatever the hell that means.

And I've learned my lesson about lust and one-night stands. Thank goodness River and I have already made it through two nights, and this marks our third. I look forward to a few more.

Autumn hands baby Ben to River, and Anna falls into the seat next to me.

"I like her," she says, smiling over at River who's rocking the baby in her arms.

"You just met her," I remind her as she admitted her guilt at not meeting River sooner.

Anna shrugs. "You like her, too," she teases.

"How do you know?" I laugh.

"Because you can't take your eyes off her." I chew my lower lip, trying to prevent my gaze from wandering to River, but I only pause on Anna for a second before the pull is too strong. Anna chuckles next to me.

"It's a good look on you."

"What is?" I ask, turning to face Anna more fully this time.

"Love."

I sputter. "I'm not in love." Anna knows my philosophy. Love is dangerous. Not only had I not loved my wife but I'd also watched my mother—who had deeply loved my father—fall apart when everything happened. My father's professions of love had been a lie. He claimed he did what he did because he loved her, but he also made his decisions sound like her fault. My mother hadn't disagreed.

Love was Anna and Ben, but that was rare and not for me.

My eyes leap to River again, finding her looking back at me.

"Not yet, maybe, but soon," Anna retorts.

I break away from River's smiling face and stare at Anna once more. "How do you know?" How does one know when they really love a person? Even Ben couldn't explain it other than saying you just know, and he was one of the sappiest guys I've ever met.

"When it feels like flying instead of falling," Anna says.

My mouth falls open. *What?* Her eyes fill with concern at the surprised expression surely written on my face.

"What?" she asks.

Is this some weird Ben-Anna voodoo? "Nothing," I mutter. "It's nothing."

Anna reaches over and pats my arm. "She's amazing with the boys."

I sigh and pinch the bridge of my nose. "I know."

"It's a gift to love other people's children. She told me she's a pediatric oncology nurse. I don't know how she does it." Anna glances up at River. "I only lost Ben. I can't imagine how many she's lost."

"Anna," I whisper. I'm not discrediting River and her patients but losing one's husband had to be worse.

"Don't let her get away," Anna warns, her voice softening.

"Where is she going to go? She lives next door." I scoff, trying to lighten the conversation.

Anna narrows her eyes. "You never know how much time you have, Zack. Cherish it with the right people." She squeezes my wrist and stands to approach River, reaching out her hands to signal she wants to hold baby Ben next.

Eventually, we sit around the outdoor table on Logan's new deck. The night continues with good food, an abundance of alcohol, and lots of tall tales. Most stories shared are about the four of us in college and out. The memories are ones often repeated, but Logan and Mason embellish them, laying it on thick with River.

"There was the time Zack was stoned and wanted to break into the football stadium."

"And when Zack thought he could sing and took over the mic during a concert at the bar."

"And remember when Zack wanted to run naked through the park." This one certainly had River's attention, and the exaggerations went on and on. Nothing was too damaging, only embarrassing, and each tale made River's brows rise higher. She was definitely seeing another side of me. One I'd actually forgotten. Between my partnership at the law firm, the divorce from Jeanine, and suddenly single parenthood, I no longer remembered that guy who did all the crazy things they mentioned.

Then Logan says, "So what's it like living in Zacky's old house?"

My arm has been around River's chair, occasionally touching her hair and absentmindedly wrapping strands around my finger. My friends haven't missed my constantly touching her. Her hip. Her wrist. Her hair. Like the positive-negative pull of magnets, I'm drawn to this woman so opposite me.

Only, this question stills my movements, and River chokes on a sip of wine. I peer at Logan, wondering why he'd ask such a question.

"Find any secrets in there about our boy?" Logan teases until he cries out, "Ow," and looks at his wife, who sits perpendicular to him.

River doesn't look at me as her shoulders stiffen. "I'd never share his secrets." She winks at Logan, who chuckles, but tension rolls down her back. She's a bit quieter the rest of the night.

When the boys are drooping, and it's time to walk home, I carry Oliver, who feels like a sack of sand against my chest. Trevor stumbles between River and me like a drunken sailor. We could have gotten a ride with Anna, but River and I needed a moment to clear the air, and I didn't want to burden Anna with my boys.

"Why didn't you say anything?" River asks as we stumble down the road.

"It isn't important. It was a long time ago."

"How long?" she asks, not letting it be.

"More than twenty-five years."

"And your family decided to move?"

"Not exactly." I side-eye her and then focus forward on the dark street ahead, occasionally lit by the soft glow of a rare streetlamp.

"What does *not exactly* mean?"

"It means, we didn't decide to move. We just . . . moved." This is not a story I want to tell River, especially with the boys in tow, even if one is sleeping and the other is practically sleepwalking. The night is alive with the chirp of cicadas, and the light, late summer breeze chills the air. River goes quiet again.

"Look, it's not something I like to talk about," I say, my voice sharper than necessary. She doesn't respond.

Finally, we near her house.

L.B. Dunbar

"Why don't I walk you home?" she suggests, noting Trevor leaning on her and Oliver continually sliding down my weary arms. *Jesus, when did he get so heavy?*

I nod in gratitude, once again finding I'm either saying I'm sorry or thank you to her. When we eventually stand before Anna's front door, River lowers to hug a sleepy Trevor, who collapses against her and probably doesn't realize she's hugging him. Standing upright, she kisses the back of Oliver's head, rubbing a hand down his back afterward. In only days, she's been sweeter to my boys than their mother had been in seven years.

Last, she looks at me. "Let's negotiate."

My brows lift. "What do you mean?"

"You tell me your story, and I'll watch your boys for a day."

"No deal." I scoff. That's not even a trade-off.

She leans in, lowering her lids. Her gaze lingers on my lips. "What would you like instead?"

"You," I admit. She wants my story, and I want her, even if it is only a ten-day fling, or eight, or wherever we're at. After watching her interact with my friends and love on my boys all night, I know there hasn't been anyone like her in my life.

Anna's words haunt me. *Spend time with the right people.*

River is the right person.

"I'll seek counsel and get back to you." She winks as I jostle a heavy Oliver to halt his slide down my body.

"You're terrible at negotiation," I say with a laugh.

"My grandfather would say, *never settle for less than what you want*." Her voice drops to imitate the male figure she mentions. Then she leans forward to kiss my cheek before backing away. "I had fun tonight. I really needed that."

The comment surprises me, but I don't have the chance to ask for details before she's finger waving at Trevor and retreating down the driveway.

Damn, Anna's right. I really like this woman. I *might* even be able to love her.

+ + +

Later, the boys are in bed, and I'm pacing my bedroom when I decide to text River, unable to wait out her *seek counsel* comment.

Me: I couldn't take the deal. It wasn't fair. I wouldn't want my boys to spend a day with you when I haven't had the chance.

I have River's number because I left her mine on the day we began building the tree fort. I didn't want my boys wandering into her yard uninvited, and I especially didn't want them messing with the tree fort before we had it safely restructured.

She sends me a text in response. Immediately, I glance out my bedroom window like the creepy stalker I've become with this woman.

River: Come spend the day with us tomorrow then. I promised the boys a maiden voyage in their new tree fort. Although a voyage suggests a ship, they seem to have a good imagination.

I had a good imagination as well, but it is nothing compared to the reality of my mouth on her. Her lips. Her skin. Her sweet pussy. My dick hardens, and I swipe a hand through my hair. I'm becoming a mess over this woman, but I can't seem to stop myself. I want her in the time I have here at Lakeside.

Scanning her dark yard again, I don't see her outside, but suddenly, I need five minutes with her. Maybe ten. I didn't get a decent good night kiss, and I need one.

Me: I have an imagination, too. I imagine us meeting in your yard in ten minutes.

River: You have quite the imagination then. I'm almost ready for bed.

Dammit, I want to join her there. Even if all I do is wrap myself around her and kiss her, I want to feel her body against mine. It's been almost twenty-four hours, and that's been too long.

Me: Just ten minutes. I can be quick. I recall how quickly she came last night, two times, and I want a repeat. I'll give her ten orgasms if she'll just meet me in her yard.

River: Just took my clothes off. A smiley face emoji follows, and I realize I might need a little longer than ten minutes with her.

L.B. Dunbar

Me: Clothing optional then. I respond with my own winky face emoji and wonder who I've become. I don't emoji. I don't do smiley faces, and I don't think I've ever tried to flirt through text messages.

Only for River would I do such a thing.

River: 10. For half a second, I wonder if she's read my thoughts about those ten orgasms, and then I realize she means minutes. She'll give me ten minutes, and I'm racing for the door, shooting off a text, begging Calvin, Anna's oldest, to listen for my boys. The older boys have been exceptional at dealing with my younger ones, and I owe Bryce and Calvin. Hell, I'll pay for their college education if it buys me time with the woman next door.

When I enter River's yard, I find her near the cliff. There's a sharp drop off the property but a staircase nearby with roughly the same number of stairs to descend to the beach below as Anna's next door. I would know. I helped my dad repair them year after year.

River's back is to me as I approach, and I place my hands on her hips, leaning in to kiss her neck. Unfortunately, she's dressed, but I'm not complaining.

"I didn't get a proper good night kiss. I'm here to collect."

"I think you're the one with poor negotiation skills." She spins in my arms, and her hands land on my chest. She immediately drops her gaze to my lips.

"How's that, angel?" I tease, licking my lower lip before biting it, and observe her eyes widen as she watches me.

"You shouldn't be jealous of your boys."

This surprises me. "I'm not."

"Lawyers shouldn't lie." She tilts her head, glancing up to my eyes as she calls me out. I peek up at the lake in the distance behind her. She's right. I am jealous. She promised time with them and hadn't asked me to join.

If you want something, you should ask for it. Hadn't I been doing that? Maybe she's the one who doesn't want time with me.

"You're so good with them, and they adore you."

"Well, I adore them."

I adore her, and I want her to like me, too. "I suck at flirting," I say instead of my actual thought and recall our first kiss and how she turned me down for more that night. I'm still fucking up if she likes my kids but isn't so certain about me.

"You're getting better at it. Like anything, it takes practice." Her hands have slid upward, and her fingertips massage the back of my neck.

"Mason's good at flirting."

"I don't want Mason," she says, her tone clear.

"He was flirting with you at Logan's." I sound like a jealous teenager, but I don't want River falling for Mason. It occurs to me that Mason presently lives next door, and he'll be sticking around for longer than ten days. I don't like the possibility that River and Mason could have more time. The proximity is too tempting. Then again, Mason already said River wasn't his type, and if it wasn't that I knew *who* his type was, I'd call out his bullshit.

"That's just who Mason is. I have his number," she knowingly states. I imagine many men have hit on River over the years. She might have a whole little black book of numbers.

"And what number is that?" I question, tugging at her hips to pull her tighter to me.

"Zero." She slowly smiles. "He has zero chance with me."

"And what about me?" What are my chances of getting more from her? Getting to know her better? Being more than zero with her?

"It's up for negotiation." She laughs after her statement, and I join her laughter.

"I don't have long tonight," I say, getting back to my purpose.

"Where are your boys?"

"In bed. I bribed Calvin to listen for them. I told him I'd only be half an hour tops." I pause, biting my lower lip and watching her repeat the motion. "But I couldn't sleep without a good night kiss from you. I want to feel your lips on mine and smell your scent on my fingers."

She blows out a breath. "You might be getting better at this flirting thing."

"You think?" I tease, lowering my voice.

Her response is to chew at her smile.

"Then how about this?" I release her hips and cup her jaw, bringing her mouth to mine in a searing kiss. The last twenty-four hours slam into me as too much time apart from this mouth. It's been forever since I've really kissed anyone, but River's lips are an endless well I want to drink from. Her name is appropriate. She's quenching a thirst I've had for too long.

My hands quickly roam down her body. Shaky fingers slip to her neck, cascading down each side of the column. My palms caress over her shoulders and down her arms to her wrists. Jumping to her hips, I slide my hands up the front of her, palming each breast in a needy squeeze. She isn't wearing a bra, and the heavy globes fill my palms.

She yelps against my mouth, but I don't break the kiss. Instead, I massage the swells, pressing them together before lowering my forefinger and thumb to pinch her nipples in tandem. The sharp nubs poke at the thin material of her dress. I release her mouth and lower for one breast, nipping at her over the light fabric.

"I need to touch you." My voice strains. That magnetic force is so strong, and I can't fight the attraction. I don't want to fight it. One hand fists the side of her dress and scrunches up the fabric. The other outlines the swell of her hip before sliding forward and slipping between her thighs. Her hands clutch at my shoulders for support as I discover she isn't wearing underwear.

"Sweet Jesus, tell me you weren't bare down there during dinner?"

"And if I was?" she teases, kissing the side of my neck.

"I should have taken you around the house and fucked you senseless."

The sharp intake of her breath hints she might have liked that. The warmth of her soaked center confirms my thought. Slowly, I dip a finger inside her.

Her breath catches again, but she still speaks. "I wasn't bare, but you know me, I can't keep my clothes on." During dinner, my friends razzed her with their knowledge of her naked time in her yard.

"I hate that they saw you naked," I hiss, drawing my finger back before rushing deeper inside her.

"Why?" She gasps, and her eyes lower as I retreat and stroke my thumb over the spot that will set her off.

"I want you all to myself." A second finger joins the first, and I slam into her, filling her.

"That's a bit caveman." Her complaint is choppy. Her body rocks against my fingers. My thumb finds that nub again.

"Call me a scalawag," I whisper in her ear. "This treasure belongs to me." I nip at her neck as my fingers surge in and out of her.

She laughs, and the pleasing chuckle flips my insides. She's so . . . fun.

"Getting your pirate on?" Her voice continues to strain, and I twist my wrist, reaching deeper within her. She groans, and the throaty sound is rough and deep like her pirate imitation earlier in the day.

"Plan to plunder the seven seas and one beautiful, ravishing *River*." My mouth seeks hers as my fingers work through slick folds. Her hands slip down my chest to my waist, and she's dipping into my shorts before I can stop her.

"River," I warn.

"Compromise," she whispers. Reaching into my shorts, she wraps her fingers around me. I'm hot and stiff in her eager palm, and she squeezes me with confidence as my fingers fuck her. She strokes and tugs while I slide through her channel. My hips buck forward, and hers match mine. I want to be inside her, but I don't want to stop touching her. I don't want her to stop touching me.

"You're gonna make me come," I groan, nipping at her neck again while my fingers slip through her moisture and my thumb flicks over her clit. My hand on her. Her hand on me. It's too much. She's a pirate seeking buried treasure, and I'm so close to exposing it. She could easily find my heart, and I'd have no way to protect myself.

Her fist moves faster, swiping her own thumb over my seeping slit, using the liquid against me. My fingers retreat to the brink of her entrance before rushing upward to fill her again and again. Her head tips to the side, and I scrape my teeth along her neck. My hips thrust, forcing my dick against her palm and my fingers deeper into her.

"Zack," she whimpers in warning, and I love the sound of my name mixing with the catch in her throat.

"That's it, angel." Her legs stiffen as they did the other night, and then her knees give. Holding her around her waist, I keep her close, allowing her to lean on me. My fingers ride the tide of her falling apart, and her hand works faster over my swollen shaft. I don't have time to warn her before I'm spewing like a geyser.

"Damn," I mutter, making a mess on her fist and my shorts. When I pull my fingers free, I lift them to my lips, catching the scent of her, and then suck them clean in my mouth. She removes her hand from my dick and licks across her palm. My mouth falls open in shock before she smiles, and I cup her jaw, crashing my mouth over hers. I want to mix the combination of her flavor with the taste of me on her tongue. Swirling around hers, I blend us together, savoring everything about her. This woman shocks me to my core, but I love it, and I'm at great risk of falling for her.

Or flying, as Anna called it, just as Ben had. I still think they've both misspoken, but it doesn't matter.

Sensing my time is almost up, I reluctantly pull back from River's mouth and press my forehead against hers.

"River, you're amazing," I whisper, closing my eyes with our heads together. My hands still hold the edge of her face.

"You're not so bad yourself, counselor. Your art of negotiation is improving, too."

I chuckle. She's the one I thought needed improvement in this area, but I realize there's a lot I could learn from her.

"Would tomorrow be too soon to spend a day with you? Me *and* the boys?" I sheepishly ask, not wanting to break her promise to my sons but inserting myself into the plans.

"Tomorrow sounds like a date," she teases, pulling back to look me in the face. "And bring your story with you."

She winks, and I'm captured. I'm going to confess all my dark secrets, and then she's no longer going to adore me as I'd hoped.

12

[River]

It's barely nine in the morning when a sharp whoop and a loud holler pull my attention to my backyard. Running across the lawn are two T-shirt-clad pirates, complete with eye patches, bandanas, and pirate hats. One carries the telescope. Another holds a plastic sword.

Oh boy.

I exit into the yard through the sliding glass doors and find a sheepish father rounding the house, scratching at the back of his neck.

"I'm sorry it's early. They've been up for hours. I held them back as long as I could."

"It's fine," I say with a wave. "Coffee?"

Zack shakes his head. "I've already had two cups."

"Be right back then," I say, pointing at the house and then pause. "Want to come in?"

Zack turns to look at the back of the house before glancing at me. "Another time." He points toward the tree house. "I better watch them."

As I enter the house to make myself a cup of tea, I watch Zack stand below my tree, gazing up at his boys tipping over the low walls of the tree fort. Trevor holds the telescope outward as if scanning the lake. Oliver drops through the entrance and scrambles down the new ladder. A swing was added as the platform was extended, and Oliver climbs onto it. He pumps his little legs while Zack slips his hands into his pockets and watches his son.

I don't suspect he's speaking to them. He's such a strange man when it comes to his boys. I don't understand why he isn't more affectionate with them. Then again, some people just aren't. Quincy admitted he was a distant father. A disciplining man. He let his wife be the soft one in their parenting. His children are even older than me, and I'm grateful I'm not technically related to them.

I continue to hold on to the hope that Zack can be different.

Returning to the yard with my tea, I stretch out on the chaise. The day will be warm, and I'm dressed in shorts and a tank top. This is my day off, and I plan to devote the entire day to the Weller men.

"Kept my clothes on for you," I tease, and Zack turns around. Slowly, he makes his way to the lounger and crawls up next to me.

"I wish you would take them off."

"Now?" I flirt, tilting my head and giving him a teasing smile.

"Definitely not now," he says, pouting in that way he does.

"So, no *friends*-cation activities today." From my understanding of things, the group is gathered in both memorial to their friend and a new tradition that began a year ago. It sounds like roughly the time I moved into the house. Their days are packed with activities for the crew that includes adults and kids ranging from teenagers down to an infant.

"The only rule is dinner together every night. Ben didn't want us to feel confined to schedules, but he also didn't want us each going our separate ways, especially Mason, who has a tendency to wander and shack up with random women."

"And Zack would never do that," I tease, shaking my head, knowing enough about this man that random isn't his style. However, I am curious if he's been with anyone since his divorce.

"Zack doesn't do that," he admits. "I've already told you, the last one-night stand I had turned into my wife."

"And how long have you been divorced?" It's the perfect opening to learn more about father and sons.

"Since March." Zack squints up at his boys. "It was this time last year that I learned of Jeanine's affair. It'd been going on for a while with some young intern in her office. She said she couldn't come on vacation with us here because she had a business trip in France. Paris. Conveniently romantic for business. Turns out, she took her own vacation with the boy toy."

"And you're not bitter," I sarcastically tease, although I'm being harsh. No one wants to be cheated on.

"I'm not. Not really. It's hard to be bitter about her because then I'd have to say I had feelings for her, which I didn't. I'm only bitter that I lost out on time and love with someone else."

"Really? Is it too late to fall in love? You're only . . . forty, if that."

"I'm forty-one now."

"Thirty-eight," I say, pointing at myself. "And I'm not a mom." I tip an eyebrow to suggest I'm jesting. The statement reminds us both of what I had to explain to the boys yesterday. "But I'm still holding out hope for one day." I refuse to believe I'll never find love or have children of my own. It's just taking me longer than the average person.

"I'm sorry about what Oliver said. He shouldn't have said that."

"He shouldn't have told me I should be a mom?" I ask to clarify.

"It was rude."

I huff. "I'm flattered that he thinks I'd do a decent job of it." I am honored. Not everyone is worthy of the title mother, and I'm thrilled Oliver sees the potential in me to be one.

"And then Trevor asking you to be his mom." Zack closes his eyes and swipes a hand through his hair. "It nearly broke my heart."

I bump his shoulder. "Well, I'm flattered again that I could be his, according to him. I'm sorry about their mother, though. I don't understand. Does she not see them?" It's invasive to ask, but I'm invested in these boys. I want to know about them.

"She has supervised visitation."

"Supervised? That sounds extreme." My first thought is she physically hurt them. As a trained mandate reporter, I'm grateful I've never had to suspect parents of abusing their child. The bruises I see on a kid come from blood draws and repeated punctures from needles, ports, and tubes.

"I didn't trust her not to use them against me. I had a great divorce attorney who knew how to negotiate. I wasn't willing to compromise when it came to them."

His protective tone is surprising but welcome. He'd fight to the end for his boys, and I'm happy to hear it in his voice. I glance over at the boys. Oliver has returned to the fort and holds the telescope while Trevor swipes the plastic sword at something imaginary within the fort.

"What did she do to them?" I whisper.

"She didn't love them. I have no forgiveness for that." His voice turns colder, edged in ice, and I twist my neck to look at him. The Zack of our first meeting has returned. His jaw clenches, and his expression hardens. His eyes crackle instead of sparkle.

"And you do?" A lump forms in my throat, and I find myself holding my breath for his answer.

"Of course, I do." He nods in confidence without looking at me. "They might be hellions, but they're my hellions. As their father, I will not abandon them." His tenacious tone should be a comfort, but there's something laced beneath the sound that raises the hairs on my neck.

"Do they know you love them?"

"I . . ." He can't answer, and the thought makes me sad.

What did your father do to you? It's the only explanation I have for the questioning glare and tight jaw. Was his father as standoffish as he is? Or did his father abandon him like his wife did their boys? I turn back toward the boys, and we watch them in silence for a minute.

"I didn't know my own father." I shrug, opening up to this man I hardly know. "I'm not bitter about it. Can't miss what you didn't have, but I had the best grandfather. He was all the dad figure I needed." I wasn't bitter about my own absent father. My grandfather meant the world to me. He wasn't a substitute but the real deal as far as I was concerned. My only regret is he passed too soon. I could use his sage advice and encouraging quips from time to time as I age. He'd have a lot to say about Zack Weller and his sons.

"I'm sorry." Zack turns to me, his eyes roaming my face.

"Don't be." I weakly smile. "Grandpa always said a man is only worthy of what he can give, not receive. My dad didn't want me. Grandpa considered him unworthy to be my father, so he filled the position instead."

Zack continues to stare at me. "He sounds like a wise man." His slow-growing grin does funny things to my insides, and I realize my grandfather would have wanted to hug Zack and slap him on the back of the head in equal portions. He would have told him in no uncertain terms to get his shit together. *Those boys need you.* I can hear the declaration in Grandfather's voice. He was such a feisty man, and I loved the stuffing out of him.

"Unfortunately, he passed when I was a teenager." I glance over at the boys, feeling Zack's eyes still on the side of my face. "Cancer." One word explains it all.

"That's why you're a nurse."

"That's why I'm a nurse," I confirm, turning back to him.

"What about other family?" He swallows around the question, and I watch his Adam's apple bob.

"My mother was a single parent for most of my younger life. Then she met Cecil when I was a teenager. They married right after I left for college. They live in Florida, and I see them once a year." Cecil is a decent man, but we didn't exactly mesh. He wasn't a father figure but more of the man in my mother's life. I don't resent him because my mother deserves happiness. She found love later in life. I only hope it will happen for me one day.

Mom had been distrustful of people. She'd been hurt by my father, a man I never met. On the other hand, I was trusting up front and learned my lesson later. I wanted to have faith in people. *A kind heart lives longer*, Grandpa said. *Beats better*. He'd tap two fingers over his chest and pat them in a rhythm to mimic a strong heartbeat. When he died, I disagreed for a while. It seemed only the good died young and left us too soon, but later, I understood. Those who are kind live on in our hearts. We never forget a good deed.

Eventually, the boys both come down from the fort and approach the lounger.

"How goes the maiden voyage?" I call out.

"Maiden? This isn't a girl thing," Trevor scoffs. He plops down on the end of the lounger, keeping his back to us while Oliver stands beside me.

"What's a voyeur?" Oliver asks.

Zack chokes on air, and I correct Oliver while I circle his little wrist with my hand. "Voyage. It's taking a trip or having an adventure. A maiden voyage is the first journey a ship makes."

"It's not a ship." Trevor corrects me, glancing over his shoulder.

"But you're pirates?" That's what they said they wanted to be. However, a child's mind can change daily. Some of my patients are princesses one day and evil witches the next. We remind them either way, cancer is the dragon that needs to be slain.

"It's a fort that we captured," Oliver explains. "Now, we need to protect it."

"Aye. And did ye find the buried treasure, argh?"

"There isn't buried treasure." Trevor's sullen tone punctuates the air.

"Trevor," Zack warns beside me as he senses his son on the verge of being rude.

"Are you sure?" I sing-song the question, tipping up a brow.

Oliver's expression mimics mine. One brow arches as he sing-songs in response. "Is there?"

"Have you looked?" My voice drags again, hinting the boys should.

"We've been looking through the telescope for hours." Trevor pouts, looking every bit like his father but not pulling off the cuteness his dad does. He crosses his lanky arms and huffs.

"I don't think it's been hours," Zack mutters, sounding a little testy himself. I reach out for his forearm and hold my hand there.

"Sometimes, a treasure can be right under your nose. You might not need a telescope to find it."

"Is there buried treasure?" Oliver's little voice rises with excitement.

"I'm not sure." I tap my chin. "Maybe search the yard."

I sense Zack's eyes on me, but I don't look at him. Trevor has swiveled at the end of the lounger, and I stare back at him.

"What did you do?" Zack teasingly hisses beside me.

"Is there a map?" Trevor questions, finally falling in line.

"No map. You must use instinct." I point at my head. "And smarts."

Oliver speaks first. "I'm smart."

"You are not. I'm the smarter one," Trevor snaps.

"Hey," Zack barks, startling all of us. "What have I told you about insulting your brother?"

"Someday, he might be the only person I have."

It's my turn to peer at Zack, surprised by the advice he's given a child.

"My brother is my best friend. I forgive him anything," Oliver adds as if this lesson has been imparted on them repeatedly. Silence falls for a second. I have so many questions but decide now is not the time to ask.

"Okay, treasure hunting. You don't need to dig, but you do need to search. The yard is the boundary. Do not go into the street. Do not climb the fence. An X marks the spot, but you must look carefully for it." I wink at Oliver before gazing at Trevor.

"Agreed?" I question. "Give me your best argh if you do."

"Argh," Trevor grumbles.

"Aye aye, Captain." Oliver salutes me and steps over to Trevor. He taps his brother's shoulder. "Race ya."

The two take off for the front of the house, and I turn to Zack. "Do you have a brother?"

"I do. One older one." He meets my gaze.

"And he's your best friend, forgiving you everything?"

"My best friends are my brothers from another mother who forgave me for anything. That's what I want Oliver and Trevor to understand. They're twins. Their bond is unique."

I stare at him as he stares back at me. "Who hurt you?" I whisper. It's not his ex-wife. He's repeatedly said he didn't love her.

"No one," he mutters, turning his attention to the distant lake. He owes me his story about the house, but I decide not to press. My hand remains on his forearm, and I stroke his warm skin. Zack glances down at my touch, staring at my fingers tickling the length of his arm. He reaches for my hand, lifts it, and presses his lips to my knuckles, lingering there while he closes his eyes.

"You're one of a kind, River Nagle," he says for some reason.

"Don't you forget it," I tease.

"I don't think I'll ever forget you." He speaks against my knuckles before turning to face me and reaching for my face. He tugs me to him for a hard kiss, sharp with tongue and ending with a light nip to my lower lip. It's over too quickly and thankfully before the boys round the house again.

"Dad, we can't find it."

"Keep looking," he says, holding his eyes on mine.

L.B. Dunbar

"Why don't you go help them?" I encourage. It won't take long with adult eyes.

"I'm afraid you'll disappear." The statement surprises me, but whatever his meaning, his eyes quickly shutter back to their protective shield. He releases me and stands without clarifying why he'd say what he said.

"Zack," I call out. "Sometimes, the treasure you seek is right before you. That's my hint to the boys."

But perhaps, it's a hint for him as well.

13

[Zack]

We found the small treasure chest—literally about the size of my fist—with two pieces of candy and two five-dollar bills inside. Mason was right; River was going to turn Trevor and Oliver into spoiled monsters.

With a little prompting, the boys rushed to River to thank her for their find. It had taken a while to discover the placement, which was under the base of the tree fort. The boys had to look up, not down, for her gift, and it was a reminder of what she'd said. *Sometimes the treasure you seek is before you.*

I didn't miss the analogy. She was a treasure, and I see her plain as day. Unfortunately, I didn't know what I'd do about her. I was leaving in another week. Logan had done the long-distance thing with Autumn for a while until he got his head out of his ass and realized he couldn't live without her, but this was different. I was enjoying River, sure. I liked how she was with my boys and me, but my little unit of three had a long road before us.

Our maiden voyage continued, free of maidens.

A brand-new nanny was lined up to start upon our return home. I'd spoken with my law partners and requested some additional time off for the adjustment, requiring a little less time in the office. I'd make up the work from home. I already started working from home long before I went into the office in the mornings and late into the evenings after I returned home. A shift to dedicate hours at home wouldn't be difficult. I'd accepted I needed to reinvest myself in the boys. The divorce had been nasty. Then with Ben's illness and subsequent death, the past twelve months had felt like a chaotic spiral.

River's sudden presence kept up the spinning effect.

"Who's hungry?" River asks after the boys express their gratitude.

"Me," they say in unison, raising both their hands.

River lays out an extensive menu of options before the boys decide on macaroni and cheese and chicken nuggets.

L.B. Dunbar

"You don't have to do this," I say as she stands from the lounger.

"If I don't make the food for them, I'll be the one to eat it all." She pats her stomach, which shows no sign of excessively eating frozen fried foods or cheese-laden pasta.

"I'll be back in a bit." She leaves me in her yard with my boys, who settle down for what I know will be only a short respite. After lunch, they'll wind up and want the next adventure.

"Can River be our mom?" Oliver asks, climbing up next to me on the chaise.

Oh boy. "It's not that simple, little man." I tug him over my lap, and he plays with the collar of my T-shirt.

Trevor climbs up next and sits beside me. "Why not?"

"Because moms and dads need to fall in love. Then a dad asks a mom to marry him." I don't go into the whole explanation of how falling in love usually happens *before* you are a dad or mom. We'll get to that conversation later. Hopefully, years later where I'll be emphasizing abstinence and condoms.

"Were you and Mom in love?"

We've had this conversation before, and I always tread lightly around it. *Lawyers shouldn't lie*, River said, and I don't want to mislead my boys.

"Sometimes moms and dads fall out of love. That doesn't mean they don't love their kids. They just don't love each other like they once did." It's the best explanation I can give because I don't want to tell them how too much scotch and a reckless night led to their conception. Or how I married Jeanine with nothing more than feelings of friendship. I quickly learned we couldn't even be friends. I'm surprised we remained married as long as we did.

"So you fall in love with River and ask her to marry you," Oliver states as if it's that simple.

"But River isn't a mom, so Dad can't marry her. He needs to find someone who is a mom."

Oh man, I didn't expect him to take my explanation so literal.

"Guys. Dad isn't falling in love with any other mom, and he isn't in love with River."

Something clatters behind us, and we all turn to see River standing outside the sliding glass door.

"Was just bringing out the plates and forks when I dropped one," she explains, not looking up at us as she bends for the utensil.

"Let me help you," I say, shifting Oliver off me and rolling from the chaise.

"No," she says too quickly, sounding a tad out of breath. "No. I've got it." She holds up a fist full of forks to stop me before setting everything on a four-person, glass-topped table.

"River?" I question, lowering my voice as I step toward her, but she waves a hand to dismiss me. Abruptly, she turns for the house, giving me her back and slipping inside. A funny feeling fills my belly, and it isn't pleasant.

River keeps up a steady stream of conversation when lunch is served, chatting with the boys about their favorite things. Television shows and movies. Books and video games. She doesn't look up at me but smiles at them while they eat. She isn't eating macaroni and cheese or chicken nuggets after all, and I feel guilty when I do, but I'm starving.

"Let me help you clean up," I say once the boys are done and asking if they can go play.

"I've got it. You enjoy them." She nods at my sons.

"I was thinking of taking them down to the beach. We've encroached on your yard long enough."

River nods. Giving me a weak smile and a tight voice, she says, "Sounds fun."

"Come with us." I reach for her arm while she holds dirty plates.

"This is your time with them." Her eyes avoid mine.

"You offered me a day with them *and you.*" I pout, but she isn't looking at me. River bitterly chuckles while shaking her head. I don't understand the dry laughter.

"Like you said, I'm bad at negotiating."

"Let's re-evaluate terms," I suggest, continuing to hold her arm, afraid to release her. "A day at the beach. Then later, I'll tell you everything. The house. The person."

"The person?" she questions. Her piercing gaze finally returns to my face.

Swallowing around a lump in my throat, I reply, "The one who hurt me."

"Zack, you don't need to do this." Her lips purse, suddenly brushing off her request to know my story. "You don't owe me anything. You're not indebted to me. It's been my pleasure to feed your boys, give them a treasure to hunt, and allow you to fix that old tree fort. It's nothing. Really."

"Really? Because that seems like a lot to me, and I want to repay you."

Her eyes narrow at the comment, and her back stiffens. "I do not need payment for being kind." Her tone turns sharper than I've ever heard.

"I didn't mean to insult you," I defend, taken aback by her tone.

"I'm not insulted." Clearly, she is, though, and I don't know how to get out of this ditch I've dug.

"Then just come to the beach because you promised us a day together, and I'm not ready to give it up." Once again, I find I'm not done with her. I'm not certain I'll ever be finished, and it's a dangerous thought as I only have a few days remaining here.

Her mouth falls open to say something, and then she clamps her lips shut. She doesn't look pleased, and I'm definitely missing something, but she finally acquiesces after another glance at the boys in the tree fort. Without another word to me, she nudges her arm free of my grasp and enters the house, knowing I won't follow her inside. I can't bring myself to enter the place, and it's her best defense to shut me out.

14

[River]

For the remainder of the day, I try to let it go. *So, he didn't love me.* What did I expect? We'd only known each other a few days. We couldn't fall in love that quickly. I'm not interested in falling in love with a man who won't be sticking around after another week. I don't need some declaration of commitment or profession of devotion, so I don't know why I'm upset. Maybe, it's the way he said it, like he was offended. Like *of course*, he couldn't possibly consider falling in love with me.

By the time we've reached the beach, I'm more confused than ever, though. Zack is constantly touching me. Hand on my hip. Fingers in my hair. A tender kiss to my shoulder.

We dig in the sand with the boys and play in the waves. The boys eat snacks that I brought, and Zack is appreciative again. He has so much gratitude it's getting on my nerves. Eventually, the boys want to leave the beach, and I need a break. Despite the fun, it's been a long day.

After we pack things up and head toward the stairs, Zack hangs back while the boys climb ahead of us. "Have dinner with us."

"Zack," I groan.

"What? What happened? We were having such a good time." He pauses on a step while I take two more before facing him. He glances over my shoulder at the boys, narrowing his eyes as if in thought. "You heard me earlier, didn't you?" He sighs. "I'm sorry. I'm sorry if it sounded wrong, but we just met. I have the boys and just—"

"I get it." What I don't get is why I'm still upset. It isn't like I expected him to fall madly in love with me after a handful of days and a collection of kisses. This is why I couldn't do one-night stands. What did I think a ten-day fling would turn into? A marriage proposal? *Preposterous.* Yet my heart still aches. For all the warnings that single parents shouldn't get involved with others, I wonder briefly if anyone considers the *other*. The one who quickly falls in love with both children *and father*. What happens to her when her heart bursts with feelings for more than one Weller boy?

"The truth is, I don't have time for love."

I remain a few stairs above him, and my mouth falls open. Words tumble forward. "Then what do you want from me?"

In frustration, Zack turns away and swipes a hand through his hair—his signature upset move. I hate that I recognize this about him already. "I just want to fuck you." The words are quiet and low while stated so direct and indifferent. He blows out a breath and sheepishly glances up at me before taking the stairs to close the distance between us.

To say my heart fell to my feet, felt stomped on, and then kicked off this staircase was an understatement. I'd never been so . . . shocked or hurt. There was no doubt we were attracted to one another—*physically* attracted—but this felt like a little bit more than just fucking one another. In fact, he was putting in a lot of effort to spend time with me, dragging his own boys into the mix, for a man who only wanted in my pants. Which he'd already been in, twice now.

"Shit, I told you I suck at this." He reaches out for my arm, but I flinch away from his touch.

"That wasn't flirtatious, Zack."

"Let me redirect—"

I hold up a hand to stop him. "This isn't a courtroom. This is life. We're not negotiating. To be clear, we're having an argument. Also to be clear, you *make* time for love. You find it. You give it. You have a big fancy watch that dictates all the hours in a day." I pause, chest heaving as if I've run miles. "If you don't want it, then that's a different story. If you don't want love, then that's your . . . prerogative." I can hardly say the word. Then I remember that he's already told me he doesn't want anything more from me. He told me the night he arrived with a wine bottle in hand. He wanted one night, and I don't understand how we've gotten to three or four plus afternoons with his boys.

My arms have flailed out to my sides in my tirade, and Zack just stares at me. Puffing out a breath, I turn to take another step, but Zack quickly overtakes me, stopping me with an outstretched arm to block my climb. He checks over his shoulder to find his boys, noting they're taking their time ascending the stairs but aren't looking back at us. Zack lowers his face to mine, coming in too close.

"That came out wrong. I want to be with you. There's no doubt I want between your thighs and inside you, but let me be clear, it's more than fucking you. I want to know who you are and why you're so kind. I want to understand how my boys fell in love with you so fast and if I can get there too because I am falling. Definitely falling." His hand cups my jaw, and his mouth possesses mine. The kiss is so powerful, I lean backward, tipping over the railing at my back. His fingers slip along my cheek, dipping into my hair. He fists a section at my nape and kisses me harder.

"I'll make time for you." He kisses me once more. "Have dinner with us at Anna's tonight."

I'm so stunned by the fierceness of his kiss and the determination in his tone, I nod to accept, having the fight kissed out of me.

Damn, he does not play fair.

+ + +

The meal passes in Anna's dining room under a cacophony of grumbling kids and adult laughter. I drink too much. Somewhere during the night, I admit that I don't have many female friends in the area outside the acquaintances I work with at the hospital and end up invited to Monday margaritas and manicures, a new tradition Autumn created once Anna moved permanently to Lakeside. I'm actually looking forward to some girl time.

Zack walks me home, but we don't make it to my backyard before we're making out like desperate teens against the side of my house. Frantic and rushed, I'm losing my mind over this man. His lips. His teeth. His fingertips. His hands roam my body like a raised topography map, memorizing hills and discovering valleys. He's everywhere all at once. Forget flirting, this man can kiss. He's no longer holding back but ravishing me.

"I don't want to argue with you," he mutters against my mouth, hanging on to our earlier disagreement. "Ever."

"It's going to happen." Love isn't without fighting. Sometimes against it. Sometimes for it.

"As long as we make up." His mouth moves to my jaw and down my neck. His hands continue to wander. "Always make up."

"Compromise," I mutter before I nip his earlobe.

"Negotiate," he moans near mine. My skirt lifts, and his eager fingers find I'm not wearing underwear. He sucks in a breath. "You didn't."

"All night," I tease. Actually, I slipped my underwear off before he walked me home.

"Angel," he growls, slipping two fingers into me. The heel of his hand rubs at my clit. His hips thrust forward, forcing the heel harder against me. My fingers fumble with his shorts, but he swats mine away, catching my wrist firmly in his hand and lifting it above my head. "Tonight is only for you. Get lost in me."

He has no idea what he's saying. I don't know what to think of him or his boys or what we're doing, but for now, I take his mouth and feel his fingers. He pleasures me like no one ever has. I'm gasping for air and swallowing his scent when the orgasm rips through me so intensely my knees buckle. The house holds me upright because Zack doesn't relent. Dropping to his knees, he attacks with his mouth next. His tongue delves, and his lips suck. He's marking me so I'll never forget him.

"Come," he demands between my thighs, and I sway against his mouth until I break once more. Silvery stars prickle my sight in the darkness. My breath rasps in heavy gulps as Zack stands and crashes his mouth against mine again. Breathless and weak, it's too much, too fast, and I'm spiraling. The next thing I know, Zack has me in his arms and carries me to the lounger where we lay beside each other, mirroring one another. His fingers brush back my hair as I stare at him until I can catch my breath.

"I owe you some explanations," he finally says.

"Zack," I tenderly groan. "You don't owe me. If you don't want to tell me, you don't have to."

"I do."

"Orgasms for information?" I tweak a brow. "You're terrible as a negotiator. I should have given one to you, if I wanted knowledge."

"I like your way of thinking, but this is different." His eyes glance from one to the other of mine, shifting back and forth before speaking. "I want to tell you. I'm just . . . I'm worried about what you'll think when I'm finished."

"I would never judge you." I know all about being unfairly accused of something. I'd never do it to him, but curiosity at what he could possibly tell me grows.

Taking a deep breath, he begins. "My father was in prison." Zack closes his eyes. Shame washes over him. "He was an accountant and embezzled more than a million dollars from the company he worked for."

Reaching for his face, I tenderly stroke his jaw, allowing the prickle of his scruff to scrape my palm. His eyes open.

"He was sentenced to twenty years." Zack exhales. "As you know, my mother and Anna's mother were lifelong best friends. My parents were from Chicago like Anna's family but moved here around the time my brother was born. My father had been offered a job he felt he couldn't refuse. Unfortunately, they lived above their means. He'd fallen into debt and started slowly taking money from the company he worked for. We later learned he had a gambling problem."

My fingertips rub along his jaw, encouraging him to tell me more.

"I'm not making any excuses for him. There are none," he bitterly states. "We could have moved. We could have sold our home and lived more within his income. He should have gotten help. My mother defended him. She blamed herself. So did he." He frowns. "He felt he needed to keep up with Anna's parents. Her father made his money in the sausage industry, and when they bought the house next door as a second home, my father wanted to prove himself. He always wanted more, more, more. A bigger house. A better car. More money. When he was arrested, we were actually broke. He'd gambled away what he'd embezzled."

"I'm so sorry, honey," I whisper. He shakes his head free of my hand by rolling to his back. My chest squeezes. I want nothing more than to wrap my arms around him and protect him from his memories, but he's lost in his head and doesn't want my touch.

He faces the dark sky and swipes a hand into his hair. "He wasn't a terrible dad. He was a great dad actually." His voice lifts in surprise as if he's just now discovering this about his father. "We were just a normal family. Roof over our head. Food in our fridge. I didn't see any signs of trouble. My father was a dreamer. A schemer," he adds softer. "He was always talking about the next thing, a better thing. House. Car. Job."

Zack pauses, eyes upward, but I doubt he's concentrating on any one star.

"The police came to the house and arrested him right in front of my older brother and me. I was fifteen, and Noah was eighteen. My mother cried for days." He blinks. "We were such spoiled punks, and I was angry. So angry. Noah left. Dad used his college fund, but Noah found a way on his own. He left me behind to face my friends, the neighbors, my teachers, and deal with our mother. Everyone knew our story. We moved into Anna's home, the house next door, for months. My mother had never worked a day in her life. Anna's dad gave my mom a loan, which I didn't learn about until years later. I paid back every cent."

Zack turns his head to face me again. "Robert . . . that's my father's name . . . was released from prison shortly before I met Jeanine at a conference." With a shaky breath, he adds, "God forgive me, but sometimes I think those boys are my penance. I turned my back on my dad, and I was given twins to torment me as a father."

"You know it doesn't work that way," I say, keeping my voice quiet. I don't like how he's spoken about the boys as punishment and know he doesn't mean it. He's hurting, and I reach for his hand instead of his face, needing to touch him in some manner. He curls his fingers around mine, holding on tight like he did that first night.

"I know," he whispers. "I *know*."

"Did you ever see your dad again?"

Zack shakes his head. "Somehow, he found me after his release. I was a successful lawyer. I'd married Jeanine. We had the boys. He wanted to reconnect. I didn't want him anywhere near my children. I assumed he wanted money. He'd been a gold seeker his entire life. He loved money more than his family."

Zack snorts, still lost in thought. "Twenty years." He blows out a breath. "I didn't know him anymore. He wasn't the man I remembered, and I wouldn't have recognized him if he hadn't come to me."

He blows out another breath. "He divorced my mother during his incarceration. She would have waited for him if he hadn't. She would have taken him back had he not done her the favor of letting her go. The divorce was the final blow. She wanted a new life. One as far from here as she could get. She moved to Arizona."

People change, but I knew he didn't want to hear it. Perhaps his father had turned over a new leaf. Maybe he really did want to reconnect with his son. Maybe he did want money and could pay it back this time. None of it seems to matter, as Zack has no sympathy for his father. The bitterness in his tone speaks of the hurt and harm Robert caused his family.

"Where did he go? After he saw you that one time?"

"I have no idea, and I don't care." His harsh tone doesn't surprise me. His anger does.

"You've never tried to find him or contact him?" I question.

"For what purpose? So he can try to harass me into giving him money? He took everything from us. We lost this house, our pride, everything." His rising tone echoes in the quiet night, and he sits upright, bending a knee and lowering his other foot to the grass. He swipes a hand through his hair once again. Slowly, I sit up beside him and press a kiss to his shoulder before leaning my chin on the muscular curve.

"You need to forgive him. If not for him, for yourself. Maybe forgiving him will allow you to have a . . . better relationship with your boys. Allowing you to give them what you want to give them."

Forgiveness is the best medicine for a broken heart, Grandfather would say. I don't think Zack is interested in swallowing that pill, but forgiveness is part of healing, and Zack needs to heal. Zack needs to forgive his father, and maybe he'll get over the hurdle he has at being a dad. He doesn't have to understand his father's motives, although he has some version of them. He needs to let go of the hurt, which is easier said than done. Forgiveness was the only way I could let go of a man I'd never known, who hadn't stepped up to be a father. Then again, I had a better deal, and cure-all, in my grandfather.

Zack huffs, clearly upset at my suggestion, so I add, "I'm sorry all that happened to you." Then I back off from dispensing advice.

"It's the reason I could never abandon the boys."

"Would you have walked away from them to get away from Jeanine?"

"Never," he hisses, glancing over his shoulder at me. Everything in that word tells me it had never been a thought. "If she wanted a divorce, she'd have to ask me. I didn't want to ever feel like I'd given up on my family."

He would have remained in a loveless marriage instead of losing his children. This redeems him somehow, but I can't process that yet.

"But you eventually did ask her for a divorce," I softly state as clarification.

"She was on her second affair. A man can only take so much, and the boys were suffering. They needed a mother."

"They need their dad, too," I remind him although perhaps now isn't the time to mention it. I had a strong sense of Zack burying himself in work to avoid his wife but without realizing he was neglecting his children.

"That's why I have them." He had custody of them but was he involved with them? Were they his center or an axis that tipped him to the edge but never fully pushed him over?

Zack sighs. "I shouldn't have told you all this. Now, you're going to judge me."

"Why would I judge you?" My forehead furrows.

"My father *stole* money. He was a crook, a thief."

"Your father's sins were not yours." I didn't even need to quote my grandfather to come up with that statement.

"It's embarrassing as fuck," Zack huffs.

"He abandoned you," I remind him, understanding his position. But I'm also about absolution. If Quincy's children had listened to him, if they'd allowed him to ask for forgiveness, things might have turned out differently for all of them. If Zack could offer forgiveness to his father, he might feel differently about his own position as one.

"He abandoned all of us," he harshly states again and stands from the lounger, giving me his back as his hands slip into his pockets. "I'm going to go."

"Don't leave like this," I softly plea, and he cranes his neck enough to look at me over his shoulder.

"We aren't arguing," he tells me as if I need the clarification. Of course, we aren't fighting, but a wall has come up around Zack. His defensive tone, along with his body's position, tells me he's trying to avoid fight mode and opting for flight instead.

"We aren't arguing," I confirm. "But you're angry, and I don't want you walking away upset. Just let me hold you."

"I'm not a child," he snaps, shifting to face me. *Defensive 101.* "I'm over it."

Clearly, he isn't, but I don't want to discuss the blatant denial with him. I just want to hold him. Zack needs to know not everyone will walk away and not everyone will take advantage of him. Most of all, I want him to know I don't judge him for something outside his control.

"I still want to hold you." I stare up at him, willing him to look me in the eye before he walks away. If it's that easy to run, then he isn't the man I think he is. He's just preached poetic about abandonment, but he needs to understand you can abandon people right in front of you. You can be physically present but not be a participant, and Zack needs to be present. With his sons. With me.

As he stares back at me, he must read my thoughts or see something in my expression that tells him not to walk away. He folds down to the chaise, and I extend my arm out for him, suggesting he curls into my chest. He wraps his body around mine like a drowning man clinging to a buoy. His leg slips over both of mine, and his arms circle my waist. His head tucks into my shoulder, and I stroke his hair until he grows heavy against me.

Pressing a kiss to his head, I consider how we're all still children inside no matter how separate we feel from our parents. No matter how old we get. We're still someone's child, and the effects of that experience can haunt us, or comfort us, the rest of our lives.

15

[Zack]

River works the late afternoon shift, which ends near midnight. The boys and I spend the morning fishing and then the remainder of the day on final touches for the tree house. I really thought we were done the other day, but we had some trim pieces, and Mason wanted to check something with the roof.

"Looks good, man," Mason says to me. "So does that smile."

"What smile?" I ask, glancing from the tree fort to my friend.

"The one on your face since you've met River."

"I'm not smiling," I argue, biting my lower lip to fight the curl.

"It's a nice feeling, isn't it?"

"What is?"

"Falling in love." Mason's words surprise me. I'd like to argue he doesn't know the feeling, cite that he's never been in love before, but I know that's not true. As much as I always thought he loved Anna, and Ben recognized it too, Mason never admitted the truth until last summer after too much tequila.

I could argue that I'm not falling in love with River, but I know I'm doing something. Falling might be a good analogy for the sensation, but Ben wanted me to fly in love—whatever the hell that means.

"You know, my card from Ben said to fly in love. Have any idea what he meant?"

"I think it's cheating if I try to help you solve the Ben-letter mystery." Mason chuckles like he *does* know what Ben intended. "But I will say, falling sounds negative. We fall from grace. We trip; we fall. It's a downward effect. Flying sounds like . . ." Mason looks overhead. "Like soaring above the clouds or floating through the sky. It's upward. It's high." He waves his hand through the air.

"Are you high?" I question, narrowing my eyes at him.

"No." He snorts. "You asked me a question. I answered. Don't be a dick."

L.B. Dunbar

I turn in the direction of my boys, waiting to hear them reply. Thankfully, they're too busy making up adventures in the tree fort.

"Too bad the tree house is here, and you live there." Mason waves a hand toward the great, wide yonder. Detroit is on the other side of the state, more than three hours away.

"Yeah, it's not like I can tell the boys to go to River's and play for a bit."

Mason nods. "Be sad to leave this behind, especially when you want to play with her, too."

I'm not *playing* her. "You heard her. The tree house will remain, and she'll guard over it for them."

"Until she meets a man, has her own kids, and lets them play in that fort instead."

My head swivels to where Oliver looks through the telescope out at the lake and Trevor points at something above it. Will River marry again? She mentioned how she held out hope that one day she'd be a mother. She's only thirty-eight. That isn't too old. Suddenly, I imagine a little girl running around this backyard with gold-colored hair like her mother and blue eyes that match the sky. In a long, flowing dress, she giggles as she swings on the addition to the fort.

"You okay?" Mason startles me, clapping me on the shoulder, and I realize I'm rubbing at my chest.

"I'm good."

"Okay." He nods. "As Thing One and Thing Two are busy, think we can chat a bit about that second property at Lake Liberty."

"Yeah," I mutter, glancing back at my boys lost in their wonderland and missing a little girl who doesn't exist but needs to join their adventure. "Yeah, let's talk business."

+ + +

Me: I know it will be late, but do you think I could still see you tonight? Signed, pirate captain.
River: Pirate captain? Is this a demand or a request?
Me: Negotiation. I know where there might be buried treasure.

120

River: Will we need a map?
Me: Giving out clues. This is my treasure hunt.
River: Oh, I like this. What clues do you have for me?
Me: Only one – Midnight at the ship.

When midnight arrives, I'm crammed inside the tree fort that looks large and spacious from the outside, if you aren't six foot three. My ass hits one wall while my feet rest against the other. I've been sitting here for roughly twenty minutes, setting everything up first and then taking time to recall memory after memory of playing in the fort my father built.

Noah and I spent hours on that first platform when we were young, and then we hid on it when our parents occasionally fought. My brother would make up games for us to play to distract us. Only one night, we couldn't avoid the noise coming from the house. Something shattered, and Noah jumped from the platform, bypassing the ladder. I followed after him in time to find my mother holding her cheek on the kitchen floor.

He didn't mean it, she kept saying despite the fear in her eyes. Noah went off somewhere screaming at our father. I later learned his explanation was the same. He'd never meant to hit her. He had never done it before. He didn't have the chance to do it again. He was arrested months later.

Tipping my head back, I swallow around the memory and close my eyes, listening to the rustle of leaves overhead and the lake rolling against the shore at the base of the cliff. Inside my mind, I'm still that child making up games and decide my suggestion that River meet me in this new tree house seems silly.

Then her head pops through the small opening. "Hey." Her voice is light. Her smile is bright. Her eyes twinkle. "What's all this?" She finishes climbing through the hatch and crawls over to me. There isn't space for her to stand but enough area for her to sit next to me. I've spread out a sleeping bag to prevent our backsides from numbing against the hard wood and set out candles Anna had.

"They're battery operated as I didn't want to risk real flames in a freshly built fort and in a tree."

"Very responsible of you," River teases.

She thinks I'm a tight-ass at times. After my father was arrested, I was uptight, working hard to prove myself in all matters. My father might have been a criminal, but I was still smart, still athletic. I went to college and law school and graduated with honors. I owe Ben and friends for most of that motivation. They allowed me to push myself and then pulled me back, forcing me to enjoy those four years at the university, not just let them pass with my nose in pre-law texts. I was a self-made man after that and I didn't waste a dime, or barter it, or gamble it. My watch was one of the most frivolous purchases I'd ever made. After that, every nice thing I had I bought only when I could afford it. Thankfully, my profession was lucrative, but I didn't take my paycheck for granted. I worked hard to earn it.

"You okay?" River interrupts my thoughts.

"Yeah, I've been a little distracted today, but I'm better now." I slip an arm around her and tuck her into my side, pressing a kiss to her forehead. She makes things even better for me, and I wish I could bottle her up like an elixir to drink on occasion. These weeks could have been spent wallowing in Ben's loss and cursing under my breath at my boys, but I've actually enjoyed my time here.

You make time for love.

"So, buried treasure?" River questions, placing her hand on my belly. "Did you find it yet?"

"It just magically appeared," I flirt. "But there are many pieces in the treasure chest."

"Oh really." She laughs and, God, I love the sound of it. That trill alone is worth more than gold or diamonds or a fifteen-hundred-dollar watch. She has other parts worth even more.

Cupping her jaw, I turn her chin, so she looks up at me and I lower to her lips, kissing her first in slow measured sips before opening wider and taking her tongue with mine. She shifts beside me and the kiss deepens. Tongues move in unison as our lips meld together. She's wearing a linen dress so lightweight and thin, I can feel her ripe breasts through the fabric pressing against my arm.

"Treasure one," I whisper against her mouth before restoring the kiss. Gently, I maneuver her over my lap.

"Treasure two and three," I mutter, lifting both my hands to cover those swollen globes peeking at me through sheer material. She isn't wearing a bra and she has no idea what that does for me. Her breasts are large and firm, filling my hands. With her center positioned over my quickly hardening dick, her mouth returns to mine. I continued to massage her breasts, squeezing the heaviness before pinching the already stiff nipples.

Breaking the kiss, I glance up at her hair and brush it back. "Treasure four." The spun-gold color has a value all its own and curtains her face, tickling my shoulders as she undulates over me. I twirl several strands around my index finger before releasing them.

"Treasure five," I murmur, slipping my other hand, still on an ample breast, to cover her heart. Underneath her skin, the organ beats rapidly, and I like that I'm the one causing it to race. She does the same to me.

"Treasure six," I hiss, buck my hips and forcing my hard length against her soft center. I'm wearing sport shorts tonight, and the silky, track material easily slides over my shaft. There isn't much barrier between us and if I have any say in this night, there won't be any others in a matter of minutes.

"How many pieces are in this treasure chest?" she softly strains as she rocks back and forth over my hardness. Her hands cup the back of my neck as her lids lower.

"It seems endless, and I want to possess all of it." Her eyes slowly open wider, and she bites the corner of her lower lip, forcing me to lean forward and take the soft puckered skin with my own. We kiss again and again, growing warmer in the confined space. Our desire grows hotter as well.

"Are we doing this here?" she says as if reading my thoughts.

"It's our maiden journey. We need to break this ship in." I smile against her mouth.

"Do I call you captain or sir?" I love how she's playing along.

"Aye, to both, and I'll call you lass as we swashbuckle our way across the shores, as we—"

"If you say rape and pillage, this role play is finished." She good-naturedly laughs as she interrupts my enthusiasm.

"I was thinking more like plunder and pluck." My mouth seeks hers once more.

"You mean fuck," she whispers, low and seductive against my lips.

"Now, I like how you're thinking." Quickly, I scrunch up the sides of her flimsy dress and tug it over her head. It easily slips free without ties or buttons, and within seconds, she's bare within my lap.

"You're naked," I gasp. She isn't wearing underwear again.

"And in my own backyard. It's a shock, I know."

"Give me that sassy mouth, lass." River purrs at the command, and I take her mouth hard, loving how she's not laughing at our role play but falling in line with it. She's wet, and the moisture dampens the front of my shorts. I wiggle at the waistband to lower them and kick them off. When River returns to my lap, her heat hits my throbbing dick, and we both groan. She kisses me again while slowly moving her soaked folds along my steel length.

"I need to be inside you," I hiss, holding her hips and guiding her to rock faster.

"Yes," she purrs as her clit catches on my tip. Fuck, I'm so close I could slip right in, but we need to be smart. I break the kiss and fumble for my shorts, removing a packet.

"You're sure about this?" I hesitate.

"Don't argue with me," she teases as she shifts so I can cover myself.

Watching me roll on the condom and tug once at my dick, she tips a brow. "Treasure eight?"

I return her to her position, lining up the tip at her entrance. "This is treasure eight." Without further foreplay, I slide into her, and her arm circles my neck. Her head tips back, and I moan against the column of her neck. She is a million pieces of treasure, and I want to own every last gem and jewel and chunk of gold. She's everything and priceless.

We move as one. Her hips roll as mine jolt upward. Her breath catches as I surge forward. Our moves complement each other until the rhythm of our kissing no longer meets the beat of our bodies. River leans back, and I lick up her neck before lowering to a heavy breast, opening wide to swallow one swell. My tongue swirls around the peaked nipple before I clamp lightly on the nub. She squeaks, and I move to the other breast, giving it equal attention. Her thighs tighten their hold over mine, and her hips move faster.

"So good, angel," I stammer through the praise. She's everything I knew she'd be and so much more. It's been so long since I've had sex, but it's never been like this, and I'm not talking about the fact we're in a tree house. This magnetic thing between River and me is something special.

I feel like . . . I'm soaring above the clouds.

My eyes focus on where I've entered River, and she moves over me. Her breath is growing shallow. Her thrusting grows more erratic.

"Feel good?" I whisper.

"Incredible, sir."

I bite her where her shoulder meets her neck, and she cries out. "I'm so close."

In so many ways, I want her closer, closer than is humanly possible, and I wrap my arms around her waist, letting her take the lead as she's found a rhythm to get off on my body. Get lost in our connection.

Slipping a hand forward, I wedge my thumb between us, circling her clit with the thick pad, and she gasps. Once. Twice. Third times the charm, and she breaks. Her thighs clench. Then she rises on her knees and falls back down, forcing me to the hilt. Her head lolls back, and her hair cascades along her spine.

"You're so fucking beautiful," I grunt as she tightens around me. Slowly, her head lifts and her lids open, exposing those sapphire blue eyes.

"Treasure nine," I hum as she focuses on me. I want her to always look at me like she is right now. Overwhelmed by the emotion in them, my body shivers, and I hastily pull her off me.

"Zack," she whimpers.

"On your knees, lass." It's such a tight fit in this box of a house, but River turns and twists and angles her ass at me, and I scramble to my knees, spreading them wide to bring her before me. "Go down on your elbows."

Fisting my fingers in her hair, she lowers her head to the blanket. Her elbows bend and then she stretches forward as if reaching for something to hold. I can't wait and slam into her, spreading her ass cheeks before squeezing them together as I slide back to the edge.

"I want you everywhere," I warn her, and she mewls in response. The sound spurs me onward, thrusting into her as her palms flatten on the floor, and her body shudders, sliding forward with the force of me delving into her heat. Sweat drips from my forehead. My chest is slick from the night's warmth. She rocks back, chasing any attempts of my retreat.

"Don't want me to leave your body?" I hiss at her ear.

"Don't want you to leave me," she moans to the padded sleeping bag.

My fist tightens, and I ride her faster, chasing her words.

I don't want to leave her either.

16

[River]

"Angel," he groans like a battle cry before he stills. His body cages mine as he goes off inside me, pulsing, pumping, teasing me with what he could give me.

I quickly dismiss the thought of a priceless treasure—a child of my own.

Zack collapses over me, heavily breathing and spent. His slick chest glides along my back, and perspiration rolls down my neck. It's so warm in the little hut in my tree, and I start to giggle.

"I'm a mess," I mutter. My hair is plastered to my face. My thighs are slick. Zack chuckles and presses a kiss on my shoulder blade.

"Come on," he says, slapping my backside, and I yelp as he slips out of me.

What the hell? I'm not into the spanking thing, and I'm about to tell him this when I peer over my shoulder and see him smiling like I've never seen him smile. Dazzling. It's the only word to describe those white teeth digging into his lower lip while his entire mouth curves upward.

"Put this back on for a second," he says to me, holding out my dress. I can hardly move. There also isn't space to stretch, nor is there enough airflow as we are tucked behind the walls. Zack places a hand on my back to help me upright, and I slip the linen dress over my sweaty body. He struggles back into his sports shorts.

"Scoot." His cheerful voice is something I've never heard as he commands me to move so he can tug the sleeping bag out from underneath me. "Follow me." He leads the way to the exit of the tree house, and I can't help but laugh louder.

"Where are we going?"

"More adventure." The smile on his face fills his voice, illuminates our dim surroundings, and warms my insides. He sounds so . . . happy.

He climbs down the ladder, holding up a hand to help me down after him. With the blanket slung over his shoulder, he takes my hand and leads me forward.

"Careful." He guides us in the pitch dark down the one hundred and fifty wooden steps to the shore. His eagerness has him skipping steps and taking them sideways with his long feet in order to keep his hand in mine, but I'm slowing him down.

"Just go," I encourage with a laugh and allow us to slip apart.

"But you'll still follow me?" His voice hints at vulnerability again. Doesn't he realize he's the one who will eventually be leaving, not me?

"I'll be right behind you." *Following you anywhere.* Upon my reply, he continues to skip down the steps, and I watch as he reaches the beach. He snaps the sleeping bag out to lay across the dark sand and then tugs down his shorts. I reach the base of the steps and laugh loud and strong as he runs for the water, naked as the night. His white backside reflects in the dark before he marches into the water and disappears with a graceful dive.

Nearing the sleeping bag, I see him pop up and shake his head. His hair flips boyishly to one side.

"Come in!" he yells, and I tug my dress over my head. I can't ever remember skinny-dipping, and I race after him until my toes hit the water.

"It's freezing!" I call out.

"It's refreshing!" he hollers back, his voice carrying in the strong breeze. Gingerly, I enter the lake as soft waves lap up my knees, then my thighs, and eventually reach my middle. Zack meets me, and his mouth captures mine. His hands cup my jaw as they often do when he kisses me, and the grasp keeps me attached to him as he lowers us both in the water. My limbs tangle with his before I wrap my legs around his waist and my arms around his neck. We continue to kiss until he stands again in deeper water. I remain around him like a koala on a tree, and when my legs shift to release me from his body, he cups my backside.

"Plug your nose," he warns and then tosses both of us into the oncoming wave. As I sputter and laugh, righting myself, I splash the roll of water at Zack, and he splashes back like we're children. Eventually, he catches my wrist to stop me and tugs me to him, kissing me again. My legs wrap around him once more, and he carries me out of the water, kissing me as he stumbles in the sand.

"You'll drop me," I warn, laughing against his mouth.

"Never." His tone dips as he nears the blanket. He lowers to his knees while I remain wrapped around him, and then he's laying me back on the sleeping bag. We have more space to stretch and spread, and my legs do just that, allowing Zack to settle between them. As we kiss, he hardens once more and reaches for his shorts. Digging in the pocket, he finds another packet.

"So responsible," I tease.

"Actually, I borrowed these from Mason."

"Ew. I don't want to consider what *borrow* means. Nor do I want to think about that on Mason."

Zack has been sheathing himself as I speak, and his head snaps back in my direction.

"You better not think of Mason when I do this." Two fingers impale me with a sharp rush, and my breath catches. "Sore?"

"Ready." Shamelessly, I'm wet again, and it's not from the lake water. He moves his fingers in and out twice before removing them.

"And you definitely better not be thinking of Mason when I do this." In one swift move, he's slipping into me again, his dick rock hard. He doesn't rush, but the effect is still the same. Long and deep, he slides forward until he's to the hilt.

"Or this." He latches onto a breast and sucks it until the nipple nearly hurts. Between the cold water and the chill in the air, the nubs are already sharp and peaked. Zack moves within me while his tongue warms my breast and I melt under him. My fingers comb through his wet hair and down his goose-bump-covered back.

"You feel so amazing, angel," he groans, releasing my breast to look up at me.

"So do you." The words mingle with a sharp exhale from me. We rock into each other, taking a little more time to enjoy the motion that matches the waves near our feet. Eventually, his fingers move to my clit, and he rubs in short, tight circles until my lower belly flutters.

"So close," I warn almost too late as I'm suddenly cascading over him, loose and relaxed in a release that seems to drag like the water lapping along the shore. I whimper, tipping back my head and arching my back, forcing him deeper inside me with my hands on his firm ass.

"So deep," he mutters, licking at my neck before increasing his thrusts. He rocks hard and fast until he breaks, and the rush of him inside me teases me once more. He braces himself on his elbows as he comes down from the high. His forehead lowers as his chest heaves.

"Fuck. I think I see stars." He laughs as he quickly pulls out of me but rolls me to my side, so I'm tucked into his. Pressing a tender kiss to my forehead, we lay like this as our breathing settles and the night breeze flitters over us. It's a night I want to last forever when I know nothing does.

+ + +

We must doze a bit because I shift with a start when Zack sits upright.

"Shit," he mutters, swiping both hands down his face. "What time is it?"

I bite back the snark on my lips. *Do I look like I wearing a watch?*

"I told Bryce I'd be back by two."

Having no clue what time it might be, I scramble to my feet and reach for my dress, quickly covering myself. Zack slips into his shorts and shakes out the sleeping bag before flipping it over his shoulder. Still groggy and a little stiff, I head for the stairs and climb at a slower pace with Zack on my heels. He might want me to go faster, but he'll need to pass me because my legs can hardly carry me.

As we near the top but remain just under the crest of the cliff, Zack captures my wrist. "Wait. Just wait."

I turn to face him, and he tosses the blanket on the stairs behind me. Remaining a step below me, he aligns our bodies, cups my jaw, and kisses me once more. The kiss quickly heats, and an urgency takes over. *Why does it feel like he's saying goodbye before we top the cliff?* His mouth becomes desperate, urgent even. His hands slowly lower, roaming my neck and my shoulders before he breaks free of my lips and spins me.

He brushes aside my hair and sucks at the back of my neck.

"Zack?" I question. *What is he doing?*

Then he bites the juncture of my neck and shoulder, and my knees buckle. He catches me around the waist as my legs fold a bit and then lowers me to my knees on a step covered by the sleeping bag. He tugs the collar of my dress over my shoulder, sucking at my skin. A slight ripping sound hints at the strain of material before the fabric slips to my upper arm. He continues to suck at my shoulder. Down the shoulder blade. A hand rounds for my front, covering a breast.

"One more time," he whispers to my skin as he continues to kiss me with a wide mouth and soft caress of his tongue.

"I thought you were late."

"I need you one more time." With a hand on the middle of my back, he presses me forward. My knees are a few steps lower than my elbows, and Zack stands a step lower than me. He lifts my dress, shoves down his shorts, and slides inside me again.

"Jesus. You're so warm. I can't . . . it's so good . . . it's—" His voice catches. "I'll pull out." The comment stills me, but Zack is on his own mission. "I promise. I swear I haven't been with anyone in more than a year."

I don't want to think about what that means. "It's been three for me."

Zack stops moving. He knows Quincy died a year ago, but he's adding up the dates, putting together something I'm not ready to explain.

"You're late," I remind him in our awkward position, and he begins to move again, taking his time at first but quickly building to a steady crescendo. Our skin slaps in the quiet night, and Zack grunts behind me, filling the air with more words of praise and compliment.

"So wet. So beautiful. So good."

I'm in the moment with him, but I'm not going to reach any pinnacle. I'm spent. With his hands on my hips and his rapid-fire thrusts, it doesn't take him long before he rushes out of me and lays his length on my lower back. Leaning forward, I lower my forehead as I feel him pulse and pump at the base of my spine. He's breathing heavily again, and I match him. It's my heart that's racing.

"Angel, I . . ." he chokes on whatever he planned to say and kisses my back. Catching his breath, he finally mutters, "I'm flying."

I have no idea what that means other than he's high from the release. We've had sex in four positions, and he's had three orgasms. It's a lot in a few hours. Slowly, he stands, uses a corner of the sleeping bag to clean my back, and then wraps an arm around my waist, lifting me to lean against his chest.

"Did I hurt you?" he whispers into my neck, and I shake my head. "I don't know what came over me, but I can't get enough of you. I'll never have enough."

They are pretty words on such a lovely night, but something beneath his tone is unsettling. This final rush through sex feels like a farewell instead of a start. However, my foolish heart is racing, and my blood is still pumping, and I want to believe our time together is endless.

I want to believe he'll make time for me.

17

[Zack]

The next morning, Mason is in a mood. He takes one look at me and smiles big.

"Our Zacky got laid," he announces to the kitchen, which is thankfully empty of children. My boys are scootering up and down the driveway while Mila and Lorna draw with chalk. I owe Bryce double the money because it was nearly four when I snuck back in the house. To my surprise, he was still up watching some app. He assured me the boys hadn't stirred, and I asked him to keep it our little secret about how late I returned. I'm certain he will. He's not up himself, so I don't know how Mason knows shit, but he's smiling at me like a pleased father.

Then he steps up to me, clasps my face, and kisses my cheek. "I'm so proud of you."

"Get off me." I press at him while trying to suppress a laugh. Losing the battle, I catch Anna watching me. Weakly she smiles, and my chest tightens. It doesn't seem fair to be feeling all this emotion for River when Anna's so sad. However, I remember what she said. Flying is a nice feeling, and I finally get it. It's like Mason explained. Falling sounds negative, like a pit with a hard, rocky bottom is below me. But flying, it's endless up there with stratosphere upon stratosphere to keep soaring through.

"So. How was it?" Mason asks, placing an elbow on the kitchen island and his chin in the heel of his hand. He bats his eyes like a teenage girl wanting all the details. "Did it hurt? Were you scared? Did you use protection?"

He straightens, but he knows the answer. He gave me the condoms because I didn't have my own. I know most men carry them everywhere, especially if they're sexually active or actively seeking one-night stands. As it's the last thing I expected to happen during these two weeks, I was completely unprepared. I'm even less prepared for how I feel.

L.B. Dunbar

River is amazing, as I said, and it's not just a physical attraction. She makes me laugh. She's playful and good at heart. Down to her soul, she's a decent person, and it's so refreshing.

"Be careful, Zack," Anna warns. "I have to live next to her when you leave."

The weight of her words crushes me, and Mason rolls his eyes with his back to Anna.

"We aren't talking long-term commitment with a diamond and a contract. This was one night." Mason tips a brow. "Or will it be a few more?"

I don't know what it will be. I suggested a ten-day fling, but the phrase feels inadequate. Something happened when we were climbing the stairs. It was like heading upward, time felt like it was rewinding, turning back the clock, and I didn't want to give her up. I wanted time to stop.

The thought reminds me I can't find my watch. I thought I had it with me when I went to River's yard, but as I didn't have it when we went swimming or when I woke on the beach, I guess not. It also wasn't in my room on the nightstand where I place it when I'm not wearing it.

"Have you seen my watch?" I abruptly ask, changing subjects. Anna shakes her head, and Mason stares at me like I'm crazy.

"Who cares about your watch? We're talking about a woman here. Zacky got laid."

"We're done talking about me. Why don't you get laid?"

Mason stiffens, and Anna tilts her head from behind Mason, staring at the back of his neck. "Been a little preoccupied," Mason quietly states. My gaze shifts to Anna. *Shit.*

"Yeah, well." I scratch at the back of my neck. "I've had a longer dry spell than you," I tease hoping to lighten the tension. Unfortunately, it doesn't seem to happen as Mason's jaw clenches. Anna's face scrunches. Neither of them moves. Finally, Mason speaks.

"How about a run to the Lake Liberty project? We can grab Logan and take all the boys." The suggestion of work isn't exactly how I want to spend a day, but River needs to sleep. She works the late shift again, and I need her rested for another late night.

+ + +

River texts me to meet her at midnight, and I love that she wants me as much as I want her. At least, I hope the feeling is mutual, and I'm reassured when I find her on the lounger. A light somewhere in the house is on but not reflecting into the yard. A blanket is tucked up under her arms, and a glass of wine sits in her hands.

"Whatcha got under there?" I tease, noticing her arms are bare, as is her chest.

"Why don't you find out?" she flirts, lifting her glass for a sip. "But first, lose the clothes."

I tug off my T-shirt, kick off my flip-flops, and pull condoms from my pocket before dropping my shorts. Standing before her naked as the night, I watch as her gaze slowly roams up my body.

"You are one dazzling man," she hums, letting those eyes eat me up. It's a nice feeling to work hard on my body and have someone appreciate it other than myself. And not just someone, but River.

I crawl up the lounger and tug back the blanket to find her naked as well. Reaching for the glass of wine in her hand, I remove it and drink the remainder.

"That was mine," she says.

"I thought we were sharing," I state, recalling our first night together on this outdoor furniture.

"Not yet." She slowly smiles and presses her teeth to her lower lip.

I slip over River, forcing her legs apart with my hips. Her body is warm underneath mine, and I tug the blanket back up over both of us. River scoots lower on the lounger, and I cup one side of her jaw before leaning forward to kiss her. She tastes like wine and summer and things I've never thought about before, like hearts, flowers, and love.

Taking my time, I kiss River long and sweet, dragging out each pull before adding my tongue to the mix. She follows my lead, keeping us lazy and loose. Her fingers dig into the hair at my nape, and we stay like this for a long time, absorbing each other with tender kisses.

Eventually, my hand skims her body, outlining her form. I cover a breast, dip to her waist, and slip between her thighs. Taking my time with every touch, I memorize her. As my fingers slide into her warmth, her head tips back a bit, and I lick along her neck before nibbling at the cliff of her jaw. She's so beautiful, so responsive, and I don't know how I'll walk away from her.

My thumb joins the mix of fingers in her heat, rubbing her clit until she gives in to me. Less of a rush, more like a slow drag, her release overtakes her. Her thighs clutch at my hand, and her channel clenches around my fingers. Eventually, her hand finds me hard and ready, but I don't want her fist.

"I need inside you again."

"I'd like that." A soft grin curls her lips, and I quickly sheath myself. Entering her last night without protection wasn't a mistake. It felt amazing as I repeatedly told her, but it also wasn't smart. I'm safe. I believe she's safe, but there's another risk I don't need to take—a second accidental pregnancy. Still, the heat, the wet, the connection were immeasurable.

Once I'm covered, I slip into place and slowly glide home. We seem to hold our breaths as I enter her until I can't get any deeper. Then I still, kissing her long and lazy once more before her hips roll upward, and mine matches hers. Leaning on one elbow, I move over her body as I had before while we dance in a rhythm I've never experienced. There's no doubt this slow tempo is making love, and with this woman, it feels so right. I'm soaring again.

We keep the even pace as long as we can, torturing ourselves as my shaft feels every pull from her channel, and she gasps at every push inside her. Magnets attracting. I'll never have enough of her like I thought last night, yet time is ticking. My vacation ends soon.

I don't allow those thoughts to take over as I roll when she rocks, and I thrust when she bucks. In no time, she's warning me, and her legs stiffen in that signal she's ready to release. I stop moving my hips.

"What's wrong?" she asks, her eyes flipping open when they just closed.

"I want to feel you come around me." My thumb is rubbing her clit in a tantalizing circle, and her smile grows as she gives in to the release. She clenches and squeezes while I'm fully encased in her warmth, and it's more than I could ever imagine. Once she settles from the high, she's cupping my backside and forcing me to move, guiding me to catch my own release, which doesn't take long as I held off to allow the sensation of her around me. Now, there's no holding back, and I speed up.

"Zack." My name on her lips catches. "Zack, I . . ."

"Yes." I know what she's hinting at. "Again. Together. Let me feel you again, angel." When she starts to clutch at my dick from the depths of her channel, I burst like a rocket shot to the moon. It's an explosion of flames and smoke and so much more as I break through another layer of stratosphere with her.

When the sensations subside, I lean forward and kiss her once more, as if we have all night which we don't. Eventually, I curl her into my chest and just hold her, straightening the blanket over both of us and pretending time stands still, and we can stay like this forever.

18

[River]

By Monday night's manicures and margaritas, I have a serious girl crush on both Autumn and Anna. Autumn is the owner of Crossroads Café, one of my favorite local places, especially as it is an easy walk from my house. There isn't an eat-in dining section but a custom-made sandwich counter and a coffee station complete with sugary treats to satisfy my occasional sweet tooth.

Anna had been a high school English teacher outside Chicago before moving to the area. This past year, she worked as a substitute because of Ben's condition but hoped for a more permanent placement in the next school year. As she learned I was a pediatric oncology nurse, we both agreed working with other people's children took a special talent and patience.

After manicures, we go to Rudder's, a local bar that's darker and quieter in comparison to the more tourist-popular Driftwoods by the beach. There, Anna tells me more about Chicago—where she grew up, where she previously lived, and what she loved about the big city. She then explains how Lakeside Cottage was her favorite place and where she met Ben.

"He liked to joke he was the lawn boy." Her parents were the original owners of the sprawling house next door to mine and had a landscaping service handle their yard care. The company was owned by Ben's father, and Ben worked for his dad as a teenager. Anna and Ben met their senior year of high school. Autumn also previously worked for the family business as an office manager. Upon their father's death, Autumn moved on to her own business venture.

"Ben had given it all up to follow me to Chicago," Anna explains. They went to Michigan State University together, but Anna wanted to work closer to her home city. "Ben opened his own landscaping business and started at the roots, as he liked to say. He cut people's grass at first."

Anna gave me the background on Ben being diagnosed, their decision to sell the business, and move their family to a place they all loved.

"It was a big change, especially for the boys, but Ben wanted to spend his final days in a place he loved more than anywhere. Plus, he wanted the time with our family. We had opposite schedules with my summers off while his summers were the busiest season."

Eventually, the conversation shifts to me.

"Zack mentioned your husband passed as well. I'm so sorry to learn that. Were you married long?" Anna asks.

I don't want to lie to her, but the situation is too complicated to explain on a first girls' night out. "Not long. He was in a similar situation as your husband. Quincy had been diagnosed with an inoperable brain tumor."

"Oh my gosh," Autumn squeaks, covering her mouth while Anna reaches for my hand, apologizing for my loss.

"I understand." My response is all-knowing and filled with compassion for Anna's position. Losing Quincy wasn't nearly as rough as Anna's loss of Ben—that long-term, long-lasting kind of love they had—but it doesn't diminish the fact I had a hole in my heart after Quincy passed away. It almost equaled the loss of Grandpa, *almost*. Ben had also died young while Quincy was nearly double Ben's age. "He was older, though, and had lived a long life."

"Where did you live before Lakeside?"

"Just outside Grand Rapids." Fondly, I recall living in the second-largest city in Michigan. "When I inherited my house, it seemed like a good time for a change." I smile again, understanding Anna's decision to move, even if it happened under difficult circumstances. "Lakeside is turning out to be one of my favorite places as well."

"I don't suppose a certain neighbor has anything to do with that." Autumn wiggles her brows.

"You mean Anna?" I tease.

Anna laughs and adds, "Those men are thick as thieves, but this is girl zone. What's said here stays here."

Autumn gives her sister-in-law a skeptical look. "Oh no, I know that look. Do not go into matchmaking mode."

L.B. Dunbar

My eyes widen as I glance back and forth between the two women, and Autumn continues. "Anna hatched a little plan in that smart brain of hers to set me up last summer and—"

"And look where you are now?" Anna squawks. "In love, happily married, and with a baby."

Autumn blushes. "You wanted to set me up with a different man."

Anna waves a dismissive hand. "Mason. Logan. Potato, tomato. What's the difference?" she teases.

Even though I hardly know the men half as well as these women, I could think of a few differences. Autumn quickly defends her husband, ticking attributes off on her fingers. "Oh, I don't know, Logan's sweet, funny, and a family man."

"Well, I don't need to try to set River up. She's already with Zack," Anna explains as if I'm not present. Then she turns to me. "Speaking of family, Zack's newly divorced, as you know."

"Don't listen to her," Autumn grumbles.

"How do you feel about other people's children again?" Anna's teasing me as she already knows I love them but want my own someday.

"Quincy had a few," I admit, which tips Autumn's brow. "They are older than me, though."

"Do you see them?"

"Never. Quincy was not close to his children, unfortunately."

Anna's forehead furrows. When you're a loving, doting parent, it's hard to comprehend that some parents just are not loving and doting.

"Zack really does love his boys," she assures me, but I don't need her to be team Zack. "He's just had a rough time. He and Jeanine fought often, and in order to avoid confrontation, he worked too much, keeping himself distant from Trevor and Oliver. Those boys were left too often with nannies. But I know in his heart, he could be a good dad."

"I believe that as well. He's just . . . lost."

"They've all been in that position," Autumn interjects. "Well, maybe not Ben. But Logan was like that with Lorna, and Mason is hopeless."

"Oh, really? What's Mason's story?" I ask, just curious as I heard he has a five-year-old daughter he hardly sees.

"It's a mess," Anna says, and that seems to be her final answer on the subject.

"Speaking of other people's children," Autumn starts once more. *Were we speaking of other people's children again?* "Zack's sons adore you."

"I adore them." Slowly, I smile, recalling how yesterday was my day off, and I'd spent another day with Zack and his boys. They played in the tree house for hours before lunch, and then we shared an afternoon of sunshine at the beach.

"Their father adores you, too," Anna adds softly, and my cheeks heat. "Zack and I have been best friends our entire lives. He's a good man." She doesn't need to sell me on him. I already think he's dazzling but he's also a work in progress. *And* he's leaving at the end of this week.

"I really like him, too." I shrug and wave a hand to dismiss the topic. "We're just having fun."

"Oh." Anna's brows pinch again. "I didn't think . . . I mean, I wasn't aware . . ."

"What she's trying to say is she didn't know you were okay with him leaving soon. Having a little summer fling." Autumn wiggles her brows again. "Anna's only fling was Ben, and then it turned into attending college together, marriage, a mortgage, and kids. You get the picture."

I did get the picture, and it was a beautiful one. "I'm not really a casual girl, but I do realize Zack lives there, and I live here." My fingertip draws a line on the table as if a map lays on the wood.

Autumn chuckles. "Oh, sister. I've been there, then Logan got on board and moved here."

"I am not asking Zack to move here." My tone turns a little offended, but that is the last thing I'd do. Zack would have to make his own decision on whether he thought he'd like us to continue, if we are officially an *us,* and even then, I wouldn't want to be the sole reason he moved anywhere. Never again do I want to be in a position where I'm accused of causing a man to make life-altering actions against his will. My heart races with the thought.

Anna's eyes widen. "Why not?"

"Anna," Autumn mutters, hinting it's none of their business. Again, I don't want to lie, but I'm not interested in sharing the truth either.

"I once had a man make a choice with me at the center of that decision. He was a good, kind man, and he gave to me what he gave of his own free will, but I've been ridiculed for it. It hurt both me and others, and I don't want to ever be in that position again." My voice hardens as I speak, not interested in explaining myself to these lovely women. They might understand, but they might not, and I won't risk a budding friendship on my sordid past. "I care about Zack and his boys, and I'd never do anything to hurt them," I add, hoping to soften my tone and clarify my intentions. I didn't have any other objective than enjoying the moments I have with the three Weller men.

"Men are so confusing," Anna says. Autumn snorts.

"As if you'd know," Autumn quips, but then her expression shifts. "Although I know Ben wasn't perfect."

"No man is," Anna admits.

"Thank goodness women are." I laugh. "And on that note, let's drink to that." We raise our glasses and tap the rims before dipping into delicious margaritas.

+ + +

Mason comes to the rescue when we're a few margaritas in and no longer able to drive home. He drops Autumn at her place and takes Anna and me directly to Anna's house.

"Zack's been a pouty-pooper pants all night, so you might as well collect him here," Mason jokes once he parks Anna's SUV in the garage.

"Yes, but I live there," I say, stumbling out of the raised vehicle. "Oops."

"Well, he's only going to bribe someone to listen for his boys and sneak over to your place, so it was best to bring you here."

We aren't being very stealthy in hiding what's happening between us. If it wasn't evident before, the fact I had dinner at the house with the rest of the family and friends on my day off again sealed the deal. Zack didn't let me move more than a few feet before he'd be at my side, arm around my back, and hand resting on my hip. As if his palm was a puzzle piece made to fit on the curve of my body.

Anna trips on nothing, trying to exit the garage, and bumps into Mason. Surprisingly, he doesn't exactly catch her as much as stiffen. He allows his chest to be a wall Anna falls against, and she pats him before righting herself. His hands lift as if he's afraid to touch her.

"I got it," she mutters when she really doesn't. Her thin stature had one too many margaritas with the compliment of only chips and guacamole as her dinner. She takes another step forward, and Mason catches her at the waist before she faceplants on the concrete driveway.

Oh, dear.

"I got it," Anna snaps.

"Clearly, you don't," Mason mumbles, scooping Anna into his arms and groaning as if she weighs too much, which is impossible. She's thin in the I've-lost-everything manner of suppressing her appetite. Death has the opposite effect on me. I eat over my grievances. *It gets better*, I wanted to tell her earlier tonight, but there's really no way to explain such a thing. Better is relative and personal. We all grieve differently, and there's no timetable on how long it will take. Anna will never be "over" Ben, but as the song says, her heart will go on, having been better because of Ben. Anna stood beside her husband through a difficult illness, and now she'll have a year of firsts without him. The road ahead is still long, narrow, and bumpy.

"I miss Ben," Anna whines, wrapping an arm around Mason's neck.

"I know, sweetheart," he says as I follow him to the front door. His tone is tender while strained, and I have a hunch about Mason and his heart.

"River, can you do me a favor?" Mason asks. "Go in and get Zack. See if he can clear out the kids. I don't want them seeing their mom like this."

Jeez, that's sweet. "Sure."

I fumble with the front door and enter the house. "Zacky, I'm home!" I call out, teasing him with the nickname his friends occasionally use to address him. After crossing the large entryway, I wander to the open concept kitchen and sitting area. This house also has a bar off the kitchen leading outdoors, a formal dining room, a formal living room, a music room, and a den, plus a master suite on the first floor and six bedrooms upstairs. It's one of the biggest homes I've ever been in.

Zack finds me within seconds, having come through the back door off the patio. He rushes me, and his mouth possesses mine, almost knocking me off my already wobbling, freshly pedicured feet.

He hums into my mouth, cupping my jaw, and once he opens his eyes, they sparkle that brilliant silver.

"You taste like tequila and limes."

"Margarita," I purr. "She is my best friend."

Zack chuckles. "Feeling pretty good?"

"The best, but Anna is blitzed, and Mason's holding her at the front door. He doesn't want the kids to see her. He asked if you could clear the floor so he can bring her in."

Zack slips his arm around me like he does and guides us both to the front hall. "No one's down here, but I'll play lookout while he brings her inside."

When Zack opens the front door, Mason's leaning just off to the side, balancing a sleeping Anna to his chest. We've caught him staring down at her, a soft expression etched on his face, and he looks up, startled by the open door as if he expected to stand there all night holding her.

"I should have dumped her ass in a shopping cart and left her at the front step."

"*Animal House?*" I laugh, catching the reference.

"She loves those old movies."

Yay, Anna. Another thing we have in common, and I'm glad as I really want to remain friends, which might be difficult if Zack leaves, and he and I don't continue. He could return home, meet another woman, marry her, and live happily ever after. I believe in second chances for everything in life, which is another reason I moved here when the house was left to me. I also believe the third times a charm if that's what it takes for love.

Zack plays the lookout while Mason carries Anna toward the kitchen and then down the hall to the master suite area.

"Should you help him?" I ask.

"More interested in helping myself to you," he says, leading us out the front door and pressing me against a column near the front steps. His mouth is ravenous. His hands roam. "But I don't want to take advantage of you when you're drunk."

"I'm not drunk," I tell him although I am buzzed. His mouth against mine is sobering me up, though. Suddenly, we hear the slight patter of rain hitting the overhang to the front entrance.

"We should go to my house." My fingers walk up the buttons of another button-down shirt. He must own stock in them and have an extensive dry-cleaning bill because they are always freshly pressed. "We could go inside." It'd be nice to actually use a bed for once with this man.

Zack stiffens and squints in the direction of my dark house. "I don't think that's a good idea."

"Why not?" He hasn't been in my house yet. Not all the days he worked on the tree house nor the mornings the boys have spent in it. He hasn't asked to use the bathroom or helped himself to a cup of coffee. We're always outside. Even on the occasions we've fooled around, we've been in the yard.

As his shoulders stiffen even more, he stills my hand on his chest, and I'm suddenly stone-sober.

"I just don't." He pulls his gaze from the house and lowers his forehead for mine so I can't focus on his face. "And you've been drinking."

I pout, and Zack laughs. "Negotiate," I whisper, not having the energy to question why he won't enter the house. He pulls back from touching our foreheads.

"How about I make out with you here, taking some liberties with you until the rain stops. Then I'll walk you home and kiss you good night on your front porch."

"That doesn't sound like a good deal, counselor." I return to playing with the button on his shirt.

"It's called compromise." His voice is low as he speaks. "I'm learning the art of it."

When he cups my jaw again with both hands, I'm lost. His true talent is kissing me senseless.

19

[Zack]

Anna was certainly suffering a hangover the following morning, and I was worried River might as well. However, she sent me a text in the early hours before her shift.

River: Nothing a little ibuprofen and a lot of water can't cure, plus some greasy food from the hospital cafeteria.

Strangely, I was jealous of the hospital dining center. I wanted to feed her greasy food. I wanted to take care of her. I almost had a heart attack when she called out, *Zacky, I'm home*, upon entering Anna's place last night. I wanted to have her greet me like that every day after a shift. Maybe not the Zacky part, but I'd rush home myself at the end of each day just to greet her the same way. Hell, I'd work from home to be near her and spend more time with my boys. Home. My home in Detroit.

I was also envious River went out with Anna and Autumn, which was completely ridiculous, but I'd missed out on a night with her. Time seemed to be winding down, which reminded me I still hadn't found my watch, and I kept forgetting to ask River if I left it at her place. I didn't wear it as much while I was here vacationing, but I'd still put it on several times until I'd misplaced it. At least, I hoped I'd misplaced it versus losing it completely. It was sentimental, even if it was only a gift to myself. It marked the passing of time. The end of putting myself through school and the start of a new career. It was a time when I thought I'd shut the door on my father's sins. I was ready to move on. Selecting law as a profession was an easy decision. I'd been wronged by my father, who wronged others, and I wanted to make the world right. I wanted justice for those who deserved it and penance for those who didn't.

I was searching for my watch once more when I heard raised voices coming from the kitchen below. On occasion, there were disagreements within the house between children or between a parent and their child. Lord knows I'd had a few altercations with my twins, but when I really thought about it, they'd been a little less rebellious this trip. Just a little.

As the voices carried, the female strain sounded above the rest, and I took my time descending the staircase. I didn't want to intrude, but things were escalating in the kitchen.

"Why can't I go?" The whine from Calvin surprised me. As far as teens went, he was laid-back and easy to please. He hadn't protested too much when his parents decided to move the family to Lakeside. Ben checked in with him often about his feelings as he'd switched school midway through his four years of high school. To appease him in some ways, Calvin was given Ben's old truck as Ben hardly drove himself anywhere in the last year of his life. Soon, Calvin would be applying to colleges and selecting a future. He would be a senior in a month. Another change was going to happen for my dear friend Anna. Her oldest child would leave her.

"Because I said so." Her voice rose as I neared the kitchen. I held back in the entryway, listening to their argument.

"That isn't an answer," Calvin argues, and he wasn't exactly wrong, but he was a good kid who respected his parents' decisions most of the time. "I don't understand. It's only for the weekend."

"I'm not letting you drive back to Chicago on your own."

"I'm eighteen. I'm old enough."

"Yes, and at eighteen, I'd consider you old enough to clean your room, but there is that." Anna's rebuttal doesn't quite fit the crime in my opinion.

"You're being unreasonable," Calvin states, and for just a second, he sounds exactly like his father. As a matter of fact, from this distance and without seeing him, I might have assumed it was Ben disagreeing with Anna, if I didn't know better.

"I am not unreasonable." Anna's voice seethes with anger, and I imagine having an argument with her eldest child while hungover isn't something high on her list of things to handle today.

"Mom," Calvin whines, and the youth in his voice returns.

"No. I'm sorry, but I'm not letting you drive to the city alone."

"You said I could return whenever I wanted to see my friends, and I want to see Devon, Marco, and Keli."

"Keli?" Anna's voice cracks.

A pause follows before Calvin speaks again. "Is this about Keli? You don't like her, so I can't go."

"I never said I don't like her," Anna remarks.

"You know, you and Dad fell in love in high school," Calvin continues, and Anna gasps. My own breath hitches as I realize this is not a good defense to give his mother. "Dad would understand."

"Well, your father isn't here." Anna's voice rises, and something shatters. With that, I enter the kitchen to find Mason a few feet behind Anna. She remains frozen in place as she stares at the broken platter, and Calvin is equally stunned by his mother's reaction.

Then Anna breaks into tears, and Calvin steps forward, but Anna holds out a hand. "No. Go to your room."

Calvin glances up at Mason over his mother's shoulder, and Mason just shakes his head, signaling for him to do as his mother said. The teen storms away, and Anna sobs harder, leaning forward to grasp the edge of the countertop, bending in half as the wracking wails come from her. Mason steps forward and then stops, his eyes panicked. Slowly, he lowers a hand for her back, and she snaps upright, spinning to face him.

"Don't." Her bark is so sharp when Anna typically has no bite to her. She was this shy, quiet girl who captured Ben's attention, and he wouldn't let her pull back from him. He read her and knew how to bring her out of her shell just enough to draw her to him. He would tell us over and over again it was love at first sight. He wouldn't let her shyness, inexperience, or economic status get in the way of winning her heart.

Mason stills, and I draw closer.

"Anna." Her name is a low cry, and she turns in my direction. Seeing me, perhaps she realizes she had another witness to her breakdown, or maybe she's just so broken. It doesn't matter to me. I simply open my arms, and Anna walks into me, covering her face against my chest as I wrap my arms around her. Her shoulders shake. Her muffled cry hurts my heart, and I glance up at Mason. His fingers are deep in his hair on the sides of his head, tugging at the locks in frustration. I know he wanted to hold her. He wants to comfort her, and he's suffering from his own heartache in more than one manner when it comes to Anna Kulis.

With a slow shake of his head, he pivots on his heels and steps through the door leading outside. It slams behind him, and he crosses the patio, heading for the stairs lowering to the beach. Someone should go after him, but I'm only one person, and Anna needs my support most at this moment.

$$+ + +$$

Anna's breakdown happens shortly before dinnertime, and after I guide her to her room, I pick up the broken platter pieces. Before depositing Anna in her bed, she said something to me, and the words play on repeat in my head.

Hold on to her, Zack. Hold her so hard her heartbeat is actually yours.

As I'm vacuuming, Mila sheepishly comes down the stairs asking if her mom is okay.

"She's just sad, honey," I say to the child who is a mix of both parents, with Anna's dark hair and Ben's blue eyes. "How about pizza tonight?"

For now, I'd like anything to detract from the eerie silence inside the house. With Mason gone to the beach and each of Anna's children hiding in their rooms, I need to get us all out of here for a while.

"Where are the twins?" It's easiest to reference them in this manner because if I say the boys, Mila assumes I mean Calvin and Bryce, her brothers.

"I don't know." She shrugs, her own little shoulder heavy.

"Okay. Let me find them, and then we can organize dinner. Think about what kind of pizza you want."

"Can Lorna come, too?" The two girls are nearly inseparable.

"Sure. Let me text Uncle Logan in a minute, okay?"

Mila nods, her expression still full of worry.

"Can you do me a favor and put this vacuum away while I look for Trevor and Oliver?"

Mila slowly smiles like she's happy to have a task, and the grin reminds me of her mother, who is constantly busy. Anna loves to entertain, but she hates idle chitchat. She loves to be the one preparing, planning, and passing out items for whatever the occasion might demand.

As Mila has a job, I race up the stairs looking for my boys. They aren't in my room, their room, or with either of the older ones. I hate to knock on Calvin's door and don't feel it's my place to intervene, so I softly ask if he's seen Trevor and Oliver. When he doesn't answer, I knock again.

"Come in," he grumbles, and I open the door only slightly.

"Hey, man," I address him as he isn't little anymore. Calvin is the exact replica of his mother in teenage male form, but he isn't shy like she once was. "Seen Thing One and Thing Two?" Calvin loves to call them the nickname, and it certainly fits. With EarPods in, he shakes his head.

"Want to talk?"

He shakes his head again, glancing down at his phone. He's not so much ignoring me as fighting to distract himself. His fingers fly over the screen.

"Pizza?"

Calvin tips his chin, giving me his approval even though there's no smile in his expression. I'd love to tell him to give his mom a break, but they're all struggling in their own way, and I wonder once more if the addition of my family is more harm than help. We're almost to the one-year mark when Ben dropped the news on us as his closest friends. Of course, Anna already knew the diagnosis. The boys had been suspicious of Ben's behavior and eventually guessed what was happening. Their father was dying. None of us could replace Ben. We'd never live up to the task, but I wanted Calvin to understand something important.

"I'm here for you." I'm holding the doorknob and leaning against the jamb as I speak to him, wondering if he's even listening to me.

"I know," he mutters and squeezes his eyes shut, swiping at them with one hand and pinching the bridge of his nose.

Ah, little man who is now big, please don't cry.

"Can you shut the door?" It's a clear sign to leave him alone. He doesn't want a hug. He doesn't want words. He wants his father, and I can't help him with that.

+ + +

I tell myself I won't panic over the boys missing until I get to River's place. If they aren't there, then I'll go into full reckless mode. They like to wander off, typically together. I'd like to think they know better than to even consider heading to that beach without an adult, but they definitely know how to tempt fate and push my buttons.

When I enter River's yard and don't see them or her, I walk even faster to the tree house. Quickly climbing the ladder, I stick my head through the opening to the fort and pause. Trevor sits beside River, his head bent, his tongue waggling. His full concentration is on something on the floor that he's coloring in frantic motions with a colored pencil. Oliver sits between River's bent knees. She's still wearing her scrub pants with a T-shirt. Her feet are bare as if she stepped right out of her shoes and met the boys here. Oliver is also hunched over like his brother, scribbling with slower movements with another colored pencil.

"Hey," I softly greet them. River runs a hand over the back of Oliver's head. He doesn't answer me, but Trevor does with a matching greeting in a softer tone. He doesn't look up from his coloring sheet. His tongue continues to wiggle.

River glances up and tenderly smiles. "I was just pulling into the garage when I saw two little creatures crawling through a hole in my fence." Her gaze shifts to Oliver, and her hand strokes down his back.

"You should fix that thing," I tease, but there's no humor in my voice. I'm exhausted as I balance my arms through the opening and prop my chin on my crossed forearms to watch my boys interact with this beautiful woman.

"I can't afford it. I know it's ugly, and I'd love to rip it out, but even fence removal is expensive." She says it so casually, not missing a beat in her attention to Oliver before reaching over and rubbing up Trevor's spine. When he stiffens under her touch, she removes her hand, not offended or surprised.

I consider her yard for a second. The metal fencing runs up one side of the property, but the north side has a solid wood fence installed by the other neighbors butting up against hers. It's private and sends a message. On the south side, where the broken fence is located, arborvitae was installed ages ago by Anna's parents as a natural barrier to the yard.

"Everything okay next door?" River's voice remains quiet as she peers up at me. The boys must have heard. I'd like to think they're used to adults arguing as they'd heard Jeanine and I go at it often enough, but it's sad to consider they're accustomed to arguments because their parents constantly bickered. Jeanine and I were a rocket blast of insults and sharp attacks, using our attorney training to hold court in our own marriage. It was a disaster.

"It will be. Pizza, guys?"

"Okay," Trevor says without glancing up.

"Cheese only," Oliver adds, still focused on his page.

"I don't think I've ever seen them color." The admission sounds sad even to my own ears, and it's pathetic that I haven't seen my boys do such a simple task. They're so active I don't ever find them still.

"I find it soothing." She rubs a hand up and down Oliver's back as if stroking lightly up his spine is as calming to her as coloring is to the kids. As I continue to watch my boys calmly color, River touches one and keeps the other close. While Trevor doesn't like River touching him, he's near enough to her that his side presses against her hip. His proximity suggests he trusts her, he feels safe with her, and she comforts him.

She comforts all of us, and I don't know how I'll walk away from her.

20

[River]

"Angel," Zack grunts from behind me. He pulled me off the lounger later that night, and I'm on my knees, with my belly on the chaise cushion. My hair is fisted at the nape of my neck, and Zack's hand falls to my hip, where he likes to rest it.

"Can't. Get. Enough." He stammers with every thrust, and I clench around him. He's already given me his mouth, and I returned the favor with mine, but as he drew close to release, he flipped me to my belly and tugged me like a rag doll into this position. He's making up for last night when I'd had too much to drink, and he didn't want to take advantage of me. I appreciate the gentlemanly behavior.

"River," he warns. "One more." His command for another orgasm shouldn't be hot, but it is. If only I could respond on-demand as he wishes, but sensing my hesitation, he lowers his chest to my back and slips the hand at my hip forward. Flicking my clit, he hisses near my ear. "Compromise."

I chuckle, wondering what we're possibly negotiating in this position. This man already molds my body in whatever manner he wishes. He also holds my heart, which is dangerous. We're on borrowed time, and tonight I feel it more than ever.

When I finally break, and he follows in tandem, he collapses on my back, pressing his forehead to my shoulder blade.

"Holy shit," he gasps. Not terribly romantic, but definitely an understandable statement. He uses a beach towel he tossed on the grass to clean me up and then helps me rise to sit on the cushion once more. The blanket from the other night rests on the lounger as we used it to cover ourselves in part. As Zack tucks his face to my chest, he wraps a leg over both of mine, sandwiching my thighs between his. His arm wraps around my middle, and I stroke through his hair as he clings to me like a lighthouse guiding him home.

L.B. Dunbar

"How do you think she's doing?" I finally ask. We had pizza in my yard, giving the kids a change of scenery for the night and Anna a rest. Calvin didn't join us, and eventually, Autumn took half a pizza to her teenage nephew. I'd learned what happened, and my heart broke for all of them again. The tree house was a good distraction for the younger set. Even Mila and Lorna played along with pirate adventures while Logan and Zack discussed Anna. Mason wasn't present.

"She'll get there, wherever there is, but it's so hard. I mean, I'm her best friend, so it's difficult to watch. Ben was one of my closest friends as well, and I feel his loss, but it's nothing like what it must be for those kids or her." Zack rubs his nose against my skin. "I don't even want to imagine losing someone I love like Anna lost Ben."

A loss like that is difficult. The hole in my heart after my grandfather died didn't feel like it could ever be filled. But loving and losing my parent-figure was not the same as loving and losing a spouse. I'm going to lose Zack soon enough, but it won't be the same thing either. We haven't discussed any kind of future, and tonight would not be the night for the topic.

"Can I ask you something unrelated to them?" We've been silent several minutes allowing the breeze to cool our skin and the dark night to blanket us.

"Hmm?" Zack purrs.

"Why won't you come into the house?"

At his sudden stiffness, I realize we shouldn't breach this subject tonight either, yet I need to know why he's so apprehensive. Did something else happen to him in the house? How can he handle being in the yard? What is the connection or rather disconnect?

"It's going to sound stupid, but I love this house. It's where so many happy memories exist but also where some painful ones occurred. I just don't know if I want to face either demon by entering."

"How can you be in the yard then?"

Zack shrugs as he slowly unwinds himself from my body and perches up on an elbow. His fingertip traces along my collarbone.

"I just can. Maybe on that first day the boys crawled over here, I was pissed. Pissed to have to step foot over here, but . . . I just had to apologize. Sitting next to you was calming." His gaze lowers for my chest, and his finger slowly zigzags down my skin. "It's like my boys coloring earlier. Being near you is soothing."

"Your boys certainly aren't stagnant near me." I chuckle at the quickly restored energy of two rambunctious seven-year-olds once they had pizza for dinner.

"Still. I think they feel . . . safe with you. I told you Jeanine and I fought often, and I'm not proud of that fact, but my boys heard it. When Anna started to lose it tonight, they came here seeking peace and solace."

"They will always be welcome in this yard," I state, confident I would never turn them away. "That tree house is theirs as long as I live here."

His head snaps up at the comment, and his fingertip stills at the swell of my breast above the blanket. "Are you considering moving?"

"Not that I'm aware of," I tease. "But this house needs a lot of work, and I'm not certain if I can handle the upkeep. I mean, it's paid for in full, thanks to Quincy, but there are still taxes and so many internal repairs and renovations needed."

"Quincy," Zack mutters, returning the trail of his finger up my chest and over to my shoulder.

"Yes. Quincy was . . . the man I inherited the house from."

"Your husband."

I should really tell him the truth, but does it even matter? He'll be leaving in a few days, and I don't see us going anywhere other than where we are right now sitting in this lounger under a star-filled sky on a summer night.

When I don't answer, Zack shifts gears. "My brother called me."

"Noah?" I clarify.

"Yes. He says he might move here."

"Where does he live again?"

"He's in Chicago. He managed an upscale hotel there after working for years all over the world for the Magellan Hospitality Group."

"Will he stay with Anna?"

"I doubt it. Besides, the apartment over the garage where Mason has been staying technically belongs to Archer, Anna's older brother."

I'd only heard Archer mentioned in bits and pieces but nothing concrete. He sounded like a mystery even to his family.

"Is he returning?"

Zack shrugs as his finger coasts from one shoulder to the other, along the line of my collarbone. "Don't know. Autumn has an email address for him, and she passed on Ben's message, but I don't actually know if he got it or if he's coming here."

"Message?" I question.

"Ben left us . . . Logan, Mason, and Archer . . . a cryptic message for the anniversary of his death."

Oh. *Oh.*

"We have a year to complete the mission." His voice drops, and he sounds a bit like Tom Cruise in *Mission Impossible.*

"And what is your mission?" My own voice rises, a bit excited by the possibility.

Zack slowly smiles without looking up at me. "It's a secret."

"Is it like a treasure map?" I continue, intrigued by the mystery and not able to let the secrecy part go just yet.

"Something like that." His smile grows larger, and he's just dazzling to behold.

We remain silent another second before Zack leans forward and scrapes his teeth over my bare shoulder. "Spend the day with us again."

Tomorrow is my next day off. I should be encouraging him to spend time with Anna and her children. His friend needs him, but selfishly, I don't want to miss any days, and my next shift will be two nights on, cutting back my time with the boys.

"Okay," I whisper, and Zack looks up at me with those silvery eyes. My heart flutters, and my belly flips.

"As it's already tomorrow then," he moans, pressing up to his hand and climbing over my body to straddle my lap. "Let's spend some quality time together now."

With that, we head into round two for the night.

21

[Zack]

We decide to spend River's day off away from Lakeside Cottage, allowing Anna to mend fences with her son and give all of them space. Mason doesn't want to join my adventure with River and the boys although I'd invited him. After he disappeared last night, I didn't want him to be alone.

"I met someone last night. I think I'll give her a call." It wasn't like Mason to be so passive about a conquest, nor was it like him to suggest a phone call in less than twelve hours, but I didn't argue with him.

As the boys were in a pirate phase, we decided on canoeing. Robbyn's River Adventures was about forty-five minutes away, offering canoe trips and inner tube floats down a four-mile stretch of the river. Oliver opted to ride with River while Trevor went with me on our paddling excursion. At one point, we stopped and had lunch on a sandbar while the boys chased a dragonfly. I swear I couldn't think of a better day which said a lot, as every other day so far with River and the twins had been amazing. She was amazing.

Her calm, sunny demeanor was just what my boys needed, and once again, I wished I could bottle her up. Or hire her as my nanny. The thought reminds me a new one starts on Monday. I'd run out of options in people who could handle my troublesome twins. We needed a Mary Poppins figure compared to all the Miss Trunchbulls we'd had.

As I watched River interact with the boys, I didn't know how I'd leave her behind or pull my boys away from her. She'd been such an unexpected distraction on this trip, and she'd been so good for all of us. Deep inside, I knew I was making another huge mistake with my children by allowing them to get close to a woman I couldn't have, but I'd grown just as close to her and didn't want to think about giving her up until the very last second.

Ten-day fling, I'd teased her a little more than a week ago. My ten days were almost up, and I flicked my wrist to glance at my watch, which

I wasn't wearing. In some ways, it was nice not to rely on time, but on the other hand, I wondered where my watch went.

As we end our canoe trip, a man awaits us on the dock. He's an older guy with a floppy sun hat on his head, looking a bit like Bill Murray as the groundskeeper in *Caddyshack.*

"How was the trip?" His rugged voice calls out as we approach.

"Great," River responds as he leans off the dock and guides her canoe to a stop before helping Oliver out of the craft. River follows, and I watch as the helper tugs the metal boat up a divot in the sloped land next to a wooden staircase. With my hand cupped under the dock, I hold my canoe in place, and River helps Trevor exit our craft. I hop out next and drag the canoe up the designated path. Once I set it next to River's I look up to find the man standing close behind me. So close I can see his eyes, and recognition hits me. I know this man.

Fuck.

"Have a good time?" His deep voice isn't recognizable, nor is the expression on his face. A hundred emotions are written in his eyes, but I can't read any of them. I don't want to read them. Instead, I see red.

"What the hell are you doing here?" The anger in my voice cannot be hidden. *Just what the fuck is happening here?*

"Zack!" River snaps, somewhere beside me.

"Saw your name on the schedule. Had to see if it was really you."

River steps closer and offers her hand. "Hi. I'm River."

The man reaches out and takes her offering, but my body vibrates. Everything in me wants to smack his arm and yell don't touch her. Her other hand lands on my forearm, attempting to calm me.

"Nice to meet you," he says to her, but I don't believe him. Nothing out of his mouth can be the truth. He turns for the boys next. "And who are you two?"

"We don't talk to—"

"Oliver," my son announces, patting his chest.

"Trevor," he introduces himself.

River's hand remains on my arm, but I can't feel her touch. My skin burns. My throat dries. *This cannot be happening.*

"Enjoy your adventure?" this unfamiliar-familiar man questions, bending at the waist to address my sons.

"It was great," Oliver says.

"Dad had trouble steering the ship," Trevor admits, and I want to clamp my hand over my son's mouth. *I'm out of practice*, I should defend. I can't remember the last time I went canoeing. It might have been as far back as when I was a kid—when I went with my dad.

My eyes narrow on the man before us, standing too close to my boys.

"I remember canoeing with my sons when they were about your age," the Bill Murray wannabe says, and I snap.

"You aren't allowed those memories."

"Zack," River hisses beside me. She wants my attention, but my eyes remain firmly on the man standing upright to face me. A man who looks nothing like I remember, yet instantly, every memory returns to me.

"I'll keep my memories, thank you. As it's all I have."

"Whose fault is that?" I mutter. Without waiting on a response, I reach for a bag near River's feet and round him, barking my sons' names before stalking off. Waiting for them near the car, River gets to me first.

"That was so rude," she scolds, coming up to me. "Do you even know that man?"

"Nope." I don't have a clue who he is now.

"Then explain yourself," she demands, cocking a hip as she places her fists on them. My little ray of sunshine is clouded over with disgust, and if I didn't want her judging me about my dad, she'll be judging me with what I say next.

"That man was my father."

+ + +

For the remainder of the day, I'm out of sorts. A sheet is draped off the tree fort, and *Pirates of the Caribbean* is being projected in River's backyard. She worried the movie was a little graphic for seven-year-olds, but I assured her it wasn't. I didn't even care about the movie after the

159

earlier run-in with my father, and I wanted nothing more than to be alone. However, River would not disappoint my boys, and she filled her yard with the *friends*-cation crew as she called us.

Anna held Trevor at her side while River had Oliver in her lap, and I've clearly misjudged my boys' reaction to the movie. I couldn't be bothered, though.

"Dude, what is your deal?" Mason hissed near me as we sit further back from the group. I'm nursing a scotch.

"I saw my dad today," I mutter, lifting the glass tumbler I commandeered from Anna's bar when I took the bottle. I would replace it. I wasn't a thief.

"Fuck. Where?" Mason understands issues with fathers as he wasn't close with his despite working for him. It's one reason he wanted Four Points to take off so badly. Logan's dad passed when he was five, and Ben's dad had been awesome, so it was only Mason and me who could commiserate on shit fathers.

"He was hanging out at some canoe rental place." I sigh, leaning forward to balance my elbows on my thighs. "What was he doing there?"

"Does he work there?"

"I have no idea." I hadn't a clue where my father has been these past years. Noah had been in contact with our dad, but I didn't understand how he could even speak to the man.

"You didn't know he was in the area?" Mason adds.

"I had no clue." When dear old dad came to see me in Detroit, I never followed up on where he went next, and although Noah had talked to our father, I didn't ask questions I didn't want answers to. I'd blocked most thoughts of my dad out of my mind. Back then with a new marriage and baby twins, I might have needed my father, but I didn't want him. He had nothing to offer me as he'd canceled his marriage and walked out on his family.

"What are you going to do?" Mason prods.

"Pretend I didn't see him," I state, bringing the glass to my lips and emptying the liquid in it. Then I pour myself another half glass.

"Man, this is not the way to deal with that shit." Mason nods at the tumbler in my hand, and I curse at him.

"Fuck you. What do you know about it?" Mason handles liquor better than the rest of us. Tequila is his twin, and I don't know how he does it.

"I know enough that drowning in that stuff will not bring you answers." Perhaps he's right. The bottom of a liquor bottle isn't going to offer wisdom. It sounds like something River's grandfather might say if I'd ever met the man. "But it's your bed, my friend. Until someone else is sleeping in it."

Fuck Mason. What does he know?

I glance up at River, seated a few feet before me on a blanket spread on the grass. My son balances on her lap, his back to her chest, his head on her shoulder. I don't need wisdom tonight. I need to get lost. I need her, and I don't want to share her with my kids.

Only as the night wears on and the alcohol numbs me, I don't get more than a good night kiss from my angel and a patronizing pat before she sends me home with Mason.

I didn't like it. Not one bit.

22

[Zack]

The next morning, I'm still in a shit mood. As River works the afternoon shift, she sleeps in the morning to rest up, and I take a morning run, stopping at Autumn's Crossroad Café with hopes coffee and a muffin will help. The place is quaint and small with a custom sandwich bar to the left of the entrance and the coffee and pastries counter to the right. Customers need to weave around a shelving unit in the middle that holds specialty items that complement their other food options.

As I stand in line, two older women wait behind me. I'm not one to eavesdrop, but their age causes them to speak loudly. Or maybe it's just that they're nosy busybodies who love to gossip. They're talking about some woman they consider a gold digger.

"I heard she inherited the house. Married someone nearly double her age, and then he leaves her that property worth almost three million dollars."

My ears perk up for some reason, but I step forward as the line moves. Almost all the lakefront homes are two million or more in cost. The property alone is worth millions. A lake view from a cliff on Lake Michigan is virtually priceless.

"He had children older than her. Didn't you say you saw her the other night with two little boys?" the first asks. "Didn't take long for her to move on."

My eyes catch Autumn's as she crosses behind the counter. She shakes her head at how vocal these women are.

"I wouldn't be surprised if she had a man waiting in the wings. I know how these things go." Lady Two speaks like she's an expert in sabotaging men. "So sad what happened to the original couple in that house."

"So sad," the first friend echoes.

"That was years ago, though," the second adds, reinforcing her agreement that whatever happened was very sad indeed.

"Prison," the first whispers, all too loudly, and I stiffen. "Embezzlement."

Everything within me fights the desire to turn around and blast these old biddies, telling them to shut up in this public place.

"If she thinks there's buried treasure in that home, she's wrong."

Without turning around, I almost hear them silently agreeing with one another.

"Did you say those two little boys belong to one of the sons from the original owners?" the second comments, and my ears ring. There isn't anyone else they could be referencing. "What was his name again?"

"Zack." It takes me a moment to realize it's not the women behind me speaking but Autumn calling out my name. When I look up, she tips her head for me to come to her. "Got your coffee ready." I haven't ordered yet.

"Don't listen to those old bitches," she whispers as I near her.

I shake my head, still a little stunned at what I heard and what it could mean.

"Yocal and Vocal are what we call those two. Always gossiping." Autumn leans forward, handing me the to-go cup. With a shaky hand, I take the offered drink, but Autumn notices my tremor.

"You okay?" her voice lowers even more.

I nod, but I'm not. "Were they talking about River?"

"There's no way River married . . ." Autumn slows her speech. "She mentioned her husband was older than her, but it can't be her."

Autumn doesn't sound very convincing, and I stare back at her. River hardly mentions Quincy. I hadn't even known his name until the other night. How could he have children older than River unless he was . . . and she was . . . and she inherited that house. Now, she's moved on to me. The man with two little boys and the original son of the owner. There isn't anything I have, though. The few remaining dollars my father had were State's evidence and confiscated. There's no buried treasure. He'd gambled away the money. We didn't have a penny. Everything I have now is all mine, and I'm careful with it. The only frivolous thing I've ever purchased is . . . my watch.

+ + +

I cannot let this go. It cannot wait until River is awake or after she returns from work. I need to speak to her, and I need to speak to her now. Standing outside her door, I pound on the wood, rattling the old thing on its hinges. When River opens the barrier, she's out of breath.

"What's wrong?" She's wearing one of those sheer linen night dresses she likes, and there's nothing to the imagination behind the thin fabric. I'd chastise her for opening the door in such a state, but I'm too worked up about what I heard.

"Who was your late husband?"

"Excuse me," she stammers, her mouth falling open before her arms cross over her ample chest and accentuate those breasts I've become overly familiar with lately.

"I asked you a question."

"And I don't appreciate your tone."

"My tone," I huff. "My tone? Who the fuck was your husband?"

"His name was Quincy. Why does that matter?"

Swiping a hand through my hair, I hate that we're having this *discussion* on her front step. And standing here, I feel like we're on the precipice of something big, something push-me-over-the-edge, falling-into-the-pits-of-hell big.

"For a man who hates confrontation, you're rather confrontational this morning," she states, lowering her voice.

"I just want you to be honest with me." Why is she being evasive? What else is she hiding from me?

"Oh, like you were honest with me about this house." Her crossed arms fall, handsfisting at her sides. I glare back at those icy blues which are opposite the typical warmth and wonder they hold when she looks at me. "And what about your dad?"

"What about him?" We hadn't discussed him once we left the canoe excursion. Once we returned to the area, we had dinner at Anna's, and then the movie happened. River and I hadn't had a moment alone, and whose fault was that? She sent me home with a soft kiss and a pat on the back.

164

"And this," I snap, waving at the front porch. "It's only a damn house. We're talking about your marriage."

"Actually, we are not discussing my marriage. It's none of your business." Now it's her tone that sets me off.

"It is my business when people think you're sniffing up my ass for money."

"Excuse me?" Her mouth falls open again, and her eyelids rapidly flutter. She can't accentuate those words any stronger. We stare daggers at one another for thirty seconds before she says, "Get out."

"We need to discuss this," I demand, holding out a hand to stop her from slamming the door in my face.

"No, we don't. We don't discuss your marriage or your boys."

"What's that supposed to mean?" My forehead furrows as if seeing this argument already heading off course. When River doesn't reply, I continue. "You think I'm a shit dad, don't you? Just say it. Tell me how you really feel."

"Nope. Your kids, remember? You'll worry about them." I'm not certain how this has turned around on me and my fatherhood ability, but I'm spiraling out of control, swirling as the pit-falling sensation consumes me.

"Just tell me the truth. Tell me where my watch is." I have no idea where that came from, but it's worth fifteen-hundred dollars. She could use the money for the fence removal or something in the house or anything if she's the gold digger those women say she is. This land alone is worth three million dollars. I would know. I look into the property value all the time and cringe to think we lost such an investment. We lost it all because my father fucking stole from someone, and now River is stealing from me.

"I don't have your watch. I gave it to the boys to return to you."

"You gave my watch to seven-year-olds?" I huff. "Not likely." I sound like a child myself as I blow on my lips like some damn cartoon character. I'm losing control of my emotions, this conversation, and my grip on reality.

"Just tell me the truth," I yell, and River stares at me.

"His name was Dennis Quincy. He owned Quincy Grocer, and he died of an inoperable brain tumor."

"Quincy Grocer? Like the entire company?" Sweat beads across my forehead. I recognize the name Quincy Grocer all too well. They own hundreds of mega-grocery stores throughout Michigan and parts of the Midwest, think Target in scale, and my father was their accountant until he embezzled from them.

"He has three grown children who are complete assholes like you're being, but he wasn't an idyllic father either. He'd done his damage, and at the end of his advanced life, he wanted redemption. He needed kindness and compassion, and I gave that to him. I didn't judge him or accuse him of things, and I certainly didn't steal from him. He left me this house in his will as a gift, a dying wish, in gratitude for being his nurse through the last year of his life. I'm not saying I deserve a house for being a decent human being, but I'm damn well working to keep it. And you're on private property, so get off." Her tone brooks no further argument. There's no negotiation or compromise. I cast the accusations.

"River, I—" She holds up her hand to stop me.

"And not that it's any of your business, but he wasn't my husband. He was a lonely old man who befriended me. And before you take your thoughts one step into the gutter, I did not fuck him for this house. I was doing my job, which I lost because of dicks like you." She's practically screaming at me at this point. "If you have further arguments with my property rights, you can contact my lawyer."

With that, she karate chops my elbow, forcing me to bend my arm, thus freeing the door from my hand, and she slams it in my face.

+ + +

"Holy fuck," Mason says to me as I wander up to his room above the garage. "Her husband was the man your father stole all that money from?" As if things could get worse in the past twenty-four hours, the knife in my chest cuts deeper. The surprise on Mason's face does not compare to the shame I feel.

"She says he wasn't her husband. He was . . . a patient." I don't even think it's legal for patients to will items to nursing staff, but it happens, and it typically lands in court when it does.

"Do you believe her?" Mason asks, and I stare back at him. My first instinct says, of course, I believe her. *Why would she lie to me?* But in the back of my head is a phrase about liars and cheaters and people who steal things, and I just don't know what to think.

"I don't know," I say out loud.

"Do your boys have your watch?"

I'd been so stunned by the turn of the argument I hadn't gone to them. I shake my head in response.

"What would she have to gain by not telling you?" Mason asks, and I'm wondering the same thing. Why hadn't she told me about *this patient*—his condition, his position in the company, and their marital status? It didn't make sense.

"Unless she knew who I was," I say without answering Mason directly. "Unless she knew I was the son of the SOB who stole from Quincy."

Mason narrows his eyes. "And how would that benefit her? Getting revenge on you for your father's crime twenty-seven years ago? For a man she only met a few years ago? It doesn't make sense."

"How do you know it was only a few years ago?"

Mason shrugs. "How long can a man live with an inoperable brain tumor?"

Probably not more than two or three at the most, if I had to guess. *It's been three years*, she said about when she last had sex. She also said she didn't fuck him for the house.

I feel sick.

She'd have no motive in seeking revenge on me. She's been very reassuring that my father's sins do not reflect on me. She wanted to know more details about my dad yesterday, but I'm the one who shut down. I'm the one who has flown off the handle and accused her of something he'd done—theft.

Swiping both hands over my face, I stare back at Mason. "I fucked this up."

"I'd say pretty much." Mason sadly agrees with me while nodding.

"Oh my God, what did I do?"

"You accused the woman you love of stealing from you, and then you all but called her a gold digger, implying she fucked an old guy for a house." Mason makes a face that tightens his jaw and strains his neck muscles. I close my eyes.

"I need to go back there and apologize." I was always entering her yard to either offer apologies or express gratitude. Today, I'd done neither. Quickly, I stand, racing out the door and skipping down the stairs two at a time. Stepping out onto the drive, my boys are drawing with chalk on the concrete.

"Trevor. Oliver. Have you seen my watch?" Had I asked them this question before? Had I asked them a second time?

"It's in your suitcase," Trevor offers without hesitation.

"My suitcase?" I question. I've looked in my bag a thousand times.

"Yeah. The little pocket on the front." I stare at Trevor as he moves his hand to explain the pouch in relation to the bigger bag. The pocket isn't large enough for anything other than a wallet or a . . . *Fuck*. I never put things in there.

"It's like a secret flap," Oliver says. "A good place for hidden treasure."

My eyes close, and I tip my head to the heavens before glancing back at them.

"Boys. Think very carefully. Did River give the watch to you?" Why would she give it to seven-year-old children?

Trevor shrugs like he can't remember, but Oliver speaks as he draws a giant X on the driveway. "Miss River was going to work. You were out running. She said she thought you might miss it, and she was trusting us to put it in a special place where you would find it, and no one else would see it."

She'd given them a treasure to bury, and they did as she asked. She had unconditional faith in them at seven years of age, and I'd had no faith in her. *Idiot*. I stare at my boys, especially Trevor. River's trust might have meant something to him even at such a young age. She asked, and they obliged. They'd been doing it since the day they met her. They respected her, so they abided by her rules, and I'd just obliterated all of that.

Not for them, for me.

$$+ + +$$

Me: Where are you?

I don't really expect her to respond, not after the way I acted, but it's after midnight, our typical meetup time, and I'm pacing in her backyard. She hasn't answered my calls, having left her house hours earlier than her typical time for work, and she hasn't replied to a single text during her eight-hour shift.

By twelve thirty, I'm beside myself. By one in the morning, I'm thinking she isn't coming home. Either way, I make myself comfortable on the chaise lounge on the cool August night and wait. She has to work the later shift tomorrow as well. She'll be here eventually.

The quiet of the night and the darkness offer reflection. As much as I'd love to wait for River in her yard, she's made it very clear to me again—this is her property. I have no boundaries when it comes to her, but I should. I don't need her calling the police on me, which I rightfully deserve. I've barged onto this land more than once, and my eyes wander to the house.

It's only a house, Ben used to tell me. *Home is where your heart is.* It's such a fucking cheesy thing to say, but I consider the words for the first time ever. I'd left my heart in this house when I thought it was a home. Ironically, my heart seems to still be in the same place as I've given it to the woman who currently owns this house. This time, it isn't my father who lost the right to this place. It's all on me.

I still can't believe I saw my dad yesterday afternoon. What was he doing here? Why was he here? He shouldn't be in the area. Hell, he shouldn't even be in the state of Michigan as far as I was concerned. He didn't have a right to return. And did he actually work there? The T-shirt advertising Robbyn's River Adventures was enough of a hint that he did. My father, the former accountant, the ex-convict, was working at some canoe rental place.

L.B. Dunbar

Fuck my life. I tip back my head and stare up at the sky as memories flip through my mind one after another of this house, this yard, my family. Barbecues and summer nights. Snow forts and sleds. The laughter. The eventual pain. Nothing made sense.

Near two a.m., I give up and retreat across the yard, returning to Anna's with my head hung in defeat. I've paid either Calvin or Bryce every night to listen for my boys, and I wonder if that makes me a terrible father. I'd asked River what she thinks, putting words to her thoughts.

You think I'm a shit dad, don't you?

God, how many things can I accuse her of in one argument? I realize I'm projecting my own insecurities on her. I'm turning into a terrible father in my own way, just like mine.

As I enter the house, the plan is to head directly upstairs to my room. I can vigilantly watch River's yard from there. But I see a soft glow coming from the kitchen area and cross the entryway.

Anna sits on a stool at the large island, holding a mug of something in her hands.

"You're up late," I say, startling her. As she turns to me, her eyes are puffy. Her face red.

"I couldn't sleep."

Stepping up to the counter, I help myself to the stool next to her.

"Calvin?" When River showed the movie in her yard, the older boys were absent. Not that I was in a frame of mind to thoroughly pay attention, but the previous year the boys attended everything we did as a group.

"He's growing up, caught between a boy and a man. We're going to have our ups and downs. Right now, it's a down. He isn't speaking to me." The corner of her mouth weakly quirks. "But he will when he needs something like gas money or his laundry done." Her jest is half-hearted, but she knows him best. And I know he's a good kid. He'll circle back to her because he loves his mom. He's just missing his dad.

"How was your rendezvous?" Her voice attempts to tease me, but she doesn't have the heart for it. I guess she knows I've been sneaking out of the house every night.

"It didn't happen. We had a fight." Was it an argument? Or was it all one-sided? My accusations. My crime. I don't have the bandwidth in my brain to even mention the appearance of my father to Anna.

She turns to face me, giving me a sympathetic look. While I expect her to tell me River and I will work it out, she doesn't.

"There's a misconception that Ben and I never fought. We came across as the perfect couple to everyone, right?" She swipes a hand through her long dark hair, but it falls back into place around her face when she releases it. "But Ben and I weren't perfect."

From the outside looking in, it might have often seemed like they were the ideal couple. In reality, they were like many couples, and being part of their inner circle of friends, I'd known of some troubles. Finances. Sex. The top two things that cause divorce. Ben would say those issues ebb and flow through all marriages, making Anna and Ben not extraordinary, but just ordinary people. Ordinary as a couple.

"He was such a great man," I mutter, staring down at the countertop. "Ben knew how to be a husband and a father."

Anna turns her head to look at me, but I don't look up. "Zack, there's no manual. Ben didn't know how to be those things any more than I knew how to be a wife or mother. I knew I wanted those things, but I didn't really know *how* to be them until I was each in their own right."

"I was a shit husband."

"Don't say that. You were with the wrong woman."

"We fought all the time."

"Fighting is normal." Anna sighs. "It's how you handle those fights, though. Pick your battles. Apologize if you were wrong. Listen to the other side. You don't have to agree on everything. It's called compromise."

My forehead lowers for my clasped hands as my arms brace on the counter. "I'm terrible at it."

"I don't think so," Anna says beside me. "You've just never had to do it. You bulldoze into a situation and take over. You did this with your mom, and you did it with Jeanine. You married her because you thought you had to. You stayed with her because of the boys."

I tip my head still on my hands and stare at Anna. "What do you mean I did it with my mom?"

"You thought you were the new man of the house. With Noah off to college almost immediately after everything happened, you thought it was your responsibility to take care of your mother."

I slowly sit up. Had I done that? "I was only fifteen," I defend.

"Exactly. It wasn't your place to take over. You just did." My mother had never worked a day in her life, so I got a job. I worked throughout high school, applied for loans for college, and continued to work when I could. Anna's dad gave Mom the loan to set her up, but I paid it off.

"What do you know about my marriage?" I'm not stupid enough to think Ben never told Anna things I'd told him, but I still couldn't imagine them wasting time discussing my situation.

"You were afraid to walk out of that marriage. Afraid you'd be a disappointment like your dad had been."

"It was more than a disappointment," I huff.

"You were ashamed of him, and what happened and how it ultimately affected your life, but from that point on . . . you bulldozed. You weren't ever going to be in a position of no money, no home, or a broken family. No matter what."

Weakly, my mouth curves at Anna's assessment. "You do know me well."

"There's a bonus to being shy and quiet." Anna certainly was that as a child and teenager, but she came into her own with Ben. There's a saying that a couple can be the yin and yang of one another, drawing out the missing pieces, complementing the other half. Ben pulled Anna out of her shell. She kept him balanced. "It allowed me to listen and observe."

She smiles softly at me. "You're a good man, Zack Weller. River knows it. In fact, she said it when we went out for margaritas and manicures."

"What else did she say?" I sound like a desperate teen. *Does she like me?* What did she say about me?

"She said she thought you were lost."

I am, and for some reason, I think of the Lost Boys and Neverland and pirate ships floating through the sky. It might be that the boys made me watch *Peter Pan* earlier tonight, but there's someone who grounds those little boys and focuses on Peter. A mother figure in her own right. A girl who is smart, witty, and kind.

River is my Wendy, and I need her.

"She also believed you'd get there. You needed practice. Like I said, Ben didn't know how to be a father. It took practice."

Like anything, it takes practice. River was referring to my flirting abilities when she said that, but fatherhood could fall on the list as well.

Softly, I chuckle. "Is that why you have three children?"

"The first is the rehearsal child." She winks at me with a swollen lid.

"What does that say about me, then, if I had two at once?"

"Maybe you needed double the practice?" Her voice lifts before a more genuine smile graces her face.

"Seriously, how is Calvin?"

"He's sad and confused and hurt and stubborn, like his father." Her smile remains, but she glances down at her mug. "He'll get there, wherever there is, eventually. We all will." Anna turns to me. "And so will you."

"I feel like I don't know where I'm going anymore or what I'm doing. I have the law practice and my partners, and I've added Four Points. But then I've lost Jeanine, which, let's face it, wasn't a loss, and I have the boys to navigate."

"Navigate," Anna repeats the word. "In some ways, navigate implies learning." *Spoken like the teacher she is.* "But I think the best thing you can give those boys is love, Zack. Unconditional. Unwavering. It's hard work at times, like my standoff with Calvin. The rewards are in the small stuff. I've seen Oliver come to you for affection, and you've been more willing to offer it. I see Trevor hovering closer to you. They just want your attention, Zack. Your time. You work too hard." She pauses. "Sometimes on the wrong stuff."

You make time for love, River told me.

L.B. Dunbar

Anna isn't wrong either. I've known for a while that my work was my escape. I didn't want to face my home life until it imploded. Maybe my own father felt the same way. He couldn't face the disappointment or the pressure he thought my mother put on him to be like the McCaryn family. He couldn't face his own failures, so he kept at it, working harder to find the means, but only dug the hole deeper. He gambled, eventually embezzled, and went to jail.

I don't want the consequences of Jeanine and me to cause such damage to my boys. They need their mother, or perhaps just a mother. A mother figure who cares for them with trust, respect, and kindness.

"I messed up with River," I admit. "I overreacted. Or reacted. I . . . bulldozed." My lids close, and Anna's hand touches my hair, comforting me like the mother she is.

"Then fill in the ditch, Zack. Plant some flowers, as Ben's father used to say."

I softly chuckle. "What was that saying Mr. Kulis had?"

"You seed. You plant. You grow. You harvest."

"Yeah." I guffaw. "Ben had his own thing last year. Live. Love. Loss. Learn."

"It's a cycle," Anna states.

"That's exactly what he said." My head lifts, knowing the two of them might not have been perfect, but they were perfectly in sync with one another.

"What stage are you at?" Anna teases.

I consider all I've lost in the past year—my marriage and my best friend. I'm learning as I go right now, but I'm also willing to learn as I live. So that means . . .

"Ready to love."

"Your boys?" Anna tweaks a brow.

"And River," I whisper.

Anna's smile grows. "Ben would be so happy for you."

I lick my lower lip and bite the flesh.

"I know." *Ben*. He would have been so happy that I'd fallen in love. *Excuse me*, flying in it or ready to fly. First, I need to focus on the "second star to the right and straight on till morning," as Peter Pan said earlier tonight.

River is that star. Morning couldn't get here fast enough.

23

[Zack]

Although I sat in a chair with my feet propped up on the windowsill for the remainder of the night, I'd fallen asleep until I heard a car door slamming. Subconsciously, I didn't know if I really heard the door or imagined it, but I flinched, and my feet fell to the floor, completely asleep. Pins and needles cripple my legs as I try to shake them out so I can stand.

When I finally have enough circulation to move, I'm limping, but I'm picking up speed, certain River must be home by now. I check the time as I found my watch in the pocket where the boys securely *hid* it. Roughly after eight, it shows, and my mind races with thoughts. *Where had River been all night?* I didn't want to believe she'd run off for a one-night stand as she'd already told me it wasn't her kind of thing, and I didn't know if she had friends in the area where she might have stayed. I did know her family was limited.

As I exit the front door of Anna's house, I hear raised voices coming from next door when I round the garage. I don't typically tuck through the hole in the fence where my sons first crawled to River's home. I've always taken the long way down the drive and around the fence to her driveway and then along the side of the house. However, I'm in a hurry today, and when I hear those voices grow louder, I skip the hole and jump the chain fence, struggling with the shrubbery before I break free to her driveway.

A man stands near River's front stoop, where she's posed and defensive in her body language. Arms crossed. A scowl on her face. She looks like she's holding herself back but ready to pounce on the man. He's roughly my height and size but dressed in suit pants and a crisp button-down. They both peer in my direction, and the man smooths his hand down the length of his tie.

"Everything alright?" I immediately ask, brushing off loose leaves that cling to me as I fought the mighty arborvitae.

"Who's this?" Suit-man asks while River simply closes her eyes a second.

"He's the neighbor." I halt at the label said with disdain. *Neighbor?* I'll tackle that comment second. First, I want to know who this guy is and why River has her hackles up with him.

"I heard voices," I state, and River twists her lips.

"Probably should get that checked then," Suit-man says. *Smart-ass.* Ignoring me as if I'm a squirrel crossing the yard, he turns back to River.

"You really should reconsider," he states to her.

"I've told you before. I'm not giving up the place. It's what Quincy wanted."

"His name was Dennis, and he wasn't of sound body and mind." Suit-man slips his hands into his pockets. "We've been through this before. You have my lawyer's contact. Talk to them."

This is when I step forward, feeling a strange sense of déjà vu from the day before.

"Everything alright, River?" I repeat, sensing nothing is right about this man standing near her front stoop, hinting at her giving up this place.

"Who are you again?" Suit-man turns to me, and I have a better view of him with his glossy hair and paunchy cheeks. His assessing gaze covers me in less than a minute, and disgust fills his face. Do I look like that when I look at people? I'm certain I do when I'm in lawyer mode.

"Zack Weller." I step forward, offering a hand, and River's mouth pops open but quickly shuts. Suit-man reaches out to shake mine although he hesitates a second, considering my hand might be unclean after wrestling the bushes.

"Daniel Quincy." My hand freezes mid-shake, and I crane my neck to look at River for clarification.

"Quincy's son?" I ask her.

"His name was Dennis," Daniel hisses, and I face him once more, releasing his hand.

"And to what do we owe the honor of your visit?"

"*We?*" he sputters. "It's a private matter." He turns back to River, who hasn't moved from her crossed arm stance.

L.B. Dunbar

"I'm her attorney." Daniel's gaze swivels back to me, taking another roam over my attire. Rumpled T-shirt. Sports shorts. Flip-flops. He shifts back to River.

"Well, this ought to be good." He gives me a salacious smile as if he sees the writing on the wall. Like I'm some local dumbass he can beat in the game he wants to play. Glancing up at River, I give her a cautious shake of my head. *Don't argue with me.*

"So, what can we do for you?" I repeat.

"Your *client*," he hisses, "stole my house."

"Is that so?" I ask, tipping back on my heels. "Would that be under inheritance laws where she was gifted this property, or did she pick it up and slip it in her pocket to steal it?"

His all-knowing expression slowly starts to wither.

"Because according to Michigan law, it's legal to leave a house to a person. And as inheritance implies someone has passed away, as is the current case, it's difficult to prove sound body and mind on a dead person."

Daniel's mouth slowly drops open.

"In simple terms, if there was a will, there was a way this house was given to Ms. Nagle. Gifted, but not stolen." I hate to even ask if the will had been contested, and I'm thankful when Daniel offers the information.

"I'll contest the will."

"You've already tried," River answers.

"Was it in probate?" I ask River despite the distance between us.

"Quincy had an estate."

I turn on Daniel. "If Dennis Quincy's affairs were in an estate, then his will is solid." The issue of a nonfamily member inheriting a sizable gift can be suspect. In the case of River, because she was the nurse slash caregiver to a dying man, it's possible the family questioned the decision in the will. They might have believed she coerced Quincy into giving her the property upon his death. If she had married him, there wouldn't have been a question—equitable property and such—but River admitted they weren't married. *Why had she told me they were?*

Running the scenario through my head, if the family already contested the will once, a judge isn't likely to repeal the decision already determined. There would have to be suspicion of foul play, and although I've accused River of such a thing with my watch, I was a damn fool. She hadn't coerced a dying man to do anything.

"We'll see," Daniel states, turning more fully to face me. "My attorneys will be in touch." Suit-man walks to his convertible parked near the middle of the driveway, and I approach River on her stoop. She doesn't address me but keeps her eyes on Daniel as he reverses and pulls out of her drive. Then she turns, giving her back to me.

"River, please." She pauses but doesn't face me. "We need to talk."

"*We* have nothing to say."

I sigh, swiping a hand through my hair. "I misspoke. I'll talk. You listen. Please."

Her shoulders fall, but she doesn't turn around.

"I fucked up. I'm sorry." The words are not enough, and River spins to face me again.

"Where did you hear it?"

I glance up at her, confused for a second by what she's asking.

"Who told you I stole the house? What was it? That I'm a gold digger. That I tricked a dying man into giving me his home. Or was it my favorite that I must have given good head to get him to gift me the house when he was dead?" Her voice rises as a tear falls. Quickly, she wipes it away. I haven't seen River cry over anything other than a sick child. Her heart is so big . . . for other people's pain.

"Someone said something at Crossroads Café. I-I misunderstood."

"And instead of approaching me like a sane person, you show up to attack me and my character." River shakes her head, crossing her arms once again. "I thought you knew me better than that. But I know you, and you make assumptions. You assumed I'd kidnapped your boys that first afternoon you barged into my yard. You didn't want to hear an explanation. You just wanted to make accusations. Well, I've heard enough."

"What was he doing here?" I nod toward the driveway.

"Just wanting to harass me again for what they feel is due to them."

"Please, tell me what happened. I want to understand."

"You had your chance to understand, Zack."

"I made a mistake," I say, my voice catching at her dismissal.

"So did I." Her face saddens as her gaze lowers, coasting along the length of my body. *I'm her mistake?*

"Don't-don't say that. Please don't hate me."

River glances up at me, her head shaking slowly from side to side. "We aren't ten-year-olds. I don't hate you. I was at risk of loving you. That might have been worse. And now, I'm tired. I worked a double shift and have another shift in a few hours. Get off my property, Zack."

She turns again, leaving me stunned on the stoop before she enters her house and closes the door on me once more. For the first time, I understand what falling really means. It wasn't falling in love but cascading into a pit of despair—utter, hopeless despair—that I just lost the perfect woman for me.

A woman I desperately need and trust.

24

[River]

I was exhausted. After the double shift, the morning altercation, and then another shift, I just wanted to sleep for weeks. Unfortunately, on my day off, my body said, get up, be productive. *Never waste a good day, and today is a perfectly good day*, Grandfather would say, wanting every moment in life to count for something. I originally had plans to spend time with Zack. Those plans were now a bust.

As I was at risk of two little boys rushing into my yard, I decide I need to get away from the house, so I went to a local farmers' market, then hit up a flea market. It was time to start renovating this old house where I could. Some new decorations along with a paint job in a few rooms might be a start.

Going to dinner by myself at Driftwoods or even Rudder's felt pathetic, so I bought takeout and took it to the public beach where I knew I wouldn't see Zack or any of his *friends*-cation crew. I ate alone, watching the sun lower in the sky just a touch earlier than it had two weeks before. Mid-August still brought the heat during the day, but a chill at night warned that summer was coming to a close.

I'd been reflective as I ate, recalling Zack's response to the sight of his father. I imagine it was quite a shock if he hadn't seen the man in over twenty-five years. His reaction, while understandable, wasn't attractive. Zack didn't need to be a perfect man, but he did need to be a decent human being. Oliver and Trevor hadn't known how to respond to the sharp snarl in his voice as he told a complete stranger he wasn't allowed to have memories. Sometimes memories were all we had, especially when the physical person was no longer in our lives for whatever reason. Not wanting to disappoint the boys because of their father's crappy mood, I carried on with the plan to show a movie in my yard, however inappropriate that movie might have been for his sons. *His children. His concern.* The thought hurt considering all I'd done for them, but then again, I didn't do things for others in hopes of a return investment. People weren't banks. You didn't make a deposit only to withdrawal more than they could give. And I was spent on thoughts of Zack.

When I finally return home under cover of darkness, I find a bouquet in a glass vase on my front porch.

Wildflowers for my wild girl. Her generous spirit is endless.

A bushel of roses couldn't have brought forgiveness for the hurt Zack caused me yesterday morning. My heart felt removed with a dull scalpel and no anesthesia. He hadn't trusted me. He thought I tricked Quincy and believed I was only after money. The accusations were familiar because Quincy's children thought the same thing. The will had been contested but found authentic. I inherited the house through Quincy's generosity. In some ways, I understood how Daniel and his siblings couldn't appreciate the gift. They didn't seem to have a decent bone in their bodies.

I hated feeling like a coward, but I didn't trust myself to wander into my own backyard. The *friends*-cation clan planned a beach fire for their last night. The men would be staying up late for a toast in memory of their friend who passed away. Zack told me about the message, although not the message he'd specifically received from Ben. I'd been invited to attend the early portion of the evening, and Zack planned to meet me after their new ritual. That would no longer happen.

It was difficult to accept that I wouldn't be seeing Zack for one more night. I really thought we were headed in the same direction, even if we hadn't discussed a future. We were moving forward, not stagnant. However, I'd been wrong before in my assessment of a relationship. Is a ten-day fling grounds for a relationship anyway? I didn't have answers. Before Zack, I thought my only focus was work and this house. He was something I had not expected and was not ready to give up. However, it certainly felt like decisions had been made. I couldn't be with a man who didn't trust me, believe in me . . . love me.

Love. It hadn't been on my radar. It wasn't that I didn't want it. I definitely did. I just hadn't foreseen it happening anytime soon. I was still adjusting to my new position—a new city, a new home, a new job. I also hadn't seen myself falling so hard for his children, which widened the hole already in my heart when I thought of the twins not being next door.

I wasn't just losing their father but losing them as well, and although they weren't my children, as Zack reminded me, I still had strong feelings about them. Oliver was so affection-desperate, and Trevor just ached. I knew I couldn't cure them of the ailments inflicted by a missing mother, but I'd been willing to try. I'd been wanting to try, and it was all a foolish thought after only ten days.

I carry the flowers into the house and set them on the kitchen table as the doorbell rings. My head hangs. I can't take another argument with Zack. I can't even handle an apology from him. I just need to be alone with my thoughts. Still, I wander to the door, wondering who would actually ring the bell. To my surprise, it is my neighbor but not the one I expected.

"Anna?"

"It's a long-overdue housewarming gift. Welcome to the neighborhood." She holds up a wine bottle and smiles.

"Thank you. That's very sweet of you." I reach out for the housewarming gift, remaining in place.

"Would it be bold of me to ask if you'd share a drink with me?" She nods at the container in my hand.

I sigh. "You don't need to do this." I stare down at the red wine. "You didn't have to come on his behalf or even pretend to be my friend. I swear it won't be awkward." I had been alone for so long I was used to the silence of my own company.

"I'm not pretending, and I'm not here for *he who shall not be named*."

I laugh at the reference.

"I'm here for me, actually." My head pops up. "I thought we could talk."

The suggestion was similar to Zack's last words, but I didn't want to talk about him.

"I need someone to talk to," Anna softly admits, holding her gaze on me. "But I understand if you'd rather not because of *him*." She hitches a thumb over her shoulder, pointing at the house next door.

L.B. Dunbar

"Don't be silly. If you need to talk, I'm a good listener." Stepping back, I give a wide berth for her to enter my home. *Lending an ear is sometimes better than offering your heart.* Grandfather 3:20-million.

As Anna walks through the house, she glances around the family room, and I follow her to the kitchen. She's obviously familiar with the layout of the place.

"In some ways, it's so different yet exactly the same." She stands beside my kitchen table, and I walk around a peninsula cabinet to retrieve wineglasses.

"I know your mother was best friends with Zack's, so I assume you've spent time in here." I didn't know if I should mention Zack's dad and decided against it. His father was his business and the story of their meeting wasn't mine to tell.

"I have, but it feels like a lifetime ago."

I nod for her to sit, and she takes a seat at the kitchen table as I open the wine bottle and pour us each a glass.

"But I'm not here for Zack," she repeats. "Although he mentioned what happened. He's an idiot. It's none of my business, though, but if you'd like to talk, I can listen as well."

The door is open for the truth, and I feel a little nauseous, but I need her to know it. "I wasn't married, and I'm sorry I said I was."

She doesn't seem at all shocked by my revelation. Tipping her head, she asks, "Why did you then?"

"It was easier than explaining the truth."

Anna waves a hand in a circle, signaling I should continue with my tale.

"Dennis Quincy was my patient. The prognosis was bleak; however, his spirit was strong. My God, that man was stubborn, but in his advanced age, his body wouldn't handle surgery. He didn't want to end his days in some vegetative state. He'd gone blind, and he liked me to read to him. He said I had a soothing voice." I chuckle with the memory. My voice is scratchy, but Quincy complimented me often on it. He said it brought him peace.

"He asked me to marry him." I laugh a little. "I thought he was joking. An old man trying to be flirtatious is risky in our days of hashtag me too, but I let it pass because he was innocent enough. What was he going to do to me? Then one day, he told me he was serious. He wanted to gift me something, and he thought it best if I was his wife. I couldn't agree. I declined." It's actually against most codes of ethics for a nurse to receive something substantial as recompense for simply doing my job. But Quincy wasn't a job for me. He reminded me so much of my grandfather minus the snarky tongue, or maybe at times, because of it.

Anna softly smiles. "It's still a little romantic."

I suppose it could have been, had I been even remotely attracted to my patient, but I wasn't. Still, it was sweet.

"Then he tried to *tip me*. He wanted to reward me for my service. I refused again. I couldn't accept money, and I didn't need it. I wasn't being kind out of some obligation. I liked the old coot, even if I didn't agree with the way he'd lived his life. Who was I to judge him? We all make mistakes." Sometimes people make bigger ones than others, like Quincy's experience as a father or Zack's dad. "He'd alienated his own children, and then he wanted them back."

Anna nods.

"When he died, I was terribly sad. I had a fondness for the man, but I wasn't having relations with him. I wasn't in love with him. He was an old man who had charmed me into liking him. He reminded me of my grandfather, a man I did love dearly." My voice cracks mentioning the comparison.

Anna softly smiles. "I don't know how you do it. I've lost Ben, who was the love of my life, but it still must be difficult to lose multiple patients. One person was enough for me."

Anna is correct. It was never easy to lose a patient, but they also weren't my family. I'd already lost someone important to me from the disease I worked amongst. I was conditioned to separate myself just enough, so the travesty of my profession didn't completely drag me under. Still, it hurt. Each loss chipped at my heart.

"Quincy's children came forward and accused me of manipulating their father once the will was read. Trust me, no one was more shocked than me. I didn't even understand why I'd been invited to attend the reading. I almost didn't go, arguing with the attorney who represented

Quincy that it was a family matter. The attorney told me I'd want to be present. The accusations flew. Daniel, Quincy's eldest, can really sling the insults." I blow out a breath. "Eventually, the hospital *had concerns*, as they termed it, and I was asked to leave. If I left without a scene, I could quit versus being fired, but I was essentially let go. The Quincy Corporation was a major contributor to the hospital."

"And that's why you decided to move here."

"I moved here because I'd inherited a run-down house with tons of potential, but yes, I had no reason to stay in Grand Rapids as I'd lost my job. I needed the change. Working with children had less risk than working with the elderly from a personal position. The difficulty is that losing a child is so much harder."

I consider Jessica, my young patient who had a difficult night. She's why I decided to take the double shift. When another nurse called in sick, I offered to stay. The sad truth was Jessica wasn't going to make it. Her parents were taking her home soon.

"What you do is so remarkable," Anna quietly says with awe, and the somber tone of this conversation pinches at my chest.

"But you didn't come here to talk about me, and I just word-vomited all over you."

"Better than real vomit," she teases.

"I've had my experiences with that."

"So have I." She laughs before the sound fades to regret.

"I'm sorry I lied."

Anna shakes her head and waves off the apology. "No need. I actually understand. That was too complicated to explain. Saying he was your husband kept it simple."

"It doesn't dispel the rumors, though, which is how Zack heard a sliver of the truth."

"Zack misinterpreted what he heard, and then he overreacted." Anna's voice turns stern, even disappointed in her friend. I don't want to discuss Zack, though. "So, what did you want to talk about?"

"Well, at first, I thought I wanted to talk about losing my husband. Does it get any easier? Will this ache in my chest ever subside? But now, I see that your case wasn't quite like mine." Anna sits up a little straighter and turns her head toward the front of the house. Maybe she's thinking she should leave, but I don't want her to go.

"You can still talk to me about him. Tell me about Ben." She's already told me some things when we first went out, and I've heard bits and pieces from the men as they've spoken about their wild friendship throughout the dinners I've shared with the group. "Tell me something unique about him. What was his favorite color? What did he love to eat? What was a song he loved to sing?"

For the next hour, Anna speaks, giving me the mundane details about her husband. We finish the bottle of wine she brought, and I open another one. The following hour passes with her telling me more about the ache in her chest and the emptiness in her bed.

"That might have been too much," she says, as a way of apology for explaining how much she missed sex and the feel of his hands on her. She missed kissing him and took it for granted that she'd have years to continue pressing her lips to his.

"You can tell me anything you wish." What I offer is the truth. I'm happy to hear about how wonderful they were and how they were not-quite-so perfect at the same time.

"I'm not close with my younger sister. Fortunately, I have an amazing relationship with Ben's sister, Autumn. She's become one of my best friends, but I feel weird discussing intimate details with her about her brother. The truth is most of my friends are in Chicago. Over the past year, I haven't kept in touch as well as I should, and I worry I've made a big mistake agreeing to move our family here. I don't have those friendships to support me." Her voice grows quieter as she speaks, and her fingers trace along the edge of my table.

"I don't have any girlfriends here either." I have work companions and a few nursing friends in the larger city, but with our chaotic schedules, we don't have the opportunity to see each other often enough.

"I just needed someone impartial." I understood. Anna needs a friend without a connection to Ben. She needs to take those baby steps to move forward without every detail of her future life revolving around her loss.

"I totally understand, and my door is always open. I've enjoyed talking to you. I want us to be friends, Zack or no Zack."

Anna sighs in relief. Her shoulders fall, and her hands stop moving along the table. "Agreed. Zack or no Zack, I'd love a new friend."

"I'm only curious, but why aren't you part of the bonding ritual?" I don't need to specifically reference the fire for her to know I mean tonight's memorial.

"Ben wrote them letters. Each of them has a mission to complete in a year. Even my damn brother has a directive, and he hasn't been home in years." Anna sighs. Her voice saddens as she asks, "Why do you think Ben left them a letter and not me?"

"It sounds like you and Ben were very open in your relationship. Perhaps he said everything he ever needed to say to you. He knew you'd be able to carry on, but those fools needed a final word of advice." It was a stab in the dark at the thoughts of a dying man I didn't know. Anna softly smiles, and I can only hope I've hit the mark or at least dispelled the question.

"You're a strong woman to have been through what you went through, River. And I'm sorry Zack added to the grief of your situation. It wasn't right of him. You're a survivor." She pauses a beat. "I'm not as strong as you."

"Yes, you are." I mean every word. "You'll make it through this. You just take it day by day. Some days will be good, and some won't be, but you make it through the day and do it again the next day and the next. Days will turn into weeks, but there is no rush. There isn't a finish line. Day by day, my friend," I repeat, holding out my hand across the table.

"Day by day," she echoes and reaches over for mine. She swallows hard and adds, "Thank you for listening."

"Listening is what friends do."

She squeezes my hand, and I know she'll get where she needs to be. It's just going to take time.

25

[Zack]

"Flowers?" Mason snorts. "That's how you wanted to win her back? You can't woo a woman on flowers alone."

I've spent most of the evening glancing up the cliff in hopes of seeing River at the edge of her property or even coming down the stairs to the beach, and I can't seem to help myself. I peer upward again before looking at Mason.

"And how would you know about wooing a woman? You've never wooed anyone in your life."

"I do, too, know how to woo."

Logan breaks into hardy laughter as the three of us remain around the beach fire. We've let it dwindle to low embers so we don't get in trouble for a full blaze in the dark. The wind is low tonight, and it's a perfect evening for what we need to do soon.

"And I don't need to woo when I have all this." Mason draws a hand down the length of his body as he sits in a chair opposite me.

"Fuck off," I mutter, and he laughs. "I don't know how else to apologize. I've said I'm sorry. I gave her flowers." I sound like a chump, but I honestly don't know what else to do. When Jeanine and I fought, we fought. There weren't passionate apologies or vigorous makeup sex. We silently went about, tiptoeing around one another until the boys needed something and the next fight began. I told River I didn't like confrontation, and I didn't want to argue with her ever. She told me it was inevitable, but she assured me we'd always make up.

We hadn't made up. "She doesn't want me within ten feet of her," I remind them.

"When has that stopped you?" Logan teases. "You need a grand gesture."

Oh God. Not more romantic bullshit. Logan has gone so soft and squishy for his new wife and their baby boy that he practically has heart emoji eyeballs. It's sickeningly sweet, and I'm so fucking envious it comes naturally to him.

"Like what?" I ask Logan instead of Mason, who wouldn't actually know how to woo a woman.

"Something big. Something she wants that says you agree, you want that too, and you want her."

"Jesus, that sounds more complicated than Mason's words of wooing."

Mason snorts and tips back a bottle of tequila. I swear we are too old for this shit, but I hold out my hand, wiggling my fingers. I need the strong stuff again tonight. We remain silent as I take my burning sip, shaking my head at the sharp tang on my tongue.

"We really need to find a fourth point for Four Points," Mason says, sobering our conversation a bit. We're leading up to what's to come next, and I sense it in the lowering of his voice.

"It doesn't feel right to ask someone outside of us to take over the landscaping portion," I say.

"We still have his crew." Logan, Mason, and Ben have been using the old Kulis Landscaping offices as the new headquarters for Four Points. With Ben gone, the landscaping manager has continued the position he's held for years. We need to make a decision whether we keep him on and add to the general contracts they have for our special builds or add a new addition to our business.

"We could ask Anna," Mason suggests. I've thought the same thing, but Anna is a teacher, not a landscape designer. She knows some basics but not the intricacies that Ben did. Ben had a financial investment in our new venture with a specific amendment that stated Anna receive his proceeds or sell his position. We all agree we cannot be the Three Points. It doesn't make sense, and we aren't willing to dismiss that Ben was our True North. He brought us together. In his name, we plan to keep our number at four.

"What about Archer?" Logan asks.

"We don't even know where he is." Somehow, I don't think landscaping will be of interest to him. I'm convinced that Archer isn't just some wayward vagabond but possibly something greater, something risky. He hadn't been home in years, and when he has appeared, Ben said he always looked a little rough, a little tough, and a lot beat up.

"What about your brother?" Mason asks.

"I don't think Mr. Magellan Hotel has landscaping in his blood. He's a hotel manager, catering to the rich and famous. Champagne bars and nightclubs are more his speed."

Mason huffs as if agreeing, and Logan nods. "We'll find somebody."

For another minute, we silently watch the low glow of the fire and listen to the soft breeze whistling around us.

"Well, should we do this?" Logan asks.

As Ben wrote each of us a message, Logan suggested we write one back to him. It was actually Autumn's idea and a little New Age for me. Not surprisingly, River loved it. The idea was we write our own thoughts on a notecard and toss them into the fire, allowing the ash to carry the message to our friend. The concept reminds me of Japanese lanterns, and I don't know why we didn't purchase a few of those instead. Then again, we couldn't easily write a personal note on them.

Mason doesn't answer Logan but adds another log to the fire and restokes the embers by placing twigs against them to ignite the wood. The fire builds, and we each reach for our notecards. So much had been said to Ben in those final months, and he hated it, always feeling like people were saying goodbye. We were. He would be leaving us forever.

I hadn't really known what to write on my card. Did I thank him for his friendship? Did I promise him I'd look after Anna and the kids? Did I acknowledge he was like another brother to me? All these things had been said to his face before he passed. It was actually River who helped me come up with something.

"What's one word you'd use to describe Ben?"

"Kind." It was that simple and reminded me quite a bit of River herself. *"Understanding. He had this way of reading people, seeing something in them that others did not. Maybe even seeing something in a person the individual didn't see in himself."* What had Ben seen in me as a friend? I was dedicated and loyal. I'd do anything for any of them. Beyond that, what was I missing that he saw?

It's strange to think Ben might have seen a teenage boy who needed people to love him unconditionally. A boy who'd lost his pride and his home, who only wanted to feel safe and seen for himself, not his father's crime. Ben had done those things. River was doing it too.

"You could always tell Ben how you are doing," River also suggested. *"Respond to his note. Tell him how you'll work on his message."* I hadn't told her what Ben had said. She didn't ask me to share it after the night I told her about it. Yet she'd still given me the best advice.

I wasn't eloquent with my emotions. Reflecting on my multitude of apologies to River, my vocabulary was severely lacking. Still, I wrote what I thought Ben might want to know about me.

"Ready?" I ask, leaning forward in my seat. Mason already sits on the edge of his.

"How do we do this?" Mason asks next.

"I think we hold the card until we can't anymore, letting it burn to nothing, then allowing the wind to take the rest," Logan suggests.

I do not know what kind of voodoo Autumn feeds Logan, but it made sense. We each dip our note into the flame and watch it instantly ignite. Holding the notecard at one corner, I wield it slowly from side to side as the flame lowers and the paper disappears. As the heat nears my fingertip, I toss the last corner into the air and watch it dance before fluttering into the larger flames. Mason and Logan do the same, and we continue to stare at the orange and yellow pattern crackling around the darkening log.

"To friendship," Mason states, lifting the bottle of tequila for another swig. He easily swallows and passes the bottle to Logan.

"To family." Logan raises the bottle in salute as well but doesn't drink. We allow him a pass.

"To forever," I say, finding my eyes cloud with thoughts of our lost friend and hope that I haven't lost the woman who helped me write a note to honor him.

I'm learning to fly. It's frightening and fantastic, and I only wish you were here to see me.

+ + +

The next day, I wake with a nasty hangover, but it's time to leave. I've missed another night with River, and as much as I long to cross into her yard, I don't know what to say to her. She works the morning shift as yesterday was her day off, and I'm sad that she hasn't had final words with the boys.

To my surprise, I find them each digging into a paper treasure chest full of things. It's an explosion of books, Lego sets, another eye patch for each of them, and plastic hand hooks.

"What's this?" The sound of my own voice is too loud for my pounding head.

"Miss River gave us each our own treasure." Oliver holds up a book about pirates. Trevor slips the hand hook over his fist. Sadly, I want to ask if River left anything for me, but I know she didn't.

"Maybe you need to go over there and steal her booty," Mason mutters, coming up beside me as the boys have littered the floor of the sitting area off the kitchen.

"You're so inappropriate," I mumble as he hands me a mug of coffee. "But I could kiss you for this." What I should do is kick his ass for always bringing out the tequila when I'm at my lowest. At forty-one, you'd think I would've learned my lesson.

"My booty doesn't swing that way, but thanks for the offer." Mason winks at me before laughing, which rattles my teeth. Why is everything so loud today?

"Okay, boys. We need to pick up and pack our stuff."

Oliver stills before looking up at me. "We didn't say goodbye to Miss River."

"I know, but she has to work today, and we need to head home."

"Why can't we live here?" Trevor asks. "We're leaving the tree fort."

"It doesn't belong to us. It's in River's yard. We can build our own at home."

"But Miss River said it was ours," Trevor says, his voice winding up. "She said it would always be ours."

"And it will be, but it stays here with her." I hate that I'm giving them an empty promise. I don't know that River will honor what she told the boys.

I'll be guarding it for you.

My thoughts race to her marrying someone and having those babies she wants. Her children will play in that tree fort. Or maybe she'll move. Maybe she'll sell the place, and my boys won't ever be allowed to enter the yard next door again. Panic seizes my chest, but I tell myself it's only the reflux of a queasy stomach after a night of drinking.

"I don't want to go home," Oliver says, his voice quivering. "I don't want to leave Miss River."

Man, I understand his pain, but instead, I grow angry. "I said pick this shit up. We need to get going."

Trevor's head pops up, and if a seven-year-old could maim with a look, I've just lost my head. Oliver swipes at his eyes, and Trevor tips his head as he glances at his brother. He offers a protective hand to his twin's back before slowly beginning to place items back in his box.

My heart sinks to my belly, and I can't blame the alcohol for the acid roiling in my stomach.

That's shame, and it's all my fault.

+ + +

The packing of cars is chaos, and there isn't enough ibuprofen in the world to tame my headache. Every vehicle door slam rattles my brain. Still, we load my car as Logan and Autumn linger with baby Ben and Lorna. Anna and Mila come outside. Calvin and Bryce have already said their goodbyes to the boys and me yesterday. As I place the final bag in my trunk, Mason stumbles out of the garage apartment with a bag of his own.

Anna glances up at him, and the expression on her face looks like panic. Mason heads to the trunk of his car and opens the hatch.

"Where are you going?" she finally asks, a tremor in her voice along with the demanding edge of curiosity.

"I think it's time I leave, too."

The air around all of us stills.

"What about Four Points?" Logan asks, and Mason stills with his hand on the trunk. He's the one who pushed this venture. He can't back out. What is he doing? What is he thinking? He hadn't mentioned leaving last night.

"Let's talk tomorrow." He glances over at Logan for support. Logan looks at me and then back at our friend and nods.

I step over to Anna as my car blocks the drive, and I'll need to pull out first for Mason to follow.

"Take care of you," I tell my friend, pulling her into a tight embrace.

"Take care of you," she says back to me, mumbling into my shoulder. I press a kiss to her temple and pull back. "You need anything, call me."

Anna nods. I know she won't call. She knows she won't call. The boys hug everyone next before piling into the car. Mason steps up to Anna, and I wait for some reason. The tension on his face is something I've never seen before.

"Ask me to stay, and I will."

Anna doesn't look up at him but toys with the hem of her shirt. "No, you need to go." Her head nods as if convincing herself, and Mason's hands slip into his pockets. He nods once to agree, but the pain in his face says it all.

"Archer's coming home," Anna states. That could mean tomorrow or Christmas or next August, but if Anna thinks her brother is an answer to something, I can't argue with her. The eldest McCaryn needs to get here.

I give a final glance in the direction of River's house. I can only see the upper half with the height of the arborvitae. The tree fort isn't visible from here. In my head, I say a final goodbye and then climb into my car to head for home.

26

[River]

I worked both the day Zack left and the next, so it's on my day off that I'm awakened by the sound of a utility truck of some sort in reverse. The annoying blare—*wheet, wheet, wheet*—grows louder, and I realize the noise sounds as if it's coming closer to the house. As I scramble to the window that faces the road, I see a truck is indeed in my driveway. A second truck follows the first. Doors slam shut as I race down the staircase. I open the front door in a rush and step into the yard.

"Excuse me!" I holler over the whirling noise. "I think you have the wrong house."

A man approaches me with a tablet in hand. "Are you River Nagle?" I stare at the man a moment, noticing he looks up and then quickly glances to the side.

"I am."

He isn't looking in my direction but lifts the tablet to eye level and reads off my address.

"That's correct." My arms cross over my chest. "And?"

A swift shift of his gaze occurs, then he looks back at the tablet. I peer down at my attire and realize I'm wearing a rather thin nightdress. My nipples and more are on display through the sheer material, and I cross my arms higher over my breasts.

"We're here to remove the fence."

My mouth gapes open, and I glance over at the metal chain link.

"I didn't order fence removal."

The man doesn't blink but reads off his tablet again. "Says here removal of chain link fencing around property. Ordered by your husband."

"My husband?" I stammer. As those closest to me know the truth, and those distant only know rumors, no one I know could have done this.

"Mr. Zack Weller. Strange you have different names and all, but who am I to judge. I can see you're a modern woman."

I don't even have time to unpack that comment before I'm simply muttering, "No boundaries." *The man has no flipping boundaries whatsoever.*

"Speaking of boundaries, he mentioned that I'm to pass along this message. *He doesn't want any boundaries between you.*" The foreman's eyes shift right and then back to his tablet, which I'm certain he's no longer reading, just staring at. "Strange message, but he said you'd understand the meaning."

Silence falls between us for a moment as I glance back at the fence. It really is ugly. I'd have a natural border along Anna's property and a solid wood structure on the opposite side of the backyard. Removal would open the front as the fence went all the way to the street, surprisingly blocking in the front yard.

"Ma'am, do we have your permission to begin?"

I scoff. It's the first time I've been asked for such a thing regarding my yard when it comes to Mr. Zack Weller.

"How much is it?"

"Says already paid in full."

"My husband used the wrong credit card. Can you just confirm the amount and I'll get the correct one?"

The man scratches the back of his neck. "We let the office handle such things, but I'll give you the number both for the amount and the manager." When he tells me how much the fence removal plus cleanup will cost, I almost fall over. I should deny the damn gesture, but something stops me.

"As long as you're here, proceed. I'll call your office, so I can clear up the credit card issue."

Looks like I just bought myself fence removal, eliminating all barriers around me.

+ + +

The day turns into quite an exciting event. Anna's worried about me and asks me to join her for dinner at her house. I think she also wants the company. I quickly learn Mason had left.

L.B. Dunbar

"Last year was the first time we'd had everyone here in a long time. My siblings and I own the place and used it as a vacation destination. My younger sister, Amelia, never visits, though, and my older brother, Archer, comes and goes on his own schedule without notice. After the other families left last year, Ben and I returned to Chicago, packed up our house, and moved. It was a whirlwind from that moment on. I didn't realize how quiet it would be once everyone was gone."

Despite dinner at her house, we came to my yard to enjoy the view and after-dinner wine. Anna gazes out at the sunset, which arrives a little sooner each evening as the calendar creeps toward September. We're sitting together on my chaise lounge.

"Did you want Mason to stay?" There was a certain something in her voice when she told me he'd left.

Anna's forehead furrows, deep in consideration. "No, he needed to leave." She takes a deep breath. "Still, it's almost too quiet with just the boys and Mila. Calvin and Bryce are busy with football practice beginning and their final days working with the landscaping company. Most days, it's just Mila and me, and even she's gotten used to going down the street to see Lorna, or Lorna comes to our house, and they disappear into Mila's room." She sighs. She doesn't need to say it, she's lonely.

Anna glances at the side of her property along my yard. "It really does look better." She pauses a beat. The removal of the fence left perfectly spaced holes with a fresh circle of sod to fill in the missing posts. It does look better, but it takes some getting used to. It's definitely a cleaner look.

"I can't believe Zack's father showed up," she adds.

"Yeah, that was unexpected." When Mr. Weller surprisingly showed up in my yard today, I saw the resemblance between father and son better. His silver eyes. His edgy cheekbones. His charming smile. It was a bold move to drop by the house. Perhaps he intended Anna's place, but the ruckus in my driveaway drew him here. He was looking for his son. Zack's disapproval of his father stems from resentment and hurt and a grieving heart, but still, he had been too harsh, in my opinion.

Anna glances at me. "I assume you know Zack's history with his dad. It was an awful time for him. He really struggled. He was used to being popular and top alpha, much like little Trevor. He felt stripped of everything good when it happened, and then he had to face it every day. The rumors. The gossip. The judgment."

I knew the feeling as I remained at the hospital after Quincy's passing, his generous gift, and the unwarranted accusations. Although I wasn't there long before they let me go.

"He meant well," she says, nodding back at where the fence once stood. It feels weird without it although I never liked it.

"I didn't exactly accept the offer, though," I remind her, having maxed out my credit card to cover the cost. Guess the yard will continue to be my focus, and I'll save the inside renovations for another year.

"River, I'm going to say something, and I don't want you to take it the wrong way." Anna pauses, taking a deep breath. "But don't run from him."

"I'm not the one who had to leave," I remind her.

"I mean his love. Don't shy away because of a silly misunderstanding. Everything has an explanation. It can be repaired." She waves her hand toward the new, lush sod and open space between the yards. My eyes lift to the tree fort, where the old platform was removed and a new one built along with a beautiful square structure including windows and a roof.

"Broken trust is hard to repair," I tell her. He didn't trust me, and that was hard to accept.

"Yes, but it's still something mendable." There are cases when trust is irreparably broken, but Anna is correct. "It can be fixed and forgiven."

My grandfather would have adored Anna Kulis.

I stare off at the lowering sun myself, questioning so many things. Zack hurt me. I don't need that kind of pain in my life, but then again, I'm fortunate Zack is still here, alive. Anna will never have the opportunity to fight and make up with Ben again. She will never have the chance to mend fences between them or remove boundaries. She's alone, and as much as I hate to admit it, I'm lonely as well without the boys having tree house adventures and Zack hoarding my chaise lounge.

27

[Zack]

"Mr. Weller, just wanted to let you know the job is complete, and your wife settled up with the mix-up in credit cards," the fence company worker says through the phone.

"What mix-up?" I question, tipping back in my leather desk chair, staring out my office window at the river separating Detroit from Canada.

"The incorrect credit card. Your wife paid with her card."

"She what?" I lean forward, and my feet hit the floor with a thud. *What was River doing?*

"Also, wanted to let you know your father was very helpful. There'd been some old footings from another fence he had us remove."

"My father?" I choke and drop my elbows to my thighs, hanging my head.

"Nice guy," the man adds.

You have got to be joking. What the hell was Robert doing there? Did he come to threaten River? Did he try to harass her as Daniel had? Did he ask her for money?

"How does the yard look?" My voice isn't as steady as I'd like it to be in asking such a casual question. The removal of the fencing included filling any holes from the posts and covering the fresh dirt with new grass. By next summer, no one would even know an ugly fence was once present between the properties.

"Looks great."

After thanking him for his call, I quickly call River. Four attempts with no answer lead me to contact Mason before remembering he isn't at Anna's. Next, I call Logan. I want someone to check on River. I want someone to physically lay eyes on her, and I don't want to bother Anna. She has enough to worry about.

Leaving my office early, I tell my assistant I'll be working remotely the next day and head out without a care for all the work that's piled up over the two weeks of my vacation. I quickly call the new nanny and then I have my brother on the phone.

"Why the hell didn't you tell me Dad had returned?"

"And hello to you, too." My brother chuckles into the phone. We just spoke less than a week ago, and he'd never mentioned our father being in the area I was visiting.

"Noah, cut the shit." I loved my brother, and we'd been close as far as brothers went, but I count him as one more person who abandoned me when I was young. We worked it out, but sometimes that resentful kid in me still flares up. Noah knows I can't handle even the mention of our father. He's been the contact on all things regarding Robert, especially after our father divorced our mother from prison. "Did you know he was here?"

"Maybe." Noah pauses. "How did you find out?"

"I had the wonderful surprise of seeing him at a canoe rental place."

"You went to Robbyn's River Adventure?" He scoffs, but Noah doesn't sound half as shocked in stating the canoe place as his surprise in me going there.

"I took the boys and River."

"Why does River sound suspiciously like the name of a woman?" Noah laughs.

"Noah, focus."

"It is a woman. Does my Zacky have a girlfriend?"

How is this man in his mid-forties? He sounds like he's still eighteen. "Noah." My teeth grind as I hit the highway heading due west across the state. "Why didn't you tell me?"

Noah sighs, long and hard. "Because I knew you were still angry. You said you never wanted to see him again, and I figured you didn't want to know his location. The last place I'd expect you to go was Robbyn's."

Even if I hadn't gone there, I might have still run into my father somewhere else in the area. I could have seen him in Union Pier, the local beach town, or worse, walked right past him and not known it was him. I recall how I hadn't even looked up when he was first talking to the boys when we approached the canoe landing. I hadn't a thought that it was him until his eyes caught mine—the same colored eyes I face in the mirror every morning.

"I don't believe this," I hiss.

"Did you talk to him?" Noah's tone drops lower, hesitating on the thought.

"No." I huff. A heavy pause fills the line as my blinker sounds through the car, echoing like a heartbeat as I pass a slow-moving vehicle.

"Maybe you should," Noah states.

"Maybe you should fuck off. There's no way I'm speaking to him."

"Don't you think it's time? It's been twenty-five years."

"Try twenty-seven, and I think hell can freeze over three times before I'll speak with him."

"That's harsh," Noah scoffs.

"He went to my . . . he went to River's house, which happens to be our old home." My voice rises louder in frustration and anger.

"Someone lives in the house?" Noah's voice rings incredulous. "I thought the old geezer was using it for company retreats and rental property."

I'd forgotten all about that. When the house was first confiscated as equity against the money stolen, it was used by handfuls of men and visitors. Parties happened next door as if they were celebrating, dancing on the grave of my childhood and the memories of my family. I hated Quincy Grocer and even refused to take a real estate case a few years ago with their name attached. *Was that case possibly River's inheritance?*

I'd rather a single woman who appreciates the place live there permanently than groups of random people traipsing through the house or, worse, lewd men doing God knows what all over the place.

My thoughts race, recalling everything I'd done to River, and all of that was only outside in the backyard, in the tree fort, against the side of the house. I'm such a hypocrite.

"It isn't a rental anymore. A woman inherited it from Dennis Quincy."

"No shit?" Noah laughs.

"No shit. But, Noah . . . Robert . . ." *Focus, dammit.*

"Dad," Noah emphasizes.

"Why would he go to the house? Why is he even in the area?" What the hell is he doing in the state of Michigan? I thought my father would want to be far, far away from the memories of where life went all wrong for him.

"It's his home," Noah states matter of fact. Our parents were actually from Chicago, much like Anna's parents, though. That's where the trouble started for my dad. Irish kid from the Southside wanting to hold his own; he was a scrapper with dreams of money and success. Most days being an accountant didn't fit his persona, nor did the family home on lake property, but he wanted it. He wanted that view and that house. He wanted to please my mother. He said it often enough.

"He shouldn't be there!" I holler into the car, blasting at the hands-free phone system.

"He can live where he wants," Noah defends, and it pisses me off even more.

"Is this why you're planning to move to Lakeside? Are you coming to see him?" Has my brother paid him visits before?

"I think we should discuss this another time when you can act like a rational adult."

I snort. *This*, coming from the man who still acts like a college guy, going to bars on the regular and hooking up with rich women in hopes of I don't know what. "Yeah, I gotta go."

"Zack, don't be like this," Noah pleads, his voice a whine, restoring him to the brother I know.

Don't listen to them, Zack. Suck it up, Zack. It's only a little longer, and then you're out of there, Zack.

Easy words for the teen who left shortly after everything blew up. He wasn't the one left behind to face it all alone with a heart-sick mother and nowhere to call home.

"I'll call you later," I mutter, acting petulant in my own right as I disconnect the line.

+ + +

By the time I'd made the three-hour trip back to Lakeside, it's dark outside. My boys are with our new nanny, and I hated to leave them behind already, but this visit needed to be done alone. I needed to see River for myself. Logan said he hadn't found River at home, which made my heart rate race even harder. I didn't really believe Robert would physically harm River. I just didn't want him anywhere near her.

Dammit, I shouldn't have left her alone. I shouldn't have left her at all. Barreling across the state, I felt an unsettling sensation ripple over my skin, and I thought about a lot of things. Number one being how I didn't want to live without River in my life.

Once I reach her front door, I hammer at the wood. Growing frustrated with the lack of response, I help myself to round her house and enter the backyard. I hardly note the missing fence that once lined her property. It wouldn't have kept me out anyway.

I find River sitting in her chaise lounge. Only . . . another body sits beside her.

"Zack?" Anna questions, noticing me first. River twists beside Anna to look at me over her shoulder. Slowly, Anna rises, says something to River, and crosses the lawn to me. "Don't be stupid." The warning surprises me as she pats my chest over my heart. I lean forward to kiss her cheek, and then Anna leaves the yard, easily walking through the space between the trees behind her garage.

"I see you've kept your clothes on," I tease, finding my voice rough as River rises next from the lounger.

"Don't have a fence to protect my privacy." The previous barrier was transparent, but in all honesty, the way I saw River was looking over the shrubbery from the second-floor next door. Now that room is vacant and dark.

"I don't want any boundaries between us anyway," I admit, and I'm not referring to a damn fence. River steps closer to me but not close enough.

"Then you'll need to let me in." She doesn't stop at that, though. She passes me, crosses her small patio, and enters her home, leaving the sliding glass door open.

The only way to mend this broken fence is to step inside.

28

[River]

I walked into the house, leaving the door open for Zack to follow. *It's only a house*, I want to say, but it's so much more to him. The child inside him feels abandoned by the rugged man who'd stood in my yard this afternoon, and watched a fence be torn out. While his face was hard, his expression was kind, resolved even to the damage he'd done. I wasn't afraid of his presence or even demanding he leave. I let him stand there, watching the men work. He didn't say much. He didn't ask about the house or Zack or the boys. He just watched. I allowed him his memories, even if Zack said he shouldn't have them.

In the kitchen, I round the peninsula cabinet and set the wineglasses from Anna's visit within the basin. Turning to the side, I watch Zack walk inside, slide the glass door behind him, and lock it. Then he pauses and looks around. The cabinets are dated. They might have been the original set from his childhood. Hardwood floors throughout the place show wear and tear from the years this home was a rental property. I personally tossed most of the rugs when I inherited the place. The kitchen dining set is definitely old, bulky, and too large for the space.

Zack doesn't linger long in his inspection. His eyes quickly find me, and he lasers in on my position. Rounding the cabinets himself, he stands before me. With his gaze focused on me, he slowly folds to his knees before me and wraps his arms around my waist. His head meets my belly, and he squeezes me tight.

"I'm sorry. I'm so sorry for what I said, for what I did."

Hesitating only a second, I seek his hair and tenderly comb through the strands.

"You hurt me," I admit.

"I know. I don't know what came over me. I'd seen my dad. Then I heard those women, and I just reacted. You aren't my father. You aren't Jeanine. You aren't like any other woman I've known."

"Jeanine?" I question.

"She was all about the buck, the bottom line, and wanting more." His voice quiets. "She was so much like my father, and I didn't see it because she was smart and successful in her own right."

I continue stroking through his hair, waiting on more from him.

"I overreacted."

Scoffing at the comment, he tilts his head and gazes up at me.

"Zack, you have no boundaries." I've used the word too many times to describe his actions. He doesn't hold back, taking what he wants, going where he pleases. If he isn't careful with this trait, he could cross a line.

"I'd like to learn. I'd like to . . . compromise."

My lip curls only a touch in the corner. "What does that even mean to you?"

"Don't leave me. I don't want to lose you." That vulnerable tone returns, and it'd break my heart if I wasn't already a little broken by him.

Sighing, I stare down at him. "You'd have to trust me, and I don't think you do."

"I don't trust myself." He takes a deep breath. "I'm afraid to love because people get hurt. People do stupid things to prove themselves."

"Zack," I whisper, accepting that he must see his mother as loving his father too much and his father trying to please her, justifying his choice to gamble.

"I'm so grateful for how you are with the boys and how good we are together." He takes a deep breath as if he's about to dive into the lake. "Ben's letter to me told me to fly in love, and I didn't know what he meant. I thought he must have miswritten his intention, but now I understand. When I'm with you, I'm soaring. It's a high I've never felt before. It's freeing and scary, but, River, I love it. I love you, angel."

I don't know what to say. My heart still aches, but sincerity rings through his apology confirmed by those pleading silvery eyes.

"Where are the boys?" I wonder.

"I left them with the new nanny. I wanted to bring them, but it was too soon. My decision was so quick." He pauses a beat. "My father was here."

The heaviness in the statement says it all. The concern in his eyes says even more as he clings to me on his knees. I continue stroking through his hair.

"He didn't mean any harm. It was all innocent," I say, instantly realizing my mistake in word choice.

"He wasn't innocent of anything," Zack snaps, slowly releasing me and rising to his feet but still crowding my space.

"Poor choice of words. I mean, he didn't do anything. He didn't really say anything either. He just stood there, watching the men work, watching them remove the fence."

Zack swipes a hand through his hair, eyes shifting to the side. "He shouldn't have been here. He shouldn't have even been breathing the same air as you."

"And what? Now you want to build an eight-foot fence around the place or place a bubble around me?" I exhale. I can't even address the fence issue yet. "Zack, you need to forgive him."

"Never," he hisses in that toughened voice he used upon our first meeting.

"Do you remember me telling you that love and gratitude are not the same thing?" Zack's eyes meet mine. "Maybe you can't love him again. Maybe it's not an option, as you say, because you don't know him, but you need to come to terms with having him at one point in your life. You need to be grateful for the father you had when you had him."

"He took everything away."

"He did." I sigh again. "But now it's time to forgive him. Forgiveness isn't for the faint at heart; only the weak can't forgive." *The world according to Grandfather number two point three seven nine.*

"I don't think I can." His voice lowers, as does his head.

"You'll be a better father if you do," I whisper, knowing that doesn't explain it well enough, but Zack needs to let go of his anger at his own father to open himself up better to his boys.

"I don't know how," he states, even lower. His lips twist, and if I didn't know he was forty-one, I'd guess him to be all of seventeen with his hesitant, strained expression.

"Maybe just talk to him. Or better yet, listen." My grandfather would say *talk is cheap, but listening doesn't cost anything*. However, I hold back that Grandpa-ism. Comparing something to money might not be appropriate for Zack's situation.

"Quincy wanted to make amends with his children as he lay dying. His children didn't. They have to live with the loss of him all over again. They'll never have answers because they couldn't listen to him." I sigh, thinking this comparison isn't getting through to Zack any better. I don't want him to regret never hearing his father's side of the story. I don't want him to be bitter like Daniel Quincy.

Zack closes his eyes for a second. "Can we not talk about my dad right now?" His exhale warns me that he has a lot going on in that head of his, and he can only tackle one issue at a time.

I have my own questions.

"What are you doing here?" I ask, wondering why he left his boys, drove across the state, and stands before me this late at night.

"I had things on my mind."

"Like what?" I whisper.

He licks his lower lip and bites the corner. "Why did you do it, stubborn woman? Why did you pay for the fence removal?"

"I don't need you to pay for things. You don't owe me. You aren't indebted to me. Not apologies, not gratitude, nor any other thing you've worked up in your head."

"I just want to take care of you." His face shifts, his expression confused.

"Then take care of *me*." I point at my chest, and Zack's eyes follow the motion. "I don't need your money. I only want you."

His fingers reach for my jaw, and his mouth lowers, brushing over mine as they did during our first kiss. He's holding back again.

"Don't be afraid to ask for what you want," I whisper against his mouth after another swipe-of-a-kiss I hope to never receive again. This isn't my Zack. This isn't how we kiss. As much as he needs to learn about respecting boundaries, he also needs to learn it's okay to want things. All he needs to do is ask for them. *Hell*, even take it in this situation. *Take the kiss.*

He reads my thoughts, and his mouth crashes to mine. Teeth and tongue. Lips and licks. We meld together in apology, forgiveness, and desire. His hands drop to my hips, and he lifts me to the countertop. My knees spread, and he steps into the space, pressing us together while our mouths continue to speak for us. His hands return to my jaw, and mine wrap around his head. For a moment, it feels like there's no beginning or end between us. We are one, and this is love. A circle that goes round and round, in dips and lifts, spinning, spinning, *spinning*.

He called it flying instead of falling, and I love the difference. Flying feels freeing while falling sounds fearful. I'm not afraid to love him.

"Let's go upstairs," I say, needing our circle more complete. Our connection to be deeper.

Zack helps me down from the counter, and I lead the way. If he wants to inspect the house, investigate as we go, he doesn't. His gaze is on me as I cross the family room and head up the staircase. Down the hall, we go to the last door. I pause outside the room, knowing this was once Zack's parents' space.

"Will you be okay going in there?"

"I'll be okay, as long as anywhere we go, you're by my side. I've already lived too long without you, and I don't want another day to pass without us together."

"You're getting better at this compromise thing," I tease.

"I'm better because of you."

At his words, I leap upward, and he catches me under my thighs. Wrapping my legs around his waist, he steps forward, and I turn the knob at my back. We enter the room with Zack's mouth on mine. He stumbles. He trips, and then we're both floating down to the bed. I bounce on the mattress and giggle while Zack catches himself over me.

"Please let me in," he whispers, moving his hand to my shorts and unsnapping the button. Assisting him, I unzip them and push them over my hips. Zack stands back and removes them, admiring my skimpy panties and the tank top I'm wearing.

"You're so beautiful, angel," he says, reaching behind his head for the collar of his shirt and tugging it over his head. It's another dress shirt unbuttoned a few buttons at the collar. This one is crisp and white, and more business attire than his other ones. He's also wearing suit pants and dress shoes.

"Did you come here from your office?" I question.

"I didn't stop until I was here."

"Zack," I whisper, reaching for his belt. He kicks off his shoes as I work at his pants. Then he's shoving them down and removing his socks. Pressing me back, he kneels on the bed and balances over me again.

"I need to be inside you, but I understand if you want to go slow. I understand if you want to back up a bit, and I'll understand if you only want me to hold you. Just don't ask me to leave."

My fingers hook into the waistband of his boxer briefs.

"I need you inside me," I say to his lips before they crash over mine, taking me with more urgency and passion than I thought possible. Breaking free, his hands roam my body, over my shoulders, and down my arms to my wrists. He retraces his path before jumping to the hem of my tank top and removing it. Quickly, my bra follows, and Zack lowers for a breast. His teeth scrape the soft flesh before he nips at the peaked nub. Then his tongue swirls, and he opens to latch on to me. His pace is leisurely, dragging out the suction and forcing my back to arch.

Need builds quickly, and I awkwardly push at the edge of his briefs.

"Want something, angel?" he teases before moving to the other aching swell. My thighs are spread, and his abs rest against my core. I buck my hips, seeking friction against him.

"I want you." Zack bites my nipple, and I squeak. He soothes the sting by sucking at the tip. With open-mouth kisses, he moves down my body, taking his time to reach my center. He blows over the cotton strip covering where I want him most, and then he removes my underwear. His eyes devour my body as he admires what he's already seen before. Only this time, the lights are on. We aren't under the dark sky but in the dim light of my bedroom. A small lamp illuminates the space, and Zack's eyes worship all he sees.

"My God, you're sunshine," he says, glancing at my hair before scanning my body once more. Then he dips his head and laps at folds seeping with need. My hips surge in reaction to the sudden warmth of his tongue. He takes me to the brink like only he can, licking and kissing like the unquenchably thirsty man he is. Eventually, I break, spilling open over his mouth, and even then, he's still drinking me in.

I whimper his name because I need him closer. My fingers tug at his ears to remove him, and I crunch upward.

"Inside me," I murmur. Zack sits back. "Condoms in the drawer." I nod to the nightstand, and Zack freezes. His eyes widen. "They're for you. Only you."

"Damn straight," he hisses, reaching over for the nightstand and hastily working the drawer. I hear rustling, and the box fumble. A packet is produced, opened, and Zack covered. "I'm wearing this tonight, but soon we're going to talk about going without this barrier. I want to give you that *someday*, River. The one where you wanted babies and more."

He can't mean it. We've jumped from a ten-day fling to I love you to children in a matter of a few weeks. My head is spinning until his tip rests at my entrance. Then he's slowly filling me, and all thoughts dissipate. There is only him and me. Zack slides to the hilt, taking his time as he did that night on the lounger. He made love to me under the stars, even if he didn't intend to do such a thing. It was romantic and sweet, and one of many moments when I felt the flying sensation of love he mentions.

"I'm soaring for you," I say as he pulls back to the edge of my channel, teasing me with retreat before surging forward to fill me once more.

"Soaring?" he questions as he balances over me, watching himself disappear into my body.

"Gliding. Flying. Getting higher."

His gaze moves to my face. "What are you saying, angel?"

"I love you, too."

Zack stills, watching my eyes before lowering to kiss me. With his thickness buried inside me, he delves into my mouth with his tongue. "Say it again," he mutters as his lips remain over mine.

"I love you."

Zack pulls back as if he doesn't believe me at first. As if he isn't certain he heard me correctly or understands what I've said. Then his expression shifts, and those white teeth show. His mouth curls wide. He bites his lower lip, giving me a knowing smirk. *Dazzling*. The happiness written on his face is truly breathtaking.

"I love you, too. I love you so much." His mouth returns to mine until his hips need to move. He pulls back, pressing inward once more before moving at a faster pace, thrusting with more determination. He wants to mark me inside and outside, but there's no rush. He's already staked his territory. I am his. He is mine. There are no barriers between us. We are a circle, on repeat, of love, and love, and love.

Zack's thrusts match the rhythm of my heart, and together, we climb. We fly, and when we burst like fireworks or summer showers, we don't see it as a fall but a glide back to earth. Drifting. Floating. Free.

He collapses over me and buries his face in my neck. "I love feeling you come around me."

"I love to come around you." Softly, I chuckle.

Zack lifts his head, pressing up on his elbows. "You're really mine."

"I'm really *mine*, but I belong with you." I smile to assure him where I stand. Beside him, with him.

Zack shakes his head with a laugh. "You're terrible at negotiation."

"What's to negotiate?"

Staring down at me, he grins again, slow and wide. "Nothing. Absolutely nothing."

After we clean up, we remain naked with only a light blanket over us. Zack lays on his side, perched up on an elbow while his hand lazily glides over my body. His palm skims down my middle, between my breasts, and over my belly.

"Why did he do it?" he asks.

"Why did who do what?"

His hand returns up my center, and a fingertip circles my breast. "Why did Quincy leave this place to you? It had to be more than your kind spirit."

His fingertip distracts me, and I lick my lip before I speak. "I brought him here to see a sunset. He'd received this place as a settlement. I had no idea it came from your family." Eyeing him, I want him to know I didn't know his history. He nods, and I continue.

"He wanted to die someplace beautiful; instead, he passed away in a small hospital room with only nurses at his side." We didn't get to stay here. It was a little like springing an inmate from prison, but I don't use the analogy with Zack.

"I thought he was blind."

"I described it to him." Quincy had been in excellent spirits that night. He claimed he could feel the warmth on his skin. As best I could, I explained the brilliance of the half-circle sun, lowered behind the water. The cool glow like a rainbow of golds and oranges effervescing outward. The clouds as they broke off in thin strips like cotton and the deep blue of the water as it rippled like folds of denim with a frayed hem of white as it touched the shore. Thinking of that night, I see it all in my mind's eye. "Two days later, he died."

Zack's forehead furrows as his finger dips down to my belly button, circling the puckered skin before dragging back to the valley between my breasts. "Wills take time. He must have already gifted the property to you before that night."

I shrug, as I don't have an answer. "In the will, he said a beautiful place should belong to a beautiful soul. He didn't mean the house. He meant the view." I could have returned the house to Quincy's children. They argued it wasn't ethical for me to take it, and some would agree, it wasn't. I was his nurse. He was my patient. Being gifted a large property . . . just isn't done, yet it happens. I didn't want it, but after an ugly fight with Daniel, I didn't want him to have the place either. This was a special spot to Quincy, and as he reminded me of my grandfather, I couldn't pass on his generous gift. It was the new beginning I didn't know I needed.

"Quincy reminded me so much of my grandfather in some ways. In others, he wasn't. Losing him was like losing Grandpa all over again, though, and it was difficult for me."

Zack nods, considering something. "So just to be clear, you haven't been married to anyone before him?" He tips up a brow while his finger stills on my skin.

"I haven't ever been married."

His forehead furrows again. "Why not?" His voice softens, expressing concern he'll hurt my feelings.

"I lived with someone for years in my twenties. We grew comfortable with one another, which can lead to being complacent. We just didn't see it going any further than what it was." Roommates who occasionally had sex. "We were both too busy. He was an emergency room doctor. After him, I'd been on dates, but nothing serious. I didn't have the time."

Zack's quiet for a moment before he speaks again. "But you make time for love."

Slowly, I smile. "You make time for love." Our eyes meet before his expression turns serious.

"I'm grateful Ben was able to come home, be here, although it was difficult for Anna. He stayed in a guest room on the second floor because he didn't want his illness tainting the master bedroom with haunting memories. He only wanted Anna to remember the good times in their bed." Zack softly chuckles and looks around my room for the first time.

"It's different in here. New paint," he observes. "Different bed and furnishings." His review moves to the window with sheer coverings. "No haunting memories," he whispers, and I wonder only briefly if he could ever live in this house again. Would it be too much for him? We've only just declared our love so moving in together seems like too much to mention.

"You okay in here?"

"I will be." He pauses as he glances back at me. "Remember when you asked me to keep my eyes to myself, and I denied I could." Zack smiles, and I chuckle at the reminder of our first encounter. "You said whatever makes me feel better. And somehow, I knew right at that moment, you, just being with you, would make me feel better."

"Zack," I whisper, overwhelmed by him. His gaze roams over my body once more. My shoulders. My breasts. My belly. His look alone is a soft caress. "You do have a beautiful soul. You are sunrise and sunsets, and I want to see them every day with you."

Deep inside, I light up because I want the same thing.

29

[Zack]

Unfortunately, I had to leave early the next morning, speeding across the state once more to get home to my boys and return to work. I had so much to do and so little time, but I took a deep breath, knowing River and I promised to make time for one another.

When the weekend drew near and Jeanine canceled her scheduled visit with the boys, it didn't take any coercion to convince Trevor and Oliver we should return to River's home, even if she had to work the morning shift both days. Her absence would actually give me time to assess the house and see what it needed. I'd noted little things on my too-short visit, like the scuffed floors and awful furniture. Entering her bedroom was like entering a different realm compared to the rest of the house, and I was grateful it was so changed. Not a drop of my parents' existence in there remained. The wall color. The sheer material covering the windows. Even the placement of the bed made it feel like a new room.

As I wander through her place, I hear voices coming from the front yard, recognizing both Trevor and Oliver's tones but not the third. Quickly, hackles rise on my neck. We've talked about not speaking to strangers, especially after the surprise of seeing my father at the canoe rental place. I didn't tell the boys who the man was, other than a rough lecture about not offering information to people they didn't know.

As I race down the stairs and out the front door, a man I newly recognize stands in the front yard.

"No!" I yell out, pointing a finger at him. "Get out of here."

Robert freezes where he stands beside an old beat-up car. It's sporty in style, though ancient in make and model. Rusty and used, it has potential. I don't want to think about how he got it or where.

He holds up his hands in surrender, and déjà vu fills my head. His arms in the air. His calm demeanor. His voice as he spoke to the police who stood at our front door.

Robert Weller, you're under arrest . . .

"Get away from my boys!" I shout.

"I didn't know they'd be here. I didn't know you were here."

"I don't care." I don't even want to know *why* he's here. "You need to leave before I call—" *the cops.* I stumble over the words, and my brows lift. Robert must hear the unspoken, and his forehead furrows as well. His arms remain in the air. *Could I call the police on him?*

We remain in this position—him with his arms up, me with a scowl on my face—when a car pulls into the drive.

River? She's home early.

As she parks, I rush to her. "What happened?"

Glancing from me to Robert, she hesitates. "I could ask you the same thing."

I gaze over my shoulder. "I don't know what he's doing here. I'm trying to get him to leave." Before I turn back to her, a hand comes to my forearm, and I peer down at it before looking up at River.

"Listen," she whispers to me. Her eyes softening. "Just listen." Her eyes well with tears.

"What's wrong?" I step closer to her, brushing her cheek with the back of my knuckles.

"It isn't me. We'll talk later." She nods at Robert, and I glance at him once more. "He's here for you."

Shaking my head, I bring my attention back to River, trying to catch her eyes. I can't do this. I don't want him here. I want to know why she's about to cry.

Too quickly, she slips around me, though, and approaches Robert.

"Hello, Mr. Weller. It's nice to see you again."

"I told you to call me Robert, honey."

Closing my eyes, I'm ready to lose my shit. I spin on my heels, and my entire body vibrates. I want him out of here. I want him gone, but River has her arm around Oliver. He's looking up at her, questioning what's going on, while at the same time, he looks comfortable and comforted pressed to her side. Trevor glares at me, his eyes filled with questions.

"Why don't we all go to the backyard for a bit?" River's eyes meet mine, and she tips her head. Silently, she seems to say, *I'm right here. I won't let anything happen*. Whether she means to the boys or me, I can't be certain. She's that Wendy character, taking care of her lost boys.

She shifts her gaze to Robert and offers him a genuine smile. I see he's captured under her spell, and he silently moves forward, following River and the boys around the side of the house toward the backyard. I have no choice but to follow as well.

The boys head for the tree fort, and River disappears into the house but quickly returns with a pitcher of iced tea and some glasses. I want to snark that this isn't some social visit, and she doesn't need to entertain him, but I bite my cheek. Personally, I could use something stronger than iced tea. River glances at me, offering me a glass, which I accept while Robert declines. Giving us space, which I don't want, she wanders into the yard, still wearing her scrubs and her clogs. With her back to us, she allows us privacy while her position suggests she won't go far.

"Just say what you came to say so we can get this over with," I snap, pinning my eyes on a man I no longer know. He leans forward, elbows on his thighs, and I notice the tattoos on his knuckles. I don't want to know what they mean or where he got them or why. He shakes his head.

"Your mother—"

"You leave Mom out of this," I immediately growl.

Sitting upright, he swipes a hand through his thin hair which is more silver than dark brown now. He looks toward Anna's house, and I want to demand he shouldn't look in that direction. He shouldn't look toward the family who took us in, told us over and over we were their family, and cared for us. I glance at River's back, drawing strength from her presence.

"You're right," he says, his voice rough. "I had a problem. I didn't think I was good enough. I wanted to give her more. I didn't want her to ever be sorry she chose me."

Robert has my attention now.

"In the end, I lost her. She was the best thing I ever had, and the best I could do for her was give her up."

I turn my head. Silence falls, awkwardly wrapping around us, before I peer back at him.

"I've got a girlfriend now."

"I do not want to hear this," I quip. *Jesus, what is he thinking?*

"Her name is Robbyn," he continues.

"Cute." Sarcasm coats my tone. *Robert and Robbyn*. The name hits me—Robbyn's River Adventure. "Did you con her into giving you a job? Buy into her business with false promises? Are you stealing from her?"

As my voice rises, River turns her head but doesn't fully glance at me over her shoulder. She approaches the tree fort, calling quietly up to the boys.

"I deserve that," Robert says, and a heavy pause follows again. "But I won't take it. She's a good woman. Smart and kind. I make an honest wage and appreciate the slower pace of life. No more hustle."

I snort at the concept and double meaning of the word. My fingers curl around the arm of the chair where I sit, feeling tied down and tortured at this . . . interview? Introduction? What are we doing here?

"I like your girl." He rolls his neck to gaze over at River.

"Don't talk about her," I snap again, coasting my shaky palms along the edge of the chair's arms.

Robert turns back to me and weakly raises a hand. "Only wanted to say you make a nice family."

The words bring me up short, but I find myself speaking. "She's not my wife." My voice is rough but not harsh. I realize my father never met Jeanine, and perhaps he thinks River is the mother of Trevor and Oliver. He wouldn't know any different, and my mind races with the thoughts I've been having since I've been separated from her.

"I'm divorced." I'm not even certain why I tell him this fact. Robert tips up a brow and gives me a knowing glance.

"We all deserve a second chance at love . . . and getting it right."

My mouth falls open, ready to retort that it's a little late for fatherly advice from him. Then I peer over at River, head tipped back, speaking to Oliver who was hanging out the window of the tree fort, and my mouth clamps shut instead.

I stare at my father. It's been almost thirty years, more than half my life, and I don't know the man before me. I don't even know if I want to know this person. The father I had is gone.

You need to forgive him, River said. It was the only way to move on. Be grateful for when I had a dad and accept that I no longer do.

"Because of her, I know I need to forgive you. For me. For them, but I'm not there yet." I don't really know if I'll ever get there. *Perhaps with River's help . . .*

Robert and I remain in awkward silence for another long moment while he lowers his head, pursing his lips in concentration. Finally, he looks up at me, weakly smiling, and says, "You should bring your boys back to Robbyn's. Next river trip is on me."

I don't think he's ignoring what I've said about forgiveness as much as bypassing it for now. He isn't looking to argue with me any more than I want to fight with him.

"Yeah, the boys would like that," I say for some reason, instantly knowing I won't take him up on the offer. My thoughts leap back to the day we went canoeing. The boys had loved pretending they were pirates searching for something hidden around every corner. River added to the adventure, calling out things she hoped to see next, yammering about buried treasure and where it might be found, and wondering if there was gold deep in the river. She was so creative. The boys ate it up.

"That's a nice new fort," Robert offers, and I notice he's been watching River and the boys during my silence. "You and your brother had quite the imagination up there."

While I recall some moments, there's so much I don't remember, perhaps blocking some memories out.

"We had to build a new one. The old platform wasn't safe anymore."

"It always was the perfect tree for a fort." My father speaks more to the tree than to me, and instantly I remember a night of laying on that platform, looking through the winter-bare branches. We were gazing up at the stars, my father and me. *Always reach for the stars, Zack. Accept no limit to what you can do, who you can be.*

Suddenly, I'm swallowing hard as more memories return to my head. I remember feeling like we were floating, flying as we glanced up at the dark sky with a brilliant display of stars.

Flying in love. I couldn't remember the age I'd been, but I'd loved my dad so much at that ancient moment. I was certain of it. But loving a parent is a different kind of love. Unfortunately, my father needed limits back then. He needed to accept what we had. He needed to trust my mother's love for him. She wouldn't have thought less of him. We would have all made changes and sacrificed like Calvin and Bryce did for Ben. That's what families do. That's what I learned from my friends. They were my family.

"People make mistakes, son." The comment draws me from my head. I want to snap at him for calling me son. I wasn't his son any more than this man was my dad, but I wasn't going to argue the term. Could we negotiate with one another? Could we compromise? I wasn't certain. Sitting here with him felt bigger than both of us.

My eyes seek Trevor and Oliver, both laughing at something River has said. With the universe as my witness, I swear I will never be distant from my boys again.

"I need to go," Robert finally says when I've taken too long to respond to him. He rubs his hands together, and I watch the motion, wondering if he'll hold out a hand to me. Will we shake like acquaintances? Will we stand and hug? The thought makes me shiver, and I quickly dismiss it. Something in my face must warn him not to reach for me, so he doesn't. He rubs his hands over his thighs next.

"Well . . ."

"Yeah." I quickly stand, scraping the feet of the metal chair against the concrete, making a sound like nails on a chalkboard. River turns in our direction and meets my gaze. Without a second of hesitation, she crosses to me.

"Leaving?" There's a question in the word, as her eyes remain on mine.

"I need to get to work," Robert says.

I almost huff but stop myself.

"We enjoyed our day at the river adventure," River offers, smiling at my father, who can't help but smile in return to her.

"You come over any time you want." He winks, and River nods, keeping her grin in place. She'll never go there again if I don't want to go. I've done what she asked. I listened. Did I absorb it? Did I forgive him? I'm not certain I'm there yet, but I let him talk.

"I'll see myself out," Robert says, giving a wave to the boys before nodding to River. "It was good to see you, Zack."

When I don't respond again, as I don't know what to say, he smiles once more at River and walks to the side of the house. Watching him disappear around the corner, I nearly collapse back to the chair, not realizing how on edge I'd been. My body aches like I've overextended myself in a workout.

"I'm so proud of you," River says, squatting beside the chair. Her hands cover one another, and her chin rests on her knuckles as she looks up at me. "How do you feel?"

"I don't know," I honestly admit, uncertain of everything. Her hand shifts to my thigh, and I quickly wrap my fingers around hers, pulling it up to my lips, lingering against her knuckle. There are too many racing thoughts in my head to process, so I'm grateful when she doesn't ask me more questions. She doesn't make me talk. She just lets me be.

"Why were you upset earlier?" I ask, recalling the tears in her eyes. "You're home early."

Her lips twist side to side as her bright blue eyes hold mine.

"Jessica died." The little girl patient she eventually told me about. The one who had her in tears the first day we were building the tree fort.

"River, angel." I reach down for her and tug her up to my lap, holding her to my chest. With her arms wrapped around my neck, her nose settles against my skin, and she inhales. Her tears are held at bay for now, but I know later that night, when we make love in the dark, we're going to cling a little harder to one another. We're going to hold tighter and never want to let go.

30

[Zack]

On Monday, after a great weekend with River, I call Mason.

"I don't know much about our project schedule, but can we add another one?" I ask my friend and business partner.

"You'd know if you moved here," Mason scoffs. We've been handling all our meetings virtually, which works but isn't quite the same as sitting in a conference room together.

"Even you don't live there," I remind him as he left Anna's and returned to his townhome in Traverse City. For a man who builds properties, it's surprising he doesn't have an individual house.

"I'd like you to take on River's house."

The line goes silent a second before Mason asks, "Are you sure about this?"

With a smile in my voice, I answer. "I've never been more sure about anything in my life." After my father left and River told me about Jessica, we were quiet but constantly touching as if afraid we'd lose the other without the physical connection. She made dinner, and I was at her side. I sat with the boys, and she held my hand. And when we finally had time alone, we made love that was a rush at first and then a slow dance second, keeping us connected as long as possible. Even in sleep, we wrapped around one another. The weekend ended too fast.

"You remember it's not your house, right?" Mason reminds me, and I grin again.

"Yeah, but going to be mine again, someday. The woman inside belongs with me." I chuckle when I consider her saying she was her own person. *I am mine.* Then she admitted she belonged by my side, and I belong by hers.

By the end of the day, I have a call from River.

"You cannot renovate my house," she huffs into the line without greeting. Her voice is full of exasperation, and I just want to see her face.

Those wide blue eyes giving me that look like I'm incorrigible, and her lush mouth chewing at her lower lip in frustration.

"Hello to you, too, beautiful," I tease. "I'm actually not renovating your house. Mason is."

"Mr. Weller, this is too much." Her calling me the formal name recalls our first meeting, but it also reminds me she called my father that name this weekend. I bite back any retort as I don't want to discuss my father again. She's made her points. I listened to both her and him. I want to move onward.

"I want to do this for you." Even without her present, I know she can see me.

"You're pouting, aren't you?"

I chuckle. I don't know what my pouting expression looks like, but she always tells me I'm too cute when I do. I wish she could see me, so she'd fall for my charm and just give in to this already. Instead, she stays quiet, almost too quiet for her.

"Zack, you don't owe me anything." My mouth falls open, and a sharp sound rushes forward, but River continues before I can speak. "Not an apology, gratitude, or a bottle of wine. I don't *need* you to fix my house."

I know this. She doesn't need me. She's one of the most independent, capable women I know, but still . . . "I want to do this for you. I want to give you everything." Suddenly, I realize I sound just like my father. He'd said the same thing. He wanted to make certain my mother never regretted picking him. I scrub my forehead, hating the comparison. My father and I are nothing alike. He abandoned the family he wanted to do everything for. He left behind the wife he wanted to give all the things.

"I don't need everything, though, honey. Time with you is all I want. Time with the boys, too."

"Just let Mason give you a quote," I fire back before her words hit me.

"No." The word is so final. "I realize it's probably something you don't hear much in your adult life, but no."

"Why not?" Doesn't she know how much I love her?

"Because I don't like to get my hopes up for things I haven't earned. I don't need this kind of gift." Her voice turns a bit colder, and I don't understand. She'd taken a sizable gift from Quincy. I want to do one better.

"Negotiate," I softly demand, scrubbing harder at my forehead.

"This is where you compromise, Zack. You honor my wishes, respect my property, and listen to me. You do as I ask. No, on a quote."

Why is she so frustrating? I just want to give her nice things, and all she wants is time.

Then it hits me. I'm still such an idiot.

+ + +

Two days later, the boys are in a mood.

"Why can't we just live with River?" Oliver whines.

"Because she isn't a mom, you dummy," Trevor grumbles back.

"Hey," I snap.

"But the tree fort is there," Oliver pouts. "I want to go in the tree fort."

I sigh. It's been a long day, and with River working the night shift while I've been at work all day, we can't talk until late. The hours are too far away, and so is she.

It isn't like the boys and I haven't been on our own since last August when I confronted Jeanine, and she immediately moved out. Then I started the venture with the guys late in the fall, hoping to have everything settled before Ben died—as morbid as that thought was. My divorce was final in March, and it's been one battle after another with Jeanine and her cancellations. Plus, there's the regular attorney work at the partnership, and suddenly, I'm recalling what my dad said about a slower pace and less hustle.

He'd thrived on the busyness, and in many ways, I did, too. It kept me going, moving forward, but I realize I might be missing a few things going at this speed. Seven years have gone by in both a painfully slow gaze and a sharp blink of the eye. My boys are growing, changing, and I still don't know them well enough. I don't want them waking up thirty years from now and never knowing *me*. I'd be no better than my father if that happened.

"Guys, I want to ask you something." I'm nervous, and I don't know why. They're just kids, but they're my kids, and I need to do right by them with the next decision I make. They'd been at the forefront of my marriage to Jeanine, but I don't want to take any other turns in life without their input.

I point at the couch, so the boys sit side by side before I take a seat on the low table before it. We've never had a formal father-son, man-to-boys chat like this, and I wipe my hands down my thighs.

"What would you think if I asked River to marry me?" I realize this is the one area I'm working fast—again. As soon as Jeanine told me she was pregnant and didn't want our babies because it would ruin her reputation as a woman on the fast track, I offered to marry her. I thought I was doing the right thing, and I immediately wanted to be there for my future children. I didn't want them to think I'd abandoned them.

River was different. This was different. I was in love with her, but I didn't need to go into all those details with my boys.

"She's not a mom," Trevor states again. "Dads marry moms."

Waving a hand at my son, I say, "Okay, forget what I said about dads marrying moms."

"Emma Peterson actually has two dads," Oliver adds in, and I don't know who Emma is or her two fathers. Yay them, but I don't want to tackle that conversation right now either.

"What if we make River your mom? A stepmom?" I realize I'm smiling too big, and my cheeks actually hurt from the force because I want them to see this is a good thing.

"Justin Stueber has a stepmom. He says she's evil like the one in *Cinderella*," Oliver adds again.

"Who's Cinderella?" Trevor asks. Oh boy, are we headed off course.

"Do you think River is evil?" Glancing from one boy to the next, I wonder what they think. She's been nothing short of wonderful with them, and I haven't had a hint they think otherwise of her.

"No." Trevor snorts like I'm crazy.

"She's great," Oliver says in his best Tony the Tiger impression. Softly, I chuckle. He's turning into quite a character.

"What makes River so great?" I'm curious. What do they love about her?

"She can talk like a pirate, build a sandcastle, and kick a soccer ball," Trevor sings her praises in the material way.

"She hugs me," Oliver says it so nonchalant, so matter-of-fact, my mouth falls open. Am I not affectionate enough with my child? Immediately, I know the answer, and my chest rips in half. *Take my heart.* Licking my lips, I rub my hands down my suit pants once more and remember how River spoke to Oliver one day.

If you want something, ask for it.

"Ollie, can I have a hug?" My voice is low, sheepish even, awaiting my own child to reject me, but just like that, he's in my arms, his little ones around my neck. Placing my hand on his back, I hold it there, spreading my fingers and keeping my palm still. I don't pat him. I don't push him away too quickly. I hold my child to my chest, and my nose prickles. My eyes burn. *What the hell?*

Looking up, I notice Trevor watching us. There's something in his eyes as well. The way he's holding back like he wants what he sees, but he doesn't ask. He doesn't trust it or himself or something. I hold out an arm, suggesting Trevor fall in next, but he doesn't come to me. Pressing a kiss to Oliver's head, I slip him to my side, keeping him under my arm. Then I shift, lift, and reach for Trevor, pulling him into my other arm before settling back on the low table. Squeezing him tight to my shoulder, I mimic my hold on Oliver. With my cheek at his temple, I inhale his little boy scent and just breathe.

"I love you," I whisper to Trevor's hair. He nods but stiffens in my arms. The words are foreign to me as well. I don't say them often. I can't recall having said them until I spoke them to River, down on my knees, begging her to keep me.

"I love you, Trevor," I say louder near his ear. His little body shudders, and I try to push him back. I want to see his face, but he keeps his head low, his forehead tucked to my shoulder. It's then that I hear the faintest sound. Just a whimper. Trevor swipes at his face, but I don't miss the tear running down his cheek. Allowing him his privacy, I tug him back to my chest, cupping the back of his head and kissing his hair.

"I love you," I say one more time, pressing him even tighter to me before leaning over to Oliver and repeating the sentiment. His head is turned so his cheek rests on my shoulder. He's been watching his brother.

Looking my son directly in the eyes, I say what's long overdue. "I love you, too, Ollie." Slowly, he smiles, and his finger swipes the edge of my nose where something liquid has seeped.

"I know, Dad," he whispers. "River told me."

Softly, I chuckle when shame should fill me. He learned it from her, just like I'm learning so many things from her and loving everything.

31

[River]

The man is so infuriating, but I love him. I exhale with the thought. It's actually sweet that he wants to renovate my house. Insufferable, but still sweet. However, a renovation is not what I want from him. I don't want him beholden or obligated, or any other thing. Then another thought occurs, which I don't even want to consider but can't help once I have it in my head.

Put a thought in the universe, and it's here to stay, my grandfather would say. He mainly meant it in reference to being mean to others. You say something, and you can't ever take it back. The same goes for thinking negative thoughts.

Like thinking a man wants to be with me for a house.

It's silly. It's ridiculous. It's extreme. He said he loves me, but that niggling doubt is there, so when he arrives the next weekend with his boys in tow, I'm out of sorts.

The Weller men get to my place on Friday evening after I've worked the day shift. I'm on again tomorrow morning as well. I offered to take the day off, but Zack tells me he doesn't want me to make any changes to my schedule. It's sweet also, but it has my questioning-thoughts feeler on high alert.

Does he want to hang at my house . . . without me? Do his boys only want to be here for a tree fort? I hate these kinds of feelings, but I trust early and learn later. I don't want to think this of Zack, I really don't, but I cannot shake the rhythm. Even when we have sex that night, keeping quiet and going at it on the floor because the bed squeaks too much, I can't rid my mind of the possibility he wants in my home because he wants his house back.

When I come home from work to find Daniel Quincy in my front yard again, I'm done.

"What the hell are you doing here?" I snap, exiting my car and hollering at Daniel before I've even made it up the drive. This cannot turn into a monthly occurrence of him arriving unexpectedly, uncalled for, and harassing me about the house. It's out of control, and it's also over. The will stated his father's intentions.

Suddenly, Zack steps out on the front porch, hearing my voice or maybe the sharp slam of my car door.

"River, we need to talk," Daniel states, and Zack is quickly at my side.

"If you have something to say, you have her lawyers to contact," Zack interjects. My mouth falls open, but Daniel steps in.

"I thought you were her lawyer."

My head turns, wondering how Zack will respond to this after he made his grand entrance through the trees the last time Daniel was present.

"I am."

Daniel scoffs. "You're just the neighbor or some other bloke looking to get in her pants and steal this house."

First, I hate how Daniel has hit on something that's been at the forefront of my thoughts this week, but what happens next, I never expected. Zack has Daniel's collar in his hand so fast, and his fist pressed up to his chin with that shirt in his fingers.

"Speak like that again about her, and you'll be hearing from me as more than her lawyer." His tone turns deadly serious.

"Meaning?" Daniel scoffs.

"I'll bury you, your career, and your company." For some reason, I'm convinced Zack can do it even though his father was the one ruined by Quincy.

"Do I need a restraining order on you?" Zack adds next. Daniel's eyes shift to me, but Zack presses upward at his chin, and Daniel has his hands wrapped around Zack's wrist. "Don't look at her."

"Zack," I whisper. Not one prone to violence, I'm surprisingly flattered by this display of possession and protection.

His head tilts to glance at me. "What? You did everything for his father in the end." He shifts back to Daniel, a man much older than Zack, and growls. "Where were you when your father needed you?"

"What do you know about it?" Daniel hisses.

L.B. Dunbar

Zack doesn't pause. "Everything." Slowly, Zack lowers his fist and releases Daniel's shirt, pushing at Daniel at the same time he takes a step back.

"Get the fuck out of here. I see you one more time on this property or hear you contacted River one more time, that restraining order will be a real thing. And that's public record, so if you're so worried about your company and scandal like I'm certain you are, you might want to think twice." Zack pauses for a second. "How are you going to explain to the shareholders you're harassing a woman who inherited your father's house because you and your dipshit siblings couldn't care enough to grant a dying man his wish?"

"You don't know anything," Daniel snaps, but Zack does know the story, and I'm curious if he might be commenting on a little more than Daniel's lacking reconciliation with his father. Perhaps he's reconsidering his absent reunion with his own father.

"Get off this property," Zack demands, pulling out his phone like he's ready to call the police. He didn't even threaten his own father in that manner, and I wonder why not?

After a final scathing glance at me, we remain on the drive as Daniel stalks off.

"What a fucking douchebag," Zack mutters under his breath as Daniel drives off in his sporty car.

"Where did all that come from?" I question, turning to him.

"I told you, I want to give you everything. That means keeping you safe and protected from assholes like him."

Licking my lips, I chew at the corner. "About that—" I'm cut off from speaking the rest of my thought when Zack's hands cup my jaw, and he kisses me fierce and fast.

"The boys are over at Anna's. We have two hours until they come back."

"I—" It's evident Zack wants to rush upstairs and have sex, but I just can't get on the same page.

With his hands sliding down to my shoulders, he pauses and ducks his head when I don't respond in agreement with his eagerness. "What's wrong?"

"I . . . Let me change. I just need to shake that off." I tip my head toward the road where Daniel exited, but I also need to get my head on straight. Zack's brows pinch, disappointment on his face, but he nods.

"I'll pour you some wine and meet you on the lounger in ten."

Weakly, I smile at him before turning for the house, feeling his eyes on my back.

When I return down the stairs, dressed in shorts and a sweatshirt because the late afternoon air temperature is shifting, I find Zack where he said, seated on the lounger. He holds a glass of wine in his hand, and when I settle next to him, he hands it to me.

"Is this mine?" I question.

"I thought we could share."

I softly chuckle at the reminder of our first night. "Do you know how?" I tease, finding my tone suggests more.

"You seem off," Zack says, keeping his eyes forward. The sun won't set for hours, but it's hanging lower in the early evening sky.

"I've had a few things on my mind this week."

"Are you breaking up with me?" He still doesn't look at me when he asks.

"Why would you say that?" I shift on the lounger to lean on my shoulder. Zack refuses to look at me.

"You know I hate confrontation." His hand swipes through his hair, a tell-tale sign he's upset.

"Why would you ask such a thing?" I question again, keeping my voice low. Zack remains quiet a second, considering something before he speaks.

"I could end up like Daniel," he states, and it's not what I expected him to say. Not one bit.

"How?"

"I could be bitter and hateful. Resentful even about my dad." He side-eyes me before narrowing his, facing forward again. "You said Quincy wasn't a good father. Whatever happened caused a wedge with his kids. He wanted to make amends at the end, and they didn't. Now, they just continue living with their anger and Quincy . . . he's just dead."

I wince at the directness of his reference.

"I don't want to be like that." He turns his head toward me. "That's why I want to be with you."

"What do you mean?"

"I know you won't let me be like that." He implies Daniel.

"Does this mean you want to make up with your father?" The concept surprises me, but I'd also be so happy for Zack. He needs something with the man.

"It means I recognize I need to let it go. The thing with my father has closed off my heart for too long. I was guarded, so guarded. Thinking I wouldn't be hurt ever again like that. I wouldn't be abandoned, but instead, I abandoned my own kids. They didn't know I loved them." His eyes focus on my face. "Until you told them I did."

Oh. "Zack, honey. They knew. They knew because you were here for them. Their mother left, but you remained in your own way."

Zack swipes a hand through his hair, looking away again. "But my way wasn't good enough."

"It's not a competition."

"But I want to be better." He turns to me once more. "With you, I'm better." His eyes search my face. "Are we breaking up?"

The vulnerable man I've seen and loved returns in those silver eyes, and I have to get this off my chest.

"Why are you with me?"

"Because I love you." Zack shifts on the lounger to mirror my position. His shoulder presses into the cushion as he faces me.

"Are you sure it isn't about the house?"

"What?! No, of course not. Why would you ask *that*?"

It's my turn to shift away, and I twist to my back, facing the lake slowly rippling off in the distance. I shrug. "You just seem so wrapped up in it. First, you didn't want to enter it, and then when you did enter, all you want to do is fix it up. I'm worried you want what it represents more than you want me."

"River," he drones. "Look at me, angel." He reaches for my jaw, gently forcing me to look at him. "I do want what it represents. I want a home with you. I want to live with you. But it doesn't have to be this house. We can burn it to the ground and build a new one. Or we can sell it and move. We can live in Detroit."

I instantly wrinkle my nose and then feel bad.

Zack softly chuckles. "I didn't think so." He turns to glance at the property over his shoulder. "I won't lie and say I'd be happy to give up this land. I would be sorry because it's a beautiful piece of property with a gorgeous setting." He shifts his attention back to me. "But it's the gorgeous woman I want more than anything. I'll live in a box with you if you want. I just want to be together."

Mr. Dress Shirts and Khaki Shorts would never live in a cardboard box, but I hear what he's saying.

"I don't want to move," I admit of the truth. I do love this house and this location.

"Would it be too bold to ask if I could move in with you?" I stare at him, surprised by the question. "I realize I'm doing it all wrong. I should be asking you to move in with me or suggesting we move in together. Your call. I just want to live in the same zip code. I don't want anything between us. Not distance or hours. I want to be with you. The boys miss you. I miss you." He gives me that sexy pout of his, knowing what it does to me.

I hold up the glass of wine in my hand. "Would you even know how to share if we lived together?" Because I want a partnership, not a man bulldozing things.

"Teach me," he whispers, lowering his eyes for my lips.

"Negotiate." My voice is cautious, uncertain if I'm hearing what I think I'm hearing.

"I want to renovate this place and give it new life. I want to freshen up everything and fill this place with love."

"Do you think I don't love it enough?"

"I think there's more love in your pinky than this house can hold, but I still want to be part of that love. I want my boys to have that love. From you. From me. In this place. I'll handle the cost of everything."

I sigh. "I can't have you do such a thing."

L.B. Dunbar

"You can't have me move in?" His facial expression drops to something I've never seen before, and his hands slip from my face. Quickly, I catch his wrists.

"That's not what I said." Slowly, I smile, chewing at my lip.

"What are you saying then? Be clear with me."

"I want to do it." My smile grows larger. "I want you here."

"Yeah?" He hesitates.

"But we do it together," I say, my heart racing. This is really happening, and I emphasize again. "Together."

"Are you trying to compromise?" He flirts. "You're typically so pushy," he sarcastically adds.

This man.

"I'll show you pushy." I press off the cushion and straddle his lap. Placing my hands on his shoulders, I peer down at him as he tips his head back to look up at me.

"Please push me," he says, his voice dropping. His hips thrust upward to emphasize his point. Then with his hands on my hip, he flips me to my back, climbing over me. His heavy length presses against my heat, and he kisses my neck. "Push me to be a better man. Push me to be what you see in me."

"You already are a good man, Zack, but I promise to try to make you better as long as you do the same of me."

"How can I make perfection better?" His nose drags over the shell of my ear.

"Together is how we are better."

"Together," he whispers.

"No holding back," I warn.

"I never hold back with you." His head pops up, and he stares down at me.

Laughing I say, "Because you have no boundaries.

"Because I love you," he retorts. "River, you once told me if I want something to ask for it." He pauses, licking his lip and chewing on the lower swell for a second. "You mentioned treasure being under my boys' nose. I saw you as the treasure you are the day we met. I've already told you how quickly I knew you were who I wanted. You've captured my heart and my boys' as well. I want the time to be with you, to love you, to share with you. . . I want you to marry me."

My mouth falls open. In the span of a conversation, we went from moving in to marriage.

"If that was too fast, it's okay. You don't have to answer me—"

"Was there a question in there?" I tease. "You normally don't ask permission."

"I'm asking—" His sheepish tone turns my insides, and my heart flutters faster.

"Yes."

His brows lift, and he draws his head back for a better look at me. "Yes?"

Swiping my hand through his hair, I look up at him. "Yes. I'll marry you."

The smile that breaks out on his face is nearly blinding. Dazzling. "God, I love you so much. I never thought I'd feel so free . . . free to just love."

"I love you, too, honey."

"Is it wrong to say I want to get naked with you?"

Tipping my head back, I glance at the house behind me, noting the second-floor window of Anna's house. "What will the neighbors think?" I laugh, drawing back to Zack's face.

"Keep your clothes on," he teases, leaning down for my neck and nipping at my skin.

"Keep your eyes to yourself." The words recall what I said to him at our first meeting.

"Never," he hums into my skin.

"Whatever makes you feel better." I squeak because he bites the juncture of my neck and shoulder while grinding his heavy length into me.

"You. You make me feel better, but what would really feel better is if you were naked under me and I was buried inside you."

Well, that's something we might be able to compromise on.

Epilogue

[Zack]

July – the following year

After losing her young patient, River realizes her heart cannot continue with the pain of her career. She's dedicated fifteen years to oncology nursing and the toll it's taken on her gentle spirit. Death has taught her to cherish life in a different way than most. She sees the simple things, loves the bigger things, and counts every day as a blessing.

She's the blessing the boys and I needed, and we moved in shortly after I proposed. Jeanine still had visitation rights, but her constant cancellations warranted another trip to family court, where I petitioned for full custody. I agreed that when Jeanine wants to see her boys, she simply had to call. She hasn't called, and I don't encourage the relationship.

If my friends think it's strange I proposed to a woman after a one-night stand—finding out two months later she was pregnant—they say nothing about my deciding to marry a woman after a month of knowing her. It was only supposed to be a ten-day fling, but I knew within ten seconds of watching her out that second-floor window I wanted her. Within ten seconds of meeting her, I knew I'd never be the same without her in my life.

"Okay, who's going with who?" I say, standing at the counter, trying to organize our crew.

"I want to go with Bryce," Trevor says, holding up his arm, and I notice Lorna's face fall. *Huh.* I glance up at Logan, who shakes his head to ignore the teenage pout of his twelve-year-old daughter. She's stuck with her father. Mason takes Mila, and I have Oliver. Bryce is a good sport at sixteen to spend the day with the gang. If he's missing his dad on this excursion, he's too old to admit it.

"Thanks, pal." I clap Bryce on the shoulder after he high-fives Trevor in acceptance of the call. Turning back for the counter, I pull out my credit card, holding the plastic to the man behind it.

"Your money isn't good here," he says, and I meet his eyes, hoping not to have an altercation with him before my friends. Logan and Mason know who he is. They're here for support as well as an afternoon of canoeing.

"I'd feel better paying," I admit, holding his eyes. "But maybe the kids could have free ice cream afterward." There's an ice cream freezer inside the shop offering bars and sandwiches. It's a concession to his offer.

"That'd be fine," he says.

"Okay, guys. Robert says free ice cream later, but that doesn't mean it's a race."

"Aw, Dad, what's the fun in that? Bryce can beat all you old guys," Trevor whines.

"Who you calling old, little man?" Mason knuckles Trevor's head.

"Alright. What do we say to Robert in case he isn't here when we finish?"

A chorus of thank yous follows with Logan droning the loudest like he's one of the younger set.

"You're such a child," Mason teases.

"Look who's talking," Logan retorts.

I simply shake my head.

"Friends?" Robert asks, tipping up a brow in a way I recognize and should hate about him.

"The best of friends. They're family."

My father purses his lips but nods once to accept what I've said. These men are my family. I've known them longer than him.

"Enjoy your trip."

"Thanks again for the ice cream," I say, slipping my card back into my wallet. "In case we don't see you at the—"

"I'll be here when you finish. I'll be waiting for you." He holds my eyes a moment before rapping his knuckles on the counter and walking to the holder of paddles and life preservers. A firm hand on my shoulder pinches it.

"You did good," Mason whispers, knowing how difficult it was to decide to come here.

"Thanks, man."

"Anything for you, my friend." He pats my shoulder blade, maybe a little too hard, and we head out for the river adventure.

+ + +

"Benjawhina," I deadpan while River is in a fit of laughter. "What kind of name is that?"

We had a good day canoeing with the guys, and even seeing Robert didn't upset me as much as I thought it might. I have River to thank for that. Everything for River.

And now, she's pregnant.

"I think it's supposed to be a take on Wilhemina." She chokes through her laughter as she tries to explain the baby's name. We know we're having a girl. River said there were so few surprises in life, she didn't want to know the baby's gender early, but we found out by mistake. The amniocentesis matched the chromosomes accordingly, and the doctor blurted out the combination although we'd told her we wanted to wait.

"It's a perfect XX."

"Next time," I told River, thinking I was accommodating. I was showing her I could compromise. She only glared at me, which I decided was rather cute on her, kind of like the pouty face she loves on me.

"Benjamina," she tries again, but I'm done with this nonsense. We aren't naming our child some construction of Ben's name, even if I appreciate the honor River wants to bestow on our future child. River credits Ben as bringing us together even though she never met him. He was the neighbor she didn't meet because the fence-lining arborvitae clearly said stay out. It wasn't the bushes that made the statement, though; it was the ugly metal chain link.

"Absolutely not," I grumble.

"The boys vote for Pirate as the name," River says, completely straight-faced.

"Well, at least they aren't asking if she can be named Kitty." Thank you, Uncle Mason, for planting that seed as an option with all the sexual implications behind it.

"What about Lake?" River's voice softens, and I do a double take, thinking she might be joking, but something in her tone tells me she's not. She's cautious, but serious.

"Do you mean Blake?" I correct.

"No, I mean Lake. Like a river flows into a lake." My wild woman shows her nature-loving way, and I like the play on her name.

"I flowed into the river." Wiggling my brows, I tease her, but I'm liking the idea. The lake was my first love, but it took River to open my heart and really soar.

"Lake Weller it will be, then."

River slowly smiles. Those blue eyes gleam like when the sun hovers over the large body of water, and I catch my breath, grateful for every day she looks at me like she is. She's sunrises and sunsets, and I'm happy to start and end every twenty-four hours with her by my side.

I never expected to be a father again at forty-one. Then again, I hadn't ever expected my heart to be so full of love.

"You know, you asked me once why I call you angel. I don't believe in mystics or kismet or any other type of voodoo, but I saw you in your yard the night of Ben's death, and again on the night I received his letter, and I swore he sent you to me. You were the angel meant to help me fly. You are the love I needed to learn to soar."

I was flying, and I never wanted to come down from the high.

Second Epilogue

August—the following year

[Jenna]

Someone's been sleeping in my bed, and she's still in it.

I thought I was dreaming. I'd been reading copious amounts of children's tales to my two little girls, and I was convinced the sentences had seeped into my subconscious. I could not get away from being a mom even in my sleep. But slowly, my brain registers that the sound of that final bear's voice was a little too gruff and a little too gravelly and a whole lot of sexy.

My eyes flip open in the dark bedroom, and my heart races. I am not alone in here. My chin is pinned by the power of a thick paw of callused fingertips and the depth of dark eyes narrowed and focused keeps me frozen in place. His nose is so close we practically touch, and I'd scream if only my vocal cords worked.

"However, she doesn't look like Goldilocks." His eyes flick up to my hair which happens to be raven black, and he chuckles, rugged and low. "So, who the hell are you?"

I swallow, feeling his wrist near my throat as his fingers hold my jaw. *Dear God, don't let him hurt the girls.* The thought speeds up my already sprinting heart.

"Please don't hurt me," I choke, and his eyes widen.

"What the fuck?" he snaps, startling me even more. "You're in my bed, 'locks." The incredulous tone mixes with his deep tenor.

His bed?

My mind flips through a mental checklist. This is Anna's house. This is Lakeside Cottage. Her folks owned the place, and she inherited it. My daughters and I are her guests. The apartment above the garage was offered to me for a much-needed break. She said her brother—

"Archer?" I croak, wondering if the man holding my jaw is the elusive older brother Anna has mentioned a time or two. He wasn't

240

expected here. At the sound of his name, his hand slowly releases my chin but travels south to my throat. The thick palm isn't squeezing. He just rests it in place like a turtleneck sweater. I can still breathe, but my breath is gone. Despite the dark room, the intensity of his eyes sucks up all the oxygen.

"Who the fuck are you?"

I struggle to find the words again. Maybe it's that strong voice or the fact he's on all fours over me. *How did I not hear him enter the apartment? Or this room? Or this bed?*

"I'm Jenna Davis, a friend of Anna's."

His hand lowers even more, flattening over my chest. I'm certain he can feel my heart thumping under my skin. I'm wearing shorts and a tank top, and loosely covered by a sheet and light blanket. But I'm all too aware of how thin the layers of material are. The heat of his hand seeps through my flesh just above the swell of my breasts which rapidly heave in fear. Maybe fear isn't the right word. Is it possible I'm also turned on? Despite not knowing Anna's brother, I was having the most wonderful dream before the gruff little bear invaded my thoughts, and that dream has my nipples on high alert that someone's hand is very near them.

However, my head says this is all wrong.

"What are you doing?" I choke because his hand is sweeping lower, and my gut reaction is to lift my knee for his balls. Which I do. Only, two things happen at the same time. First, he captures my leg between his before I get anywhere near his precious cargo, then his hand slips lower, squeezing my breast.

"What the fuck?" he says, his voice like sandpaper against rocks.

"What the frickety-frack?" I say at the same time.

"What the fuck is frickety-frack?" That incredulous tone returns, and I finally find enough strength in my arms to lift them upward and push at his chest. Speaking of rocks, he's missing a shirt, and his smooth pecs are as solid as a boulder. He bitterly chuckles at my weak attempt to move him but shifts enough for me to scramble out from underneath him. He remains on the bed, on his knees, while I slip off the mattress and back up until I collide with the wall.

"I'm not going to hurt you," he says. That rugged voice softens only a sliver, and my arms cross over my chest in a giant X, covering myself as best I can.

"You just manhandled my boob," I blurt.

"You were sleeping in my bed. Find a woman in my bed, and I get to touch her."

"That's rather assumptive and chauvinistic."

"Those are two big words I can't comprehend in the middle of the night, babe."

I huff again and then think of my girls.

"Tell me you didn't touch my daughters." My heart continues to hammer as the statement stammers from my lips.

"You've got kids?"

I roll on my shoulder, intending to slip from the room through the open door. Only, I misjudge the distance to the entrance and smack into the frame.

"Frickety, frack, frack, frack," I hiss as my nose explodes in pain and my eyes sting. Instantly, warm hands are on my shoulders, steadying me from behind.

"Where're you goin'?" The seductive sound blurs with the pain radiating across my face, and tears fall.

My voice shakes as I speak. "Just let me go. Just let me get my girls, and I'll get out of here."

His hands peel free of my shoulders, but he doesn't move. His presence overpowers me from behind. Heat wafts off his chest. I sense the strength of him, but it's no longer fear holding me in place. His breath tickles the fine hairs on the back of my neck. *Would he kiss me there?* It's the most ridiculous thought I've ever had.

"Look, there's no need to go anywhere. It's the middle of the night. I'm sure this is my sister's fuckup. It's been a long night. I'll just take the couch."

I have no sense of what time it is. I'd left my hometown of Elk Lake City, roughly three hours north of Lakeside, and arrived midafternoon. That was hours ago. The girls and I needed a change of scenery, and

Anna is a friend from college. When she moved here, we promised we'd get together more often.

"No, you should take your bed," I say, spinning to face him, bumping into the firm chest which remains too close to me. My nose throbs and tears still prickle my eyes, but those nipples of mine ache as they tenderly scrape the inside of my thin tank top.

"You gonna join me again?" The teasing shift in such a rough voice doesn't compute at first, so in all seriousness, I respond.

"I'll just sleep with my girls." I'm certain I won't sleep after all, but I'm not in the right frame of mind to wake the girls and carry them out of here. Plus, it is somewhere past midnight, and the thought of crossing the driveway to wake Anna doesn't sound great. She's been so kind to offer this garage apartment for a two-week stay.

"You weren't supposed to be here," I defend.

"It's still my place," Archer reminds me.

"Yes, but you weren't supposed to be here," I repeat as if that clarifies anything.

"Well, I am." A large arm lifts, and I flinch at the raising of his paw, preparing for a strike. "What the fuck? Calm down." Our eyes meet, and his search mine for answers I cannot give.

"Do you need to keep saying that word?"

"What word?"

"The frickety-frack word." It took years of training on my part to curb my vocabulary so I don't drop an f-bomb or two before my girls. I'm conditioned not to swear as I teach high school and need to keep a stern face when I call out kids for language. But I was no saint outside my classroom until I had children of my own. Even then, I'm still not perfect.

Thinking of my two little ones, I need to get out of this room and check on them. Taking a step to the side as Archer's presence is just so . . . present, I kick the doorframe of the opening I still cannot seem to make it through.

"Frick," I hiss as my heel collides with the edge in a fluky spot right where the two pieces of wood corner together. A definitive thud echoes in the quiet of the place.

L.B. Dunbar

"You're kind of a hot mess." He roughly chuckles again.

Don't I know it. He doesn't need to know it, though.

"I'm just gonna . . . and then tomorrow . . ." I can't seem to collect words because I inhaled as my breath caught when I kicked the door, and *sweet cherries,* Archer smells good. I can't distinguish any specific scent, but it's strong and musky, and I lick my lower lip. Even in the dark, Archer's eyes lower to watch the motion.

"Girls' room," he says, dropping his voice while focused on my mouth. I don't know if it's a question or a command, but two hands come to my shoulders, shift me to the right, and spin me to face the wide door opening. I hardly take a step through the space when the door is closed at my back, and I race across the living room, but not before bumping into the edge of the couch and then stubbing my toe on the coffee table as I'm unfamiliar with this layout in the dark. Hobbling to the bedroom where the girls sleep, I finally make it to the door and slip into their space, pressing my back against the barrier once closed, and wondering what has me so flustered.

With my head tipped back and my eyes closed, I recall Archer's heavy, thick hand over my breast. Maybe I moved, and it was all innocent enough. I did try to knee him in the balls, and squeezing my breast might have been more a gut reaction. Still, I reach for the swell and tenderly place my hand over the heaviness, feeling my nipple erect and firm, peaking the soft, thin cotton of my shirt. Then I stifle a giggle. A ridiculous teenage girl squeak at the thought of that large, mysterious man purposely tweaking my breast.

"Oh my God, I need to get laid," I quietly mutter to the darkness and the heavens. My lids flutter open, and I lower my head to face two twin beds and two little reasons it hasn't happened in years. Taking a deep breath, I sigh with exhaustion and move to one bed, pressing at Rosie's little shoulder so she'll roll over. For a tiny thing, she can take up a lot of space with thin limbs spread in all directions. I know I won't get a wink of sleep with her as she often climbs into my bed at home. I don't mind it much, as the bed feels too large without Ryan, but Rosie has no concept of head on pillows and feet toward the foot of the bed.

Eventually, little heels will be pressed into my back, and I'll be forced to the edge of the mattress, practically hanging on to a sliver of the blanket.

Still, she shifts, and I settle into the bed, pulling the blanket to my throat as if it can hide me or protect me. My head rolls to the left, and I check the other bed. Talia sleeps soundly on her side, facing my direction. Her little hands are tucked under her cheek, and her lips part, causing her to softly snore. With not a care in the world, not a fear in her dreams, my little worrier rests.

"Sweet dreams," I say to the dark, wanting only quiet and peace in both my girls' heads as they slumber.

For me, I'll be lying here wide-awake until morning before I escape the apartment of one hot Archer McCaryn.

L.B. Dunbar

Thank you for reading this work. I hope you enjoyed Zack and River's story. Please consider writing a review to tell others about them.

Read more about Archer and Jenna in *Loving at 40*.
When the prodigal son returns to find a single mother in his bed and hope at a second chance for love and family.

Do you read Logan and Autumn's story in *Living at 40?*
A purposefully planned pregnancy surrounds the start of the Lakeside Cottage collection of shenanigans.

Enjoy love over 40? Meet the Silver Foxes of Blue Ridge. Four brothers, one brewing company and a mountain town they call home. Start here: *Silver Brewer*.

And stay up to date with L.B. Dunbar through <u>Love Notes</u>.

+ + +

More by L.B. Dunbar

<u>Lakeside Cottage</u>
Four friends. Four summers. Shenanigans and love happen at the lake.
Living at 40
Loving at 40
Learning at 40
Letting Go at 40

<u>The Silver Foxes of Blue Ridge</u>
More sexy silver foxes in the mountain community of Blue Ridge.
Silver Brewer
Silver Player
Silver Mayor
Silver Biker

<u>Sexy Silver Foxes</u>
When sexy silver foxes meet the feisty vixens of their dreams.
After Care

Midlife Crisis
Restored Dreams
Second Chance
Wine&Dine

<u>Collision novellas</u>
A spin-off from After Care – the younger set/rock stars
Collide
Caught

<u>Smartypants Romance (an imprint of Penny Reid)</u>
Tales of the Winters sisters set in Green Valley.
Love in Due Time
Love in Deed
Love in a Pickle (2021)

<u>The World of True North (an imprint of Sarina Bowen)</u>
Welcome to Vermont! And the Busy Bean Café.
Cowboy
Studfinder

<u>Rom-com standalone for the over 40</u>
The Sex Education of M.E.

<u>The Heart Collection</u>
Small town, big hearts - stories of family and love.
Speak from the Heart
Read with your Heart
Look with your Heart
Fight from the Heart
View with your Heart

A Heart Collection Spin-off
<u>The Heart Remembers</u>

THE EARLY YEARS
<u>The Legendary Rock Star Series</u>
Rock star mayhem in the tradition of King Arthur.
A classic tale with a modern twist of romance and suspense

L.B. Dunbar

The Legend of Arturo King
The Story of Lansing Lotte
The Quest of Perkins Vale
The Truth of Tristan Lyons
The Trials of Guinevere DeGrance

Paradise Stories
MMA romance. Two brothers. One fight.
Abel
Cain

The Island Duet
Intrigue and suspense. The island knows what you've done.
Redemption Island
Return to the Island

Modern Descendants – writing as elda lore
Magical realism. Modern myths of Greek gods.
Hades
Solis
Heph

About the Author

<u>Love Notes</u>

www.lbdunbar.com

L.B. Dunbar has an over-active imagination. To her benefit, such creativity has led to over thirty romance novels, including those offering a second chance at love over 40. Her signature works include the #sexysilverfoxes collection of mature males and feisty vixens ready for romance in their prime years. She's also written stories of small-town romance (Heart Collection), rock star mayhem (The Legendary Rock Stars Series), and a twist on intrigue and redemption (Redemption Island Duet). She's had several alter egos including elda lore, a writer of romantic magical realism through mythological retellings (Modern Descendants). In another life, she wanted to be an anthropologist and journalist. Instead, she was a middle school language arts teacher. The greatest story in her life is with the one and only, and their four grown children. Learn more about L.B. Dunbar by joining her reader group on Facebook (Loving L.B.) or subscribing to her newsletter (Love Notes).

+ + +

Connect with L.B. Dunbar

www.ingramcontent.com/pod-product-compliance
Lightning Source LLC
Chambersburg PA
CBHW071249190726

48292CB00007B/2476